Miss Smythe and the Midnight Lord
Copyright © 2025 by Rogue Press. All rights reserved.
Published by Rogue Press

All rights reserved. No part of this book may be used or reproduced in any form by any means—except in the case of brief quotations embodied in critical articles or reviews—without written permission.

This is a work of fiction. Names, characters, places, and incidents are products of the author's imagination or are used fictitiously and are not to be construed as real. Any resemblance to actual events, locales, organizations, or persons, living or dead, is entirely coincidental.

This e-book is licensed for your personal enjoyment only. This e-book may not be re-sold or given away to other people. If you would like to share this book with another person, please purchase an additional copy for each reader. If you are reading this book and did not purchase it, or it was not purchased for your use only, please return to your favorite retailer and purchase your own copy. Thank you for respecting the hard work of the author.

Stay in touch through the C. N. Jarrett newsletter!

Miss Smythe and the Midnight Lord

RELUCTANT RECKONINGS
BOOK TWO

C. N. JARRETT

ROGUE
PRESS

To my father, for encouraging every artistic tendency he found in his kids.

Miss you, Dad.

PROLOGUE

"Fear is pain arising from the anticipation of evil."

Aristotle

AUGUST 1, 1821

Lord Aidan Abbott, the honorary Baron of Abbott and heir to Viscount Moreland, carefully wiped his riding boots before entering the family townhouse from the back garden. Riding Valor had been a boon to his recent turbulent thoughts, and his spirits had been lifted by the invigorating air.

Striding down the hall and contemplating whether he needed to change before going out again, he entered the entrance hall, where he found Lord Moreland standing rigid, staring at the letter in his hand while an unknown footman awaited a response.

Aidan frowned in consternation. His father was a composed gentleman of the highest order, and little could shake his exemplary demeanor, but his pale complexion spoke to troubling news.

"Father?"

The sound of Aidan's voice seemed to jolt Lord Moreland from a trance. Drawing a deep breath, his father looked up at the waiting servant. "We will be arriving at Ridley House as soon as our carriage is readied."

The servant nodded. "Yes, milord. I shall inform Mr. Michaels of your arrival."

Once they were alone, Lord Moreland turned to Aidan. "It is your sister. One of the footmen at Ridley House held Lily hostage and attempted to abduct her after she uncovered his involvement in the late baron's murder."

Aidan's knees went weak, and he grabbed for the banister. "Is she ..." He could not bring himself to complete the sentence, overcome by the nightmarish images racing through his head.

Is she dead?

"Their butler informs me that she is well, but the servant is ... no longer with us." Lord Moreland waved the page in his hand, but despite his reassurance, he was still pale and distracted. His concern for his young daughter was evident.

Aidan drew in a shaky breath, unaware until that moment that he had ceased breathing entirely at the thought that his little sister might be harmed. A swirl of guilt clutched at his chest, because he had been a selfish cad and left her alone when he had promised his parents to take care of her.

"This is my fault!"

Lord Moreland shook his head, as if to marshal his

composure. "Nonsense. This is the fault of the man who murdered Lord Filminster. I ... must find your mother, so we may depart for Ridley House."

Aidan nodded, but the words did little to absolve him. His selfish behavior on the night of the King's coronation had left Lily alone. It was the reason she had witnessed Brendan Ridley entering the widow's home across the street. Why she had fallen asleep in the drawing room window seat and later seen Ridley depart in the early hours. It was Aidan's neglect that had made her feel compelled to step forward with a scandalous alibi to save Ridley from the hangman's noose when the young man had been suspected of patricide. There was no denying it. Aidan's actions had forced Lily into marriage to protect her reputation.

He stepped back, already moving toward the door.

"I am not waiting for the carriage. I shall see you at Ridley House."

His father raised his brows in surprise, but Aidan ignored him, running out of the Abbott townhouse and leaving the door ajar as he headed down the street, away from Grosvenor Square, his long legs devouring the distance. He did not care if he appeared a lunatic, running as though the hounds of hell pursued him. He must see Lily with his own eyes, must confirm she was truly unharmed. Whatever had happened, however it had unfolded, this was his doing. And it was long past time he took responsibility for the part he had played in the risks his innocent sister had undertaken to save another.

This is my fault. This is my fault. This is my fault.

The litany echoed in his mind, beating in time with his thundering heart as Ridley House came into view. Without slowing, he vaulted up the steps and pounded on the heavy wooden door with his fist.

It swung open after a moment to reveal Michaels. The butler's eyes flicked with cool disdain over the disheveled, breathless gentleman on the front step, but Aidan could not spare the moment to care about appearances.

"Where is she?" he demanded, his voice rough with urgency.

Michaels sniffed, but stepped aside with professional detachment. "The drawing room at the top of the stairs."

Aidan entered without acknowledgment. Ridley House loomed around him like a mausoleum, anchored in time with its faded carpets and outdated wallpaper. Dark, brooding portraits lined the corridor. Former barons and their wives, their painted eyes severe and watchful, seemed to pass judgment on the uninvited intrusion.

He made for the dim staircase, the air heavy with age and silence. Etiquette did not even enter his thoughts. Only one thing mattered. Finding Lily. Seeing her. Reassuring himself that she still breathed, still stood upright in the world.

Bounding up the stairs two at a time, he reached the first-floor landing and swung his head from side to side, scanning the doors.

Where is she?

Determining that the drawing room would likely overlook the street, Aidan rushed to the far door without the slightest concern for the measured tread of the butler ascending the stairs behind him. Gripping the handle, he threw the door open.

Across the room, Lily and her husband sat on a settee, his tiny sister pale and trembling, with the new baron's arm protectively encircling her waist.

"Lily!"

She looked up sharply as Aidan strode into the chamber. He knew he must present a wild figure. His coat askew, his boots muddied, and his face flushed from his sprint through the streets of Mayfair.

"Aidan? How did you get here so quickly?"

Even from the doorway, he saw it. The redness around her slender neck. The blackguard had laid hands upon her. Aidan felt something crack inside his chest, an anguish so acute he could scarcely breathe.

It is my fault!

"Ran here … as soon as we heard the news … Left our parents … to take the carriage … Terrifying … to hear you had been attacked. I …" His words came ragged between gasps as he crossed the room and dropped to one knee before her. Taking her hands in his, he gave a shuddering exhale. "This is my fault! If I had taken care of you that night, instead of abandoning you to carouse with my friends …"

Lily frowned and pulled gently on his lapels before leaning forward to enfold him in a soft embrace. "It is not, Aidan. I am well. Gracious, you must have run like the very wind."

"I should never have left you alone."

"But you did. And now I am married." Her smile was small but genuine. "Life goes on."

Aidan groaned. His chest constricted, the weight of culpability pressing heavy upon his ribs. "Until it does not."

"I am safe," she insisted. "See, you are speaking with me at this very moment. The entire matter is settled."

He pulled back slightly to better study her face. From this distance, near enough to see each freckle across her cheeks, he saw the cruel bruising on her throat. It turned his stomach. That anyone could harm a girl so full of life and goodness was beyond comprehension. If the footman still lived, Aidan would not trust himself not to commit violence then and there.

"Is it over? Was the footman the one who committed the murder?"

Brendan Ridley, now Baron of Filminster, cleared his throat. "No, I am afraid not. He claims he was paid to conceal the identity of the killer. At least we know now that it was nobody in the household."

Aidan sprang to his feet. "How do we know it is true?"

Filminster rose too, stepping into the center of the room. "I suppose we shall search his things to find evidence of the payoff."

Aidan's jaw clenched. "If it is true, then there is still a killer out there. Someone who might harm my sister!"

"We will keep our guards to patrol the house—"

"What?"

Filminster looked to Lily, who had sat upright in alarm.

"They need not follow you about," he amended quickly. "Simply take care of our home until we know we are safe. In addition to that, we will have a new housekeeper and maids at the end of the week, so Ridley House will be properly staffed, along with a new lady's maid. It will be far more difficult for any attempt at intrusion once there is a full staff on duty."

Lily turned to Aidan. Her gaze was clear and steady, and though she remained pale, there was steel behind her quiet poise.

Aidan did not fully relax, but he gave a grudging nod. "See that you do, Filminster. My sister is irreplaceable."

CHAPTER ONE

"The aim of the wise is not to secure pleasure, but to avoid pain."

Aristotle

Aidan had not slept for the past two nights. Lily's encounter with the footman had been a rude awakening, a mortifying reflection of his own negligence. The thought of harm befalling his sister was more than he could bear, which was why he now sat in Filminster's study for the third time in as many days.

The room carried the scent of aged leather and the faintest whiff of pipe smoke. Heavy drapes, slightly parted, allowed diffused morning light to fall across dark wood paneling and a towering bookcase lined with calf-bound volumes. A ticking bracket clock on the mantel marked the tension with each precise beat.

"I need your help."

Filminster's declaration punctuated the silence like a dropped decanter, shattering Aidan's fixed gaze.

Aidan straightened in his seat on the embroidered settee, eager to assist. The helplessness clawing at his chest had grown intolerable. Any action, however minor, would be preferable to the gnawing guilt that shadowed his every thought.

Across from him lounged the fool, Lord Julius Trafford, in his usual ostentatious attire. The sheen of purple silk caught the muted light as he stretched his legs across a delicate footstool, utterly unbothered by his surroundings. Aidan's brother-in-law, meanwhile, stood at the window, hands clasped behind his back, silhouetted against the gauzy curtain.

"What has happened? Is Lily safe?" Aidan's voice cracked with urgency. He had been drowning in guilt since abandoning his sister, as though every misfortune that unfolded stemmed from that single wretched decision.

"I have discovered the letter that my … father … wrote. I now know what led to his murder on the night of the coronation."

Lord Trafford flicked at the lapel of his coat, the emerald in his pinky ring catching the light like a flare. He purred in a supercilious tone, "Your father … or your uncle?"

Filminster turned from the window to scowl at his friend. "You know of that?"

Trafford arched one brow in lieu of reply. Aidan leaned forward, his brows drawing tight with indignation. "What is Trafford talking about?"

Filminster sighed. "I suppose the gossip has been circulating, so I might as well speak the truth … The late baron was my uncle who married my mother to save the family from shame. My true father, his elder brother, died weeks before the wedding."

Aidan pulled a face at this unsavory disclosure. "Faugh!"

His brother-in-law chuckled dryly. "Just so."

"May I read the letter?" Trafford had straightened from his lounging position. His indolent air had evaporated, and Aidan glimpsed for a moment what it was that Filminster appreciated about his dolt of a friend.

Filminster pulled a folded page from inside his coat, walking over and handing it to Trafford to read. Aidan watched intently, noting that the other honorary lord, heir to the Earl of Stirling, grew solemn. Trafford whistled through his teeth, looking up to shake his head in disbelief, his affectation of wheat curls bouncing over his cropped brown hair. "This provides a serious motive for murder. This is both wealth and power at stake."

Aidan held out his hand expectantly, and Trafford handed the letter to him without comment. It was covered in splotches of ink, which effectively censored some of the words, as if a censor had taken a quill to it. The parchment was slightly yellowed at the corners and smelled faintly of dust and iron gall ink. But what he read made his blood run cold.

Sir Robert Peel
London, July 19, 1821
Sir,

It has come - - my attention that the true heir to Lord - - - - - - - - has not been acknowledged.

I was speaking with his lordship before the coronation, and he informed me of his recent bout of ill health. He spoke fondly of his youngest brother, informing - - of his strength, intelligence, and wit at great length. There was no mention of his lordship's middle brother, Peter, who you may be aware died near twenty years - - -.

Peter and I attended Oxford together, - - - his death was tragic - - - unexp- - - - -. I have thought of him often over the years, which is why I feel the need to pass this information - - - - - -u.

Before departing England, Peter married a wom- - of Catholic descent. She convert- - - - - - - - - were married - - - - - Church of England, before leaving our shores. I maintained correspondence with him until his death. He had written just months before his death to inform me of the birth of his son.

I cannot say for certain where the boy and his mother are - - - - - all these years, but he would be the true heir and I implore you to look into th- - matter. - - - - - - - - - is the true heir to the title of - - - - - and his father's legacy cannot be ignored.

I understand the trials of being a second son, and I cann- - allow this matter to stand. Whether - - - - terrible injustice is a mistake due to ignorance of the child Peter sired, or a deliberate obfuscation of the facts, I must speak on my friend's behalf. His son is the true heir and must be found immediately. I will locate our shared correspondence when I return to Somerset and have them forwarded to - - - - - - - - - - -.

J. Ridley, Baron of Filminster

Aidan absorbed what he had just read before slowly exhaling, the implications setting in. The letter crackled slightly as he adjusted his grip, its brittle edges catching the sleeve of his coat. "Lily is in serious danger if the killer believes his secret might be contained within the walls of Ridley House."

Trafford snorted. "And the culprit would be correct, considering the letter you are holding."

"There is insufficient information to reveal his identity!" Aidan's protest was met with a twist of Trafford's lips.

"There is enough. An elderly lord, suffering from a recent bout of ill health, with a younger brother named Peter who died some twenty years ago, and an even younger brother set to inherit his title. Who has likely killed the baron to conceal the knowledge of the true heir in order to secure his inheritance? It drastically reduces the number of suspects."

"Precisely," Filminster responded. "Lily and I spent last evening and this morning comparing a recent copy of *Debrett's* to a copy from thirty years ago to compile a list of peers. The runner, Briggs, is investigating what happened to each of the Peters to learn the circumstances of their deaths. Thus far, we have a list of six heirs who might fit the description, which is why I need your help."

Aidan was brought back to the declaration that had started this conversation. Filminster needed his assistance to secure Lily's safety. "What do you need?"

Filminster cleared his throat, twisting the toe of his boot on the bright Aubusson rug adorning his study floor while his dark chestnut curls fell forward over his brow. The room was quiet but for the creak of a leather chair as Trafford shifted beside him.

"It is much to ask ..."

Trafford smirked. "That has not stopped you before."

"This is different, Julius. My bride is in danger." Filminster inhaled deeply before continuing. "If anything happened to Lily, I would never forgive myself."

Nor would I.

Aidan could simply not imagine how he would ever recover from putting Lily at risk. If harm befell her, his guilt would consume him entirely, and there would be nothing in his bleak future to console his soul. This was a matter of life and death.

With that realization, Aidan reached a decision. It was time to stop resisting this new relationship with his sister's husband. They needed to band together for Lily. His sweet young sister deserved their cooperation and protection. Rising to his feet, he interrupted the *tête-à-tête* between Filminster and Trafford.

"Whatever you need, I will do it."

Filminster's brandy eyes flickered to Aidan, and he nodded. "Thank you ... Aidan."

Trafford heaved a heavy sigh. "I am in. What is next?"

Returning to the window, Filminster leaned against the deep sill carved with floral scrollwork. The light streaming in fell across the gleam of the ormolu clock beside him. "I need your help to investigate these six men. Lily and I are still considered scandalous for our supposed tryst on the night of the coronation. Although the scandal is abating now that we have wed, it is difficult to be discreet when all eyes are upon us. You two gentlemen, as single young bucks about Town, will be welcomed into the homes of polite society with high hopes you might make a match with their daughters or nieces. That access will allow you to search for information that might shed light on their involvement."

Aidan rubbed a hand over his face. The fine wool of his coat scratched his jaw. In the normal course of things, he would never agree to such unethical conduct. Gaining access under false pretenses was not the behavior of a man of character.

But this is for Lily.

He accepted the truth of it. A man of character would take steps to correct his mistakes, regardless of what he might be required to do. It was a matter of restoring his honor, and if he needed to dirty his hands for the greater good, then so be it.

"Where is the list?"

~

FREDERICK SMYTHE WAS the most irritating of men, Gwen decided, resisting the urge to clench her fists and stamp her slippered foot against the Axminster carpet beneath her.

"We cannot afford it, Papa! I am five and twenty! On the shelf! A spinster! Pray tell, what is the point of spending money on yet another ball when none of the young men wish to dance with me?"

Her father's lips curled into his customary grin. The one that had, for decades, dissolved the resistance of family, friends, and fellow politicians alike. Gwen steeled herself not to be affected by his charm. The late-afternoon light streaming through the parlor's tall windows gilded his silvering temples and caught the dust motes hanging in the still air.

"It is not the time to give up, Gwendolyn. It is only a matter of time before you meet a gentleman who appreciates your wit and grace."

Gwen could not help but snort. "Grace?" Twisting her face, she sang the refrain from her youth, voice dipped in mockery. "Gwen, Gwen, the Spotted Giraffe!"

Her father's grin faded. "I curse myself to this day for sending you to that school. Those harpies destroyed your confidence, but I see a great beauty when I gaze upon you, Gwendolyn. Your mother stole my very heart from my chest the moment I beheld her. And once she quoted Homer to me in Ancient Greek ..." He raised a hand to his chest, as though steadying a memory that had stirred too sharply. His eyes softened, gaze drifting toward the fireless hearth. "I shall never forget a moment of our time together."

Gwen felt tears prickling. Lifting a hand, she dabbed at her eyes with a handkerchief, giving a discreet sniff. The scent of lemon polish from the rosewood escritoire nearby mingled with old paper and dried lavender from the potpourri bowl on the mantel. "Mama was majestic."

"As are you, daughter."

She shook her head, rejecting the notion that she was the beauty her mother had been. "I am a ginger!"

"A Titian red."

"And spotted!"

"Delightfully freckled."

"Mama was an elegant auburn, Papa. I am a gangly, spotted ginger!"

Her father shook his head in denial. "You are glorious, and your mother would agree."

Gwen fell silent, biting her lower lip. She wished her mother were here with them now to settle their argument. "Mama did not like to waste money."

"You are not a waste of money. The right man will recognize your worth and value. We shall join forces with another family and grow our resources, for your future and for Gareth."

Gwen smiled at the mention of her younger brother. Having him home for the summer had revealed how quickly he was growing up with his trousers too short by the end of the month. It had been a poignant moment to wave him goodbye from the stone steps when he returned to Eton to continue his studies. "Gareth's grasp of Latin and Greek is impressive. Mama would be delighted."

"As you will be one day when you have children of your own."

Longing rose in Gwen's chest. A raw, unspoken ache that she squashed down ruthlessly. If the past few years had taught her anything, it was that no man would ever wed her. Nay, she was to be a spinster. Her only hope of progeny was to adopt a foundling to dote on. A child to whom she could pass on the love of learning, just as her mother had done with her and Gareth.

Since recent events had brought home the fragile, fleeting nature of life, and the pressing need to pursue one's dreams while still able, Gwen had undertaken a careful evaluation of what truly mattered. She planned to seek a foundling to adopt once her father admitted defeat. His lofty visions of her grand union were merely dreams. Frederick Smythe was tilting at windmills if he thought an honorable gentleman would ever take notice of Gwen, Gwen, the Spotted Giraffe.

The few men who had displayed interest were not to be considered. It was not Mr. Spalding's thinning hair or receding chin that ruled him out, but the many times he had misattributed Socrates that ensured she could never marry him. The thought of being irritated by his intellectual failings for the rest of her days was simply too much to bear.

Mr. Rutledge had been pleasant, courteous even, if a bit on the older side, but his sole topics of conversation were fox-hunting and hounds. Gwen found both subjects tolerable only in moderation. She had once endured an entire afternoon tea in Hertfordshire listening to the merits of different types of hunting horns, and she had not recovered since.

Gwen wanted what her parents had shared, a meeting of the minds as much as the hearts. And if hearts were out of the question, then at the very least, she required a sharp mind. An intelligent husband to father her children. Otherwise, she would prefer to remain alone.

"No wedding, no children."

Her tone was sharp, clipped by frustration and cool resolve. Frederick Smythe was a dreamer, and she could not afford to be drawn in by his illusions. She would not don armor and take up a lance to joust the sails of a wind machine, convincing herself there were giants where only harmless contraptions creaked in the wind.

Her father turned to her, his sympathetic blue eyes gentle. He stood no taller than Gwen herself, both of them reaching a formidable five feet nine inches, an inheritance from some long-legged Smythe ancestor whose portrait still hung in the stairwell. "You are lovely, Gwendolyn. The right man will appreciate you and provide you with the security you deserve, while you will provide him with a worthy and challenging partnership."

Gwen looked down at the toes of her kid-leather slippers, their soft blue bows barely visible beneath the hem of her dove-gray morning gown. Her shoulders heaved with a heartfelt sigh. She wanted to believe her father. She truly did. But hard-won experience told her he was deluded, blinded by paternal love to her many perceived shortcomings. Mama had been a great beauty *and* an excellent scholar. Gwen had inherited one of those traits, and it was not the one that could be seen in the reflection of a looking glass.

"Papa, we cannot waste money on such extravagances."

Her father strolled over to his desk, a man dapper for his years. His youthful energy, barely diminished by time, radiated from his every movement. A reflection of the strong interests that animated his days. The sharp cut of his charcoal superfine coat and matching trousers, along with his pristine white linen neckcloth and gleaming shirt cuffs, spoke to his fastidious nature. Yet he possessed an easy manner that endeared him to most people, be they tradesmen or titled lords.

The desk itself, a handsome pedestal model in polished walnut, bore neat stacks of correspondence and a half-written letter in his elegant copperplate hand. Though he managed their finances with considerable care, as the third son of a baron he had inherited no great fortune. They were not a wealthy family and could scarcely afford the lavish ball he insisted on holding each year in her honor, even as the male members of the *ton* continued to overlook her presence with almost comical regularity.

This brought to mind the women who tittered behind their fans, their high-pitched amusement barely muffled by lace and feathers, giggling at her unfashionable appearance, her statuesque height, and her frankly unrepentant intellect.

Gwen sighed, wondering how to explain to her idealistic father that she was a poor investment. How her mother had managed to be a graceful beauty despite her scarlet locks remained a mystery to her only daughter.

Mama was unique. Special.

And Gwen was merely an oddity.

A fact that Frederick Smythe refused to accept.

"Please, Papa. The money can be used for Oxford when Gareth is ready. It has been seven years, and I am still a wallflower. What could possibly happen this year that would be different from any other year?"

Her father cocked his head, his lips quirking into his characteristic grin. The amber paperweight on his desk caught the sun as it shifted, casting a flicker of golden light across the green leather blotter. "This year you could encounter the right man. The one who recognizes the perfection of my only daughter and falls at her feet, defeated by her magnificence."

Gwen burst into laughter despite her resolve to steel herself against her father's whimsies. She finally found the breath to respond.

"You are incorrigible, Papa."

His blue eyes twinkled in the late-afternoon light. "*Nullum magnum ingenium sine mixtura dementiae fuit* ... There is no great genius without a touch of madness."

Gwen shook her head. "Aristotle will not sweeten my temper, old man."

"Ah, but we both know that is a lie."

She bit her lip to prevent a smile, unable to argue with her father's claim. It appeared there would be no dissuading him. The ball would proceed, as declared over breakfast, and her visit to his study had not achieved a single, solitary thing.

CHAPTER
TWO

"The ideal man bears the accidents of life with dignity and grace, making the best of circumstances."

Aristotle

AUGUST 13, 1821

The past ten days in Trafford's company had been excruciating. Together, they had attended several social events, to Aidan's increasing chagrin, the pursuit of information notwithstanding. Trafford was not the kind of companion he wished to be associated with, but they had been seen together the length and breadth of Mayfair, nodding to matrons, bowing to debutantes, and shaking hands with dandies, while Aidan had been forced to endure the other man's antics with clenched teeth.

Currently, Aidan stood at the shadowed corner of a

narrow street, the limewash walls of the townhouse behind him cool against his shoulder. He observed the home of Mr. Frederick Smythe amid the loud clatter of carriage wheels, the occasional hiss of steam from coach horses, and the muffled notes of a pianoforte drifting faintly from the lit windows.

The night sky was adorned with silvery clouds and a large full moon, but from his vantage point in the street, his view of the magical evening unfolding above was largely obscured by overhanging eaves and the high hedgerows lining the Smythes' drive.

"How do you plan to get in without an invitation?"

Trafford waved his hand in dismissal, a practiced flick of indifference, though his gaze was sharp as he assessed the arriving guests. His gold silk tails shimmered faintly under the gas lamps. Aidan growled in irritation, his jaw tight. Of all the men in London, must he endure this preening peacock?

Nevertheless, he stepped back, boots scuffing lightly on the uneven cobbles, granting the other man the space he had requested.

This is for Lily.

The reminder helped to quell his resentment. He was no longer a soldier, but it felt very much like he had been ordered to serve as batman to the most aggravating officer in the regiment. He had attempted to question Lily about Trafford's involvement, but she had only chattered cheerfully about the new books she had ordered for the library, as if she had not faced death and injury less than a fortnight earlier.

"If Brendan trusts Trafford, then so do I."

That had been her only reply, which meant, surely, that she did not know the fop all that well.

Aidan cracked his knuckles, an old habit from his cavalry days, and began pacing behind Trafford, awaiting the oaf's direction with reluctant forbearance.

Suddenly, Trafford broke the silence. "I see my great-aunt, Gertrude, with her husband." With that, he took off toward the Smythe residence, his gold silk tails fluttering behind him like a banner on a battlefield.

Aidan hesitated, then cursed under his breath and followed his now-constant companion. Trafford wove through the line of carriages gathered in the crescent-shaped drive, his kid-leather shoes quick over the gravel. He skipped up to an elderly couple just descending from a town coach with polished lamps and a worn crest.

"Aunty!"

A wizened old lady with stooped shoulders in blue silk squinted up at her nephew before clapping her hands in delight. The plume on her turban wobbled with the motion.

"Julius, my boy!"

Trafford leaned down, accepting a trembling hand that emerged from beneath an embroidered shawl. She pinched his cheek between arthritic fingers, beaming with pleasure. Behind her stood the husband, an equally ancient man clad in old-fashioned breeches, white silk stockings, and buckled shoes that looked to big for the spindly legs which did little to disguise the march of time.

"What are you doing here, boy?"

Aidan suppressed the urge to roll his eyes. Trafford was anything but a boy. The man had clearly dallied with numerous women of the *ton*, attired like a coxcomb with far too much allowance wasted on foppery. Only a nearsighted great-aunt could affectionately view him as a boy.

"I was just walking by with my friend." Trafford

gestured in Aidan's direction. Aidan gritted his teeth. They were on a small but elegant estate near the Thames, private property, which belied the notion that they happened to just be passing by. "Are you attending an event?"

"It is the Smythe ball. Frederick has a daughter he has been attempting to marry off for years. She is a dear girl, but the boys do not like her, I am afraid. A wallflower."

"That is a pity. I was hoping to catch up, but if you are otherwise occupied ..." Trafford trailed off with deliberation, baiting his great-aunt.

"Come with us, Julius! Frederick will be delighted to have such strapping young men in attendance."

Without hesitation, Trafford joined arms with his relation and assisted her up the front steps, lit by twin lanterns bracketed to the columns. Aidan exhaled through his nose and followed them in with the frail husband, resisting the temptation to offer his own arm as the gentleman shuffled upward with careful, halting steps.

Soon, they stood in the long receiving line. Trafford chattered brightly to his great-aunt while her husband stared blankly about, as if wading through foggy recollections.

From his considerable height, Aidan could see over the heads of the crowd. Up ahead, his attention caught on a statuesque redhead standing beside the host, a tidy gentleman in his fifties with an unremarkable but pleasant face.

The young woman was ... luminous.

She stood with quiet poise, her bearing noble without artifice. She might have appeared to step down from the friezes of the Parthenon, like one of the Elgin Marbles recently installed in the British Museum. A veritable goddess of antiquity with Titian hair wound in artful curls, a classical profile, and skin like cream left out under moonlight. But it was the scattering of freckles dusting her décolletage—innocent, sun-kissed, and utterly unpolished—that ensnared Aidan's interest.

He had always harbored a fondness for red hair, but this ... this was something else entirely. Her tall, willowy form was clothed in a gown of ivory silk that clung modestly to her Grecian frame, the folds recalling the drapery of statuary. There was nothing theatrical about her elegance. It seemed the natural expression of a woman both spirited and serene.

This was the woman society had deemed a wallflower?

The men of London must be blind.

Rubbing a hand over his shaven chin, Aidan felt a surprising surge of anticipation. For once, the tedium of another London ball had vanished, replaced by the delightful realization that when he reached the end of the receiving line, he would at last be presented to the resplendent goddess who had stolen the air from the room.

"It is time to go."

Aidan slowly comprehended that the statement had been directed at him. Trafford was peering his way with a questioning look, his brow raised in mild curiosity. He bobbed his head toward a side hallway leading away from the receiving line.

Disappointment settled over Aidan like a damp cloak. His spirits, which had lifted in a rare moment of wonder, plummeted once more. The recollection of Lily's peril came rushing back. Her vulnerability, the danger that still lingered. Of course he could not afford the indulgence of an introduction to the young woman at the end of the hall. For the briefest moment, he had allowed himself to forget the gravity of their purpose. But it was not to be.

With a last glance toward the glowing figure in ivory silk, he turned and followed Trafford away from the chattering guests and gilt-framed mirrors of the reception chamber.

Soon, they stood together in a dimly lit library, its paneled walls lined with old calf-bound volumes, the scent of beeswax polish and aged paper thick in the air.

"Do you have any notion how ridiculous you look in this ..." Aidan threw out a hand toward Trafford's resplendent gold coat.

"Now, now, Little Breeches. There is no need to tell Banbury stories ... I am unduly handsome in my brocade, as we both well know."

Aidan snorted in disgust, though it escaped more like a sigh. It was a farce to be engaged in this investigation with the clownish Trafford, but the choice had been removed from his hands. Filminster's other trusted associates, the Earl of Saunton and the Duke of Halmesbury, were married men. Trafford, absurd as he was, remained the only bachelor man Brendan trusted to help ensure Lily's safety.

Considering that Aidan had only recently returned from his Grand Tour, he had no long-standing allies to put forward. There was no time to vet new ones.

"Did a certain young woman capture your eye out in the hall?" Trafford's tone turned sly. "You seemed rather ... bemused."

Aidan looked away, unwilling to discuss the quiet astonishment he had felt upon seeing, he presumed, Miss Smythe. It would be folly to pursue any introduction to a debutante whose father might yet be involved in murder. The entire notion was preposterous.

"Is Aunty not surprised at our departure?" he asked coolly. "I thought you were to catch up?" The sneer was a thinly veiled attempt at changing the subject, and Trafford's grin revealed he had noted it at once.

"Aunty will quite forget she saw me tonight by the time she reaches the head of the line. She and Uncle are easily distracted these days. I saw an opportunity to proceed, and I took it."

Aidan was relieved the subject of Miss Smythe had been dropped. He was still rather shaken by the sheer force of his reaction. The memory lingered like a phantom sensation. The elegant profile, the freckled skin. But there would be time to contemplate such matters later. Much later, and only after they had completed this wretched errand.

This was not a time for musings, but for action.

"What is the plan?"

"I think I shall wander about and gather information while you search Smythe's office."

Aidan wanted to argue. Sneaking through a gentleman's private places was not his idea of an excellent or honorable pastime, but he could not deny that Trafford was better at soliciting information. Not least because the idiot seemed to know almost the entire *ton* and their servants, with the exception of marriageable misses. Aidan hated being disingenuous and violating peoples' trust by searching their homes, but ...

This is for Lily. To keep her safe.

His father would have definite opinions about what Aidan had been doing these past two weeks, which was why Lord Moreland had not been informed of their informal enquiry into six heirs. To date, they had managed to rule out only one of the men on the list. The gentleman in question had been holed up in the country with his family after a serious fall, so could not have been the murderous visitor on the night of the coronation.

There were six men to investigate, but Smythe was the man at the top of their list. He was the heir to a baron, which made him a promising suspect because the murdered Baron of Filminster had been seated with other barons the day of his murder.

There were whispers of Smythe selling off assets in the clubs, and Filminster had pointed out that a suspect with some sort of financial difficulty could certainly be driven to a passionate act such as murder if the late baron had threatened his future inheritance.

"I will meet you in the ballroom when I am done," Aidan murmured, his voice low and grim.

Trafford nodded, too easily. "Have fun, Little Breeches. You might learn interesting things when you search through a man's private belongings."

Aidan frowned, unsure what Trafford was alluding to, but before he could respond, he was left alone, the ostentatious golden tails of the other man's coat the last thing one could see from the dim interior of the room.

Sighing heavily, Aidan walked over to the door to peek his head out and look about. Where would Smythe's private study be?

Gwen's cheeks ached from the smile fixed on her face. For the better part of an hour, she had stood beside her father, welcoming every guest into their home with unflagging politeness. Her posture was correct, her greetings faultless, and her tone precisely modulated. Every inch the dutiful daughter of the house.

Most of the gentlemen had barely acknowledged her presence, offering her the kind of distracted bow reserved for a footstool or a fern. Their interest had been reserved entirely for her father, whose considerable charm and irreverent wit never failed to endear him to his peers.

The ladies had been little better. Many had passed her with the faintest tilt of their heads, their painted smiles thinning behind fans of ivory and lace. A few older matrons had stopped, their eyes alight with the kind of kindness that felt like vinegar in an open wound. They had inquired, pityingly, whether anyone had begun to court her yet.

Gwen would have preferred outright rudeness. The extended conversations about her lack of prospects, delivered with matronly concern, were far worse. They left her struggling to steer the discussion elsewhere, her facial muscles straining under the weight of polite responses and feigned good humor.

How she longed to be ordinary.

Her appearance, whatever its merits, only ever served to draw attention, and not the sort she desired. She stood too tall, with the wrong shade of hair and an outspoken fondness for scholarship. It made her a spectacle. A curiosity to some, a cautionary tale to others.

Once, years ago, she had dreamed of making a match despite her peculiarities. Of finding someone who might value her wit, her mind, even her freckles. But it had taken only a Season or two to disabuse her of such notions. Her illusions had been stripped from her like petals from a flower, one indifferent glance at a time.

She had wished her mother were still alive to guide her through the ordeal. But by the time Gwen had been old enough to enter society, the family had already lost its brightest light. And Gwen had been left to navigate the treacherous currents of the *ton* alone.

She had learned to protect herself from scrutiny, to craft

a mask so carefully applied that even she believed it, at times. She no longer noticed the sidelong glances, the whispers, the pity.

Except ... it still hurt.

Gwen skirted the edge of the ballroom, her slippers soundless against the polished parquet as she wove past gilt-framed mirrors and marble-topped console tables. She admitted the truth to herself, as painful as it was.

After all these years, she remained disappointed. Disappointed that she had never found her match.

Her parents had shared a great, enduring love. When her mother fell ill, her father had made a solemn vow to care for Gwen and Gareth. They had cloistered themselves at home during those final months, tending only to each other, savoring what little time remained. Mama had passed peacefully, having secured a promise from each of them that they would attend to one another always.

And they had kept that vow.

Papa, Gwen, and Gareth had made every effort to remain a close-knit family. It had become their unspoken way of honoring her mother's memory. Gareth wrote weekly from Eton, and she and Papa would read his letters together in the drawing room after breakfast, sometimes aloud, sometimes in quiet reflection. Gwen penned their replies, recording little household events, snippets of news, and the small details their mother would have wanted them to share.

Mama would have been proud.

If only Gwen had made a match, she might now have children of her own. Sweet, clever babes who would carry on that legacy of love and learning. But it was not to be. If her mother were still alive, Gwen would have sought her counsel on how to navigate the *ton* with dignity and hope.

But after seven failed Seasons, it was clear that she would never wed.

It might have been easier to relinquish that dream had her father stopped insisting on another turn on the marriage mart each year. He simply refused to believe that his daughter was undesirable to the gentlemen of society.

She watched the dancers twirling beneath the chandeliers, a flurry of silk and muslin, the women's gowns painted in peacock hues and pale pastels. The gentlemen, by contrast, were adorned in their regulation blacks and midnight blues, the fine cut of their coats whispering wealth and privilege.

And yet, irony remained her only true companion at these balls. Her own father's events, no less. At her own balls, she barely danced.

A few of Papa's cronies, gallant and graying, sometimes filled a spot or two on her card out of affection for Frederick Smythe. But on most nights, she was fortunate to secure half a card, if that.

Gwen glanced down now at the delicate rectangle tied to her wrist with a ribbon of pale satin. Three dances remained unclaimed. It was enough time to take some air on the terrace, which would spare her the pitying stares of chattering guests and allow her to recover her composure.

Decision made, she began weaving through the press of lace and brocade near the perimeter, her hand gently brushing aside a cluster of overzealous debutantes as she made for the tall French doors at the far end of the room.

"Miss Smythe!"

She hesitated.

Every instinct urged her to pretend she had not heard and slip outside, but her mother had not raised her to be discourteous. With a practiced, gracious breath, she turned to find Lady Gertrude Hays peering up at her, cheeks flushed, feather bobbing in her turban.

The old lady was kindly, but incurably garrulous. Gwen's heart sank.

"Are you enjoying your evening, Lady Hays?"

The woman bobbed her head, her hair as white as snow and gathered in a coiffure nearly two decades out of fashion. Thick strands were pinned in loops about her head, and a once-stylish turban of faded blue silk clung valiantly to her crown. From it, a blue plume jutted at a reckless angle, trembling with each movement and threatening to poke her in the eye.

Gwen smiled softly and, with careful fingers, reached out to straighten the feather before Lady Hays did herself an injury. The old woman beamed at her touch.

"My great-nephew is here. I should like to introduce him to you, if I may." She squinted into the throng of dancers and circulating guests, her gaze clouded by age. After several moments of peering, she turned back to Gwen with a sigh. "I am afraid I cannot see him. Have you met him? Lord Julius Trafford? He is a dear boy."

Gwen shook her head, though Trafford's name was far from unfamiliar. His reputation for fashion and roguish pursuits was well known among society. What he was doing at her father's ball was a mystery. Perhaps he had taken a sudden interest in one of their guests?

"I have not had the pleasure, my lady."

"I shall locate him," Lady Hays declared with determination, the feather now once again wavering precariously.

With great relief, Gwen watched her go, her skirts trailing behind her as she disappeared into the crowd like a homing pigeon set upon its mission.

This, at last, was her moment to escape.

Gathering her ivory skirts in both hands, Gwen strode purposefully toward the tall terrace doors, propriety be hanged. Her steps were swift, decidedly unladylike, but the guests, engaged in their conversations and dancing, scarcely noticed her passage. And if they did, well, she doubted their opinions of her could sink any lower.

Reaching the doors, she wrapped slender fingers around the brass handle and opened them with an eager sweep. The music and chatter faded behind her as she stepped outside and drew the door gently closed.

Several guests were already enjoying the night air, leaning against the carved stone balustrade that overlooked her father's tidy gardens. Gwen gave them a polite nod before turning away, seeking a stretch of solitude.

Rounding the corner of the terrace, she stopped, startled into stillness by the glory above.

A full moon hung low and heavy in the sky, its light bathing the terrace in silver. The clouds, fat and plush as goose down, glowed with reflected luminescence, while countless stars sparkled across the midnight canvas. The fragrance of night-blooming jasmine drifted from the garden below, and a cool breeze whispered against her skin.

The sight stole her breath.

For a moment, her bruised feelings and weariness from the evening fell away. The sheer beauty of the night stirred something in her. A longing, tender and unspoken. A yearning for what she had never had.

It was the sort of night meant for lovers. For whispered secrets and tender laughter beneath the stars. A night for shared dreams and clasped hands, for the kind of intimacy that poetry dared to capture but never quite could.

Gwen sighed, her chest rising and falling in time with the breeze. The loveliness of the evening wrapped around her like a silk shawl, beautiful and weightless and tinged with sorrow.

Every young woman ought to share an evening like this with someone who adored her. At least once.

But for Gwen, it seemed such things were not to be.

CHAPTER THREE

"Love is born into every human being; it calls back the halves of our original nature together; it tries to make one out of two and heal the wound of human nature. Each of us, then, is a matching half of a human whole ... and each of us is always seeking the half that matches him."

Plato

"Plato is dear to me, but dearer still is truth."

Aristotle

Aidan was fortunate in discovering Frederick Smythe's study at the end of the corridor Trafford had indicated, only two doors down from the library, its heavy oak door partially ajar. The room lay in complete darkness, cloaked in the hush of early evening. After a few moments fumbling among unfamiliar furniture,

Aidan located a taper and managed to coax a flame from the tinderbox positioned atop a narrow cabinet near the door.

The single candle he lit sent warm flickers across the paneled walls and gilded frames of sailing ships that lined them. Holding it carefully aloft, Aidan advanced into the chamber, the scent of old vellum and furniture wax meeting his senses. A well-used desk stood near the cold hearth, and he made his way to it, seating himself in the creaking chair with a grunt of discomfort. Smythe, several inches shorter than he, evidently favored a lower seat, and Aidan's long legs were ill-accommodated by the narrow kneehole.

Opening the desk's right-hand drawer, Aidan withdrew a stack of loose pages, fanning them into the candlelight atop the blotting mat. As he thumbed through them, a low whistle escaped his lips.

Bills of sale.

Paintings. *Objets d'art*. Even a modest parcel of land just north of London. Thousands of pounds, perhaps tens of thousands, all liquidated in the past six months alone.

The gossip surrounding Smythe's financial instability had not been exaggerated. What could compel a man to divest himself of so much? Gambling debts? Imminent bankruptcy? Some hidden folly?

Aidan's pulse quickened. Here, perhaps, was the motive they had sought. Smythe's desperation for funds could easily have driven him to silence Filminster's uncle, perhaps fatally.

If solid proof of the act could be secured and the man arrested, Lily's danger might at last be dispelled, and this harrowing chapter brought to an end.

Drawing the inkstand closer, he selected a sharpened

quill and found a fresh leaf of foolscap in the drawer. Methodically, he began recording the entries. Names of purchasers, prices rendered, descriptions of goods, and any addresses noted. The faint scratch of quill on paper echoed in the still room.

This list would be invaluable. Briggs, the runner, could trace each transaction. And perhaps, at the end of this paper trail, they might find the evidence they needed to unravel the truth.

Finding the pounce, Aidan sprinkled the fine powder across the fresh ink, watching as it dulled the sheen of the words. With a careful breath, he blew it off, then folded the sheet with precision and slid it into the inner pocket of his coat. His lurking had borne fruit. Perhaps they had found their man. It would be a profound relief to conclude these clandestine endeavors, which continually gnawed at his sense of honor. He was not fashioned for deceit. Such duplicity sat ill with him, the ethical implications an ever-present undercurrent of unrest.

He returned the bills of sale to the drawer with methodical care, then repositioned the inkstand and quill precisely where he had found them. Producing a linen handkerchief from his waistcoat, he wiped away any smudges or impressions his presence might have left upon the surface. Rising, he pushed the chair gently back beneath the desk and padded across the thick Axminster rug toward the cabinet by the door. There, he replaced the candlestick, then leaned down to extinguish the flame with a breath that stirred the air but left the silence undisturbed.

At the threshold, he paused. Muffled voices echoed from the corridor beyond, drawing nearer. His pulse quickened.

Turning, he scanned the darkened room now bathed in

silver by the moonlight pouring through tall windows across the chamber. As his eyes adjusted, he discerned that the casements were in fact French doors leading to a terrace. The voices had grown more distinct, male and female tones, strolling and unsuspecting. He must act swiftly.

He crossed the room in a few long strides, heart thumping as he tested the latch. He looked left and right, checking for any witness to his emergence.

Some thirty feet along the stone terrace, a lone woman stood, haloed by moonlight, her attention wholly absorbed by the vista before her. Aidan inhaled slowly, sending up a prayer that the door hinges had been seen to recently. If they creaked, all would be undone.

He eased the door open, mercifully silent, and stepped out into the night. The air was cooler here, faintly scented by the clipped box hedges below. He drew the door closed behind him and moved to the balustrade, laying his hands upon the stone. It still held the gentle warmth of the departed sun, grounding him in the stillness of the hour.

Lifting his eyes, he beheld the sky above, vast and serene. The moon reigned sovereign, its glow turning the clouds to luminous gauze. In that still moment, he was nothing more than a man in awe of the heavens.

To his right, the young woman remained unmoving. Her profile was a study in elegance. The soft line of her jaw, the delicate architecture of her nose. All rendered in perfect relief by the moon's pale glow. She had not yet seen him.

She must surely be Miss Smythe. The same composed young woman from the receiving line, now revealed in ethereal majesty.

Without conscious decision, he spoke aloud the words that arose unbidden in his soul.

"Who can know heaven except by its gifts?"

She started slightly, a soft intake of breath the only evidence of her surprise. She did not turn to face him, yet her voice emerged clear and thoughtful.

"And who can find out God, unless the man who is himself an emanation from God?"

Aidan blinked, momentarily unmoored. "You have read *Astronomica*?"

"Marcus Manilius was one of the greatest poets of Ancient Rome."

Her voice, low and lyrical, held the quiet assurance of a mind well-trained. Aidan's breath caught. A scholar. A thinker. A woman of intellect and grace.

The folded list in his breast pocket mocked his romantic optimism. Did he truly believe that the heavens would reveal the other half of his soul to be the child of the man responsible for the attack on his sister two weeks earlier?

Yet, how else did one explain this synchronization, this attraction he was feeling for the young lady? He had traveled the realm and the Continent and never encountered such feminine perfection as a divinity who quoted the great minds of the ancient world. How was such a woman unwed? Undesired by the bucks of the *ton*? Was she surrounded by deaf and blind imbeciles?

If only ...

Drawn by forces beyond conscious thought, he stepped to her side. They stood together, shoulder to shoulder, as silent witnesses to the majesty of the night. His subterfuge forgotten, he beheld her as one might venerate a sacred vision, overwhelmed by reverence, by yearning, and by the unbearable ache of possibility.

Gwen was not accustomed to tall, striking gentlemen seeking her out, yet here one stood, mere inches away, his presence a quiet thunder in the hush of night. Perhaps it was the dramatic beauty of the evening that had drawn him forth. Certainly, he could not know that he was standing beside *Gwen, Gwen the Spotted Giraffe*, whose freckles were the bane of her existence and whose mirror offered no illusions of fashionable appeal.

Only moments earlier, she had sent up a silent plea to the stars, wishing she might share a moment like this, only once, with a gentleman who could see her, truly see her. And now, as though the very heavens had listened, he had appeared from the shadows, summoned by poetry and moonlight. Since their peculiar exchange on *Astronomica*, he had said nothing more, and she dared not speak for fear the enchantment would unravel.

She exhaled softly, accepting this improbable moment for what it was, a fleeting marvel spun from moonbeams and wishes. Clearly, the man believed he stood beside someone else. Likely, in the dim light, he assumed her to be a statuesque brunette with alabaster skin, not the freckled, flame-haired oddity she had always been. Still, she would not correct him. Not yet. Not when this singular moment was the nearest she had ever come to romance.

The fear of ruining the moment had her squeezing the stone beneath her fingers, as she clung to the phantasy that an eligible man wished to share the view with her. She was terrified she would ruin the moment and it would end before she had gathered every sense, every second, that she could before returning to the solitude of her real life.

Not only was he physically impressive, from what she could see from the corner of her eye, but he had perfectly translated the Latin poem and attributed it to the rightful source. He was a true scholar to engage in such a discussion, and for just a fleeting second, Gwen dared to believe that this was the man who her father had promised would appear. She released her cynicism to allow the magic of possibilities to enter her heart.

It is to savor the moment, she told herself. But despite her pragmatic nature, deep in her soul she felt that something unexpected was unfolding.

From the corner of her eye, she saw that his hand had come to rest next to hers. It was the tiniest fraction of an inch away, so close she could feel the heat emanating from his glove to soak into her skin. If she had the courage to move, she could touch him, but she was too afraid it would end their interlude before it had begun. She willed her hand to remain in place.

It was without surprise when she felt his large hand extend to cover hers, and she accepted that she was dreaming this entire encounter. That soon she would awake to find out she had dozed off on the terrace and imagined this entire circumstance but, in the meanwhile, she would bury herself in the dream. If only every slumber included such wonderful happenings.

The man gently tugged at her hand, turning to pull her into his arms ever so slowly as if to give her the opportunity to protest, and Gwen was amazed at the realism of this apparition. She could feel the strength of his arms wrapping around her waist and shoulders, smell the leather of his boots and his freshly laundered linen, as he pulled her against his hard body. Tilting her chin, she watched him lower his head and accepted the press of his lips against hers, sighing in pleasure when she was enveloped in masculinity.

She lifted her arms and let them rest lightly around his neck, not pulling, not pressing ... simply being. He drew her a breath closer, her form nestled against the solid warmth of his chest. The sensation made her dizzy, not with fear, but with wonder. Was this what it meant to be wanted? Desired ... not as a convenience, not as a social match, but for who she was in this single, sacred instant?

He leaned his head to hers, his cheek brushing hers, and Gwen inhaled sharply as he breathed deeply, just above her temple.

"Citrus ..." he murmured, his voice a low, reverent sigh.

The single word sent a ripple down her spine, not because of its boldness but because of its gentleness. It was not lewd. It was admiration. And she basked in it.

The tip of his nose brushed the curve of her ear, and the whisper of his breath made her tremble. Gwen tilted her head slightly, allowing the contact, her skin thrumming with sensation. She did not move farther. She did not have to. The thrill came from being cherished, not consumed.

His hands settled more fully at her back, fingers splayed in a protective gesture rather than one of possession. She felt safe. Seen. The very air between them crackled, not with impropriety, but with the possibility of something precious and real.

Then ... a sound.

The distinct creak of a door opening onto the terrace shattered the stillness. They froze.

Gwen's breath became shallow, her chest rising and falling in a quiet panic. Not from passion, but from dread. They parted slightly, their eyes locked. He shut his eyes briefly, as though in regret, then looked past her shoulder, his body tensing with recognition.

Please let it be her father. Please let it be no one important.

But as his eyes focused, Gwen knew. They had been seen.

Her heart sank like a stone. Her height would give her away, even in shadow. There was no hope of concealment. The single virtue she had maintained in a society that prized female decorum above all else, her reputation, was now imperiled by a single, dreamlike moment beneath the stars.

The stranger stepped forward, positioning himself between her and the direction of the sound. His movement was silent, deliberate. A shield.

Gwen took the opportunity to lift her hand, smoothing her skirts and adjusting her hair with trembling fingers. Her face was warm, not from desire now, but from mortification. Whatever came of this, the consequences would fall squarely upon her shoulders.

He would walk away with only the faintest trace of scandal. She, however, stood on the precipice of social exile.

If it was not her father who had opened that door, if it was a guest or a member of the *ton*, she would be ruined. No apology, no explanation would suffice.

She whispered a prayer into the darkness, her voice no louder than the wind.

Let it be Papa.
Please.

AIDAN WAS STILL REELING. His emotions were in disarray, his senses overwhelmed by Miss Smythe's presence, but the intoxication was swiftly giving way to the sharp chill of reality. The terrace, which had only moments ago been cloaked in moonlit intimacy, was now peopled with onlookers. Guests had rounded the corner in a murmuring cluster and come to a halt, their eyes wide, their expressions a mixture of fascination and horror. It was as though he had sprouted horns and hooves before their very eyes.

Near the back of the group, Trafford stood frozen, his face a portrait of stunned disbelief. He raked a hand through his wheat-colored curls in agitation. A moment later, he lifted both arms in a gesture of helplessness, a silent apology mingled with acknowledgment. There was no extricating themselves from this.

Several older couples stood rigidly, the ladies pressing gloved hands to their mouths, the gentlemen straight-backed and stony-eyed. Aidan recognized none of them, but their expressions revealed that they most certainly recognized him.

"It is Moreland's heir!" The impasse was shattered by a shrill voice. A peeress with graying blonde hair whose dismay pierced the night air like a bell.

"Who is that with him?" asked the gentleman beside her, clutching her arm with a mix of suspicion and curiosity.

Trafford cleared his throat and stepped forward, trying to reclaim the narrative. "I am quite certain this is not what it appears. Lord Abbott is a nobleman of unimpeachable character."

Aidan did not hear him. His gaze was fixed on Trafford, his mind turning with ruthless clarity. In his breast pocket, the folded list of sales crinkled with his breath. If their suspicions proved true, if Frederick Smythe's hand could be tied to a terrible crime, then the brilliant, self-possessed woman who had just stirred something profound in him would be doubly ruined. First by the scandal of this moment and again by her father's likely downfall.

The thought made his blood run cold. Miss Smythe—so learned, so luminous—deserved better than whispers and disgrace. She deserved dignity, protection. And that duty, however unintended, now fell to him.

The dark, he hoped, had hidden the worst of their embrace. When he had shielded her body with his own, perhaps he had spared her from the most damning implications. Yet he knew whispers would race ahead of fact.

He had kissed her. He had reached for her first. The blame lay squarely with him.

Aidan glanced once more at Trafford, who stared back with dawning horror as comprehension bloomed on his face. Aidan could almost hear the silent cry, *Do not say it. Do not make it worse.*

But for once, Aidan felt certain.

Miss Smythe was no flirt, no schemer. She had trusted him, and he had answered that trust with recklessness. There was only one path now that offered any form of justice, any protection for her name.

Drawing a breath deep into his lungs, Aidan turned toward the gathering. The air was hushed, the scent of box hedges and evening dew rising faintly in the space between them.

"I just offered for Miss Smythe's hand in marriage," he said, voice clear, firm, and steady. "And she accepted."

The declaration landed like a thunderclap. Behind him,

he heard Gwen's soft intake of breath. Trafford visibly winced, lifting a hand as though to halt the inevitable.

But it was done.

CHAPTER
FOUR

"The gods too are fond of a joke."

Aristotle

Gwen had not yet peered around Lord Abbott to behold their witnesses, though it was clear enough from the murmur of voices and shifting feet that her audience was not limited to her father. It was a veritable throng of guests. Any faint hope of discretion, she supposed, had vanished like dew in the morning sun.

Worse still, her stolen kiss with a stranger, one born of moonlight and longing, had not been with some anonymous gentleman. No. According to the collective gasps behind them, she had been thoroughly compromised by none other than the heir to Viscount Moreland.

"I just offered for Miss Smythe's hand in marriage ... and she accepted."

The words reached her in his deep, resonant voice,

smooth and certain, as though declaring the most natural truth. It took several seconds for the meaning to reach her ears, let alone settle in her mind.

And then it did.

The stranger knew her name.

And he had just announced their betrothal to half of London.

Her mouth parted in astonishment. She had been kissed by a stranger. A beautiful, magnetic stranger. And now, she was publicly his intended? The very absurdity of it made her chest tighten.

She could not possibly allow this to stand. Surely, he did not mean it. He could not. And yet ... and yet ...

"You are to wed Miss Smythe?"

The voice was unmistakable. Lady Astley. Matriarch, merciless gossip, and relentless guardian of *ton* propriety. Gwen winced. She did not need to look to know the woman's face was scrunched in polite disbelief, ready to dissect every detail for afternoon tea.

Crouching slightly behind Lord Abbott's back, Gwen rolled her eyes and pulled a discreet face, stifling the childish urge to stick out her tongue. Spinster she might be, but there was no call for Lady Astley to sound so thoroughly incredulous.

"I am," came Lord Abbott's calm reply.

"Miss Gwendolyn Smythe?" Lady Astley's voice rose a pitch, incredulity heavy in every syllable.

Gwen held her breath, but the response came unshaken.

"I was overcome by Miss Smythe's beauty and wit," he said, his voice low and commanding. "Her acceptance of my offer is a great honor that I shall cherish all my future days."

She blinked, stunned. There had been heat in his tone,

yes, but also something protective. Proud, even. And it had not sounded rehearsed. Could it be true? Could he truly see her that way?

No. Of course not. He had been caught. His sense of honor compelled him to speak nobly. Once he saw her clearly in bright morning light, without moonbeams and sentiment, he would realize his mistake. She was tall, freckled, peculiar. He would wish to take it all back.

And she would let him.

He could not be held to account for a kiss she had not only welcomed, but wanted with all her lonely heart. No man of sense should be expected to tether himself to a stranger simply for a moment of poorly timed fancy.

Yet ... he knew her name. Had he known her all along? It hardly signified. Her chances for courtship had been negligible before this evening. Her romantic future, such as it was, had long been relegated to fiction and dreams. A scandal could not ruin what never existed.

Still, she would do the honorable thing. She would not trap a gentleman in marriage to save her reputation.

"Lord Abbott misunderstood me."

The words trembled at first, but she steadied them. She would not let him sacrifice himself on the altar of her foolish longing.

With as much grace as she could muster, Gwen stepped out from behind him, spine straight, chin high. She fixed her eyes not on the crowd, but on the tall French doors behind them, focusing on the reflection of the candlelit ballroom rather than the judgmental stares.

"He made his offer," she continued, "but I turned him down."

Gasps rippled through the gathering like wind across a pond.

"You turned down the heir of Viscount Moreland?" Lady Astley's voice rang out, aghast, like a bell proclaiming a scandal too rich to ignore.

Gwen resisted the urge to sigh. Was it so impossible to believe that a woman might not leap into a man's arms, even one with a title?

"I did," she replied simply, firmly, with all the poise she could summon from her very bones.

From the corner of her eye, Gwen could see Lord Abbott cock his head slightly, the firm line of his square jaw tightening at her declaration. A subtle shift, but enough to show he had not expected her to contradict his attempt to preserve her standing.

"I confess Miss Smythe had her reservations regarding my offer," he said evenly, his voice carrying over the murmurs, "and I was attempting to persuade her to change her mind."

Gwen nearly burst into laughter, an almost hysterical sound she just managed to swallow. To his credit, Lord Abbott was doing his utmost to raise her in the estimation of those gathered, subtly implying that it was he who fell short. That he was the supplicant. That she held the power.

What he did not understand, could not understand, was how little Gwen truly had to lose.

She could not force a marriage upon any man, not even one complicit in her disgrace. A union ought to be founded upon something real. On respect. On shared truth. Not because the eyes of the *beau monde* demanded satisfaction.

Though fear coiled tightly in her middle, unspooling and tightening again like a frayed ribbon, she was not a woman to cower from the consequences of her own actions. She would not forgive herself if she used the weight of a single kiss to entrap a man into lifelong duty.

Lord Abbott deserved to choose his future freely. And she ... well, she would bear her punishment, as any woman must who lets herself be swept up in moonlight and poetry.

"I thank Lord Abbott for his offer," she said steadily, "and for his attempt to protect my reputation, but I stand by my refusal."

The gathering fractured into debate, hushed tones growing louder by the second. Gwen was certain she heard someone exclaim she was a stupid girl, most likely Lady Astley, that bitter old biddy who had never spared Gwen so much as a kind glance.

Still, she stood firm. Her principles outweighed the tittering of the crowd, and she would not sacrifice her self-respect to salvage public opinion. Her future, however lonely or diminished, must be one she could live with. The judgment of people who had never once taken the trouble to truly know her would not shape her fate.

Next to her, Lord Abbott exhaled sharply, the breath escaping him like wind against stone. Then, in his deep, deliberate voice, he cut through the din.

"It appears we cannot reach an agreement," he said, "so I believe that Miss Smythe and I shall discuss this with Mr. Smythe."

Lord Astley's head immediately bobbed up. Waving a bony hand to quiet his wife and the others gathered beside them, he addressed the situation with the thin yet commanding voice of a man long accustomed to being heard. "Agreed, young man. I think we must step inside to find Frederick so you can debate this private matter without an audience."

Gwen could not find fault with the suggestion. In truth, it suited her perfectly to end this humiliating public display. "I will be in the study," she said quietly.

Without another glance at the sea of eyes still trained on her, she turned and walked briskly away from the crowd. Her steps carried her through the open doors and into the hush of the terrace beyond, where cool air brushed her cheeks. Entering the ballroom was unthinkable. There would be no regaining composure beneath the scrutiny of that crowd. Even a woman of iron will would falter after being caught in a romantic embrace before half the *ton*.

She slipped through the French doors and into the study, grateful for its shadowed stillness. The hush was a balm.

Moving through the room, Gwen lit the lamps one by one, the soft glow of the flame casting pools of golden light against the wood-paneled walls. When she turned to sit on the sofa across from her father's desk, her brow furrowed in mild surprise.

His workspace had been neatened.

The inkstand and quill were perfectly aligned. The drawers were all shut. The desktop had been wiped clean, not a trace of pounce remaining. It was odd. Her father was meticulous in his dress, yes, but in matters of paper and pen, he had always been famously careless. He cursed under his breath when pounce dust blackened with ink collected in the carved buttons of his cuffs. An aggravation of his own making, yet one he never seemed to avoid.

Perhaps one of the servants had slipped in to tidy the room? Though it struck her as strange they would find the time, given the frenzy of preparations that had overtaken the household for this evening's ball.

Still, the thought did not linger long.

Her mind was too tangled. Her hands trembled faintly in her lap, though she clasped them tightly together in an effort to still them. She hoped her father would come soon.

That he would know what to say. That he might guide her in what must now be done.

She had thought herself strong enough to face anything. And yet ... sitting here, alone in the quiet, her stomach was a tight, aching knot, and her palms were damp with dread.

The notion of re-entering the ballroom turned her breath shallow.

What have I done?

Allowing a stranger to touch her, to kiss her in so intimate a fashion. What had she done? Was she so starved for affection that her morals, her very sense of decorum, had been cast aside in exchange for a fleeting moment of pleasure?

She frowned at the thought. No, that was not it. That was not the truth of it.

There had been something ... *more* on the terrace. A resonance. A quiet magic that had settled over them like grace from the heavens. In those moments, she had not felt reckless, but safe. Utterly and entirely herself. As though the rhythm of her soul had suddenly aligned with another's. There had been a symmetry between them, a silent understanding that required no words. Not only desire, but recognition.

Despite her current dread, Gwen knew with a strange certainty that she would carry the memory of that encounter like a locket tucked close to her heart. A cherished thing however inconvenient.

Relief stirred in her chest at the sound of approaching footsteps in the hall. The erratic parade of thoughts swirling in her mind had become unbearable. With luck, her father might bring a measure of calm. Direction. She needed guidance, a path forward through the tangle she had created. Her misstep had not endangered herself alone, but unsettled the entire household.

The footsteps halted. The door opened.

Gwen straightened abruptly, her hands clenched together in her lap, her thoughts scrambling to form some coherent explanation, some defense of her conduct, however feeble.

But the man who entered was not her father.

It was the stranger from the terrace.

Tall, commanding, broad of shoulder and straight of bearing. In the lamplight, he looked impossibly handsome. Rich brown hair, warm eyes the color of polished mahogany, and features that seemed sculpted by a divine hand. For a moment, she wondered whether her senses deceived her. Surely, such a man could not have sought her out? A man so clearly bred from privilege and elegance? It defied reason.

And yet he stood before her, hesitating, his gaze resting on hers with a depth that made her breath catch. Then he crossed the room and lowered himself onto the settee beside her.

Gwen remained stiff, hands folded tightly, the edge of the cushion barely bearing her weight. She did not move. She could scarcely believe that, even after seeing her plainly in full light, he had chosen to sit near her.

Turning to glance at the door, she saw her father enter.

And her heart dropped.

Frederick Smythe was beaming. Positively glowing with delight.

Gwen recognized the expression instantly. It was the same look he wore whenever he believed fate had gifted him a triumph. Her father did not merely approve. He was elated. No counsel of reason would come from him tonight. No quiet support if she wished to deny the man beside her.

He believed, with complete conviction, that the right man had at last appeared.

~

AIDAN WAS STILL REELING from the tumult that had played out only moments ago beyond the very doors now shut behind him. He had never conducted himself in such a reckless fashion. From the earliest days of his youth, his father had ingrained in him the value of restraint, of dignity, of upholding their name with honor. Yet he had been caught beneath the night sky, with his hands upon the person of a gently bred young lady.

The memory made him wince.

Later this evening, he would be duty-bound to confess his folly to the viscount. That, too, was a galling prospect.

Never in his life had he done anything so disgraceful.

What about leaving Lily alone on the night of the coronation?

The bitter thought pierced his reverie. He closed his eyes briefly as the weight of that night returned to him. The reason he was in the Smythe household this very evening had been almost forgotten in the swirl of other sensations.

Apparently, poor judgment was becoming a rather unwelcome theme in his life.

And yet, sitting here now, beside the very woman whose kiss had undone him, he could not deny the undercurrent of something far more potent than shame. There was excitement, yes, but also reverence. A humbling sense of awe.

She was unlike anyone he had ever met.

There was something timeless about her. A figure born not of society's artifice but of classical beauty and intellect. A Renaissance muse come to life. Perhaps *The Birth of Venus*, in all her striking singularity. The flame of her long red hair framed her delicate features like a halo, and though he tried to temper the thought, it stirred him deeply.

He chastised himself for the sudden flash of imagination. The inappropriate thought of her posed upon a shell as in Botticelli's famed painting. Just how far did that celestial constellation of freckles travel?

He exhaled slowly, willing himself to return to sense.

When he had first entered and she had turned toward him, meeting his gaze directly, he had been struck by the clarity of her eyes. Deep blue, like her father's, but softer somehow. More thoughtful. In the golden hush of lamplight, her skin had glowed like rich cream, and it had taken effort not to stare. The impulse to sit beside her had been undeniable. She drew him in not only with her appearance, but with her mind. Sharp, eloquent, composed.

And now, sitting beside her, close enough to catch the subtle citrus scent that clung to her skin, Aidan found himself tangled in a far more troubling question.

Was she involved?

Despite every instinct that urged him to believe in her innocence, he could not ignore the gravity of his mission. Protecting Lily and the baron must remain his highest priority. The stakes were too great.

If her father was indeed entangled in criminal pursuits, the truth had to come to light. It would fall to him to see it through. But perhaps, if he handled matters with care, he could shield her from the worst of the aftermath.

He could not allow sentiment to cloud his purpose. And

yet ... if he could forge some manner of alliance with her tonight, he might guide the storm rather than be swept away by it.

Frederick Smythe appeared remarkably cheerful about the turn of events. He closed the door behind him and strode across the room to settle into the chair behind his desk, as though nothing unusual had occurred.

Aidan noted with no small relief that Smythe registered no sign of disturbance in his study, no hint that a stranger had rifled through the drawers or left traces of an unauthorized visit. A small mercy, considering what was about to unfold.

"So, when is the wedding?" Mr. Smythe clapped his hands together, beaming with unconcealed glee. His eyes, so like his daughter's, sparkled as he regarded the pair seated before him.

Beside Aidan, Gwendolyn let out a groan.

"Papa, this is not a time for jesting! We have a serious situation at hand."

Her father's grin only broadened. "Levity in the face of trials, my dear, is what makes life bearable."

Aidan could not help the faint twitch at the corner of his mouth. There was something undeniably infectious about the elder Smythe's easy manner. His joviality and charm made him instantly likable. Too likable. That was precisely the danger.

Aidan reminded himself not to be drawn in. He could not afford to be softened by good humor or warm eyes. Not when there was a very real possibility that this man—this smiling, affable man—had been involved in a murder.

The thought chilled him. A necessary reminder. Lily's attacker had not seemed dangerous either, not at first. Trust could be deadly.

It was time to direct the conversation.

"I have explained to Mr. Smythe what happened upon the terrace," Aidan said, careful to keep his tone level. "And I have informed him of my intention to wed you."

He glanced ever so slightly, watching Gwendolyn from the corner of his eye, keen to gauge her response.

Now, in this well-lit room, with the fire casting golden light across her features, she was even more arresting than he remembered. It seemed improbable, and yet it was true. Her profile, her posture, even the thoughtful crease in her brow. All of it rendered him speechless.

It was difficult to reconcile this composed, intelligent young woman with the one who had moments ago stood trembling beneath the stars, clinging to him as though drawn by some unseen force.

A rush of warmth spread across his chest, stealing into his throat, as memory returned unbidden. The feel of her lips. The shape of her. The unexpected sweetness of it all.

He made a low sound in the back of his throat before he could stop himself. A brief, involuntary exhale of memory and sensation.

Gwendolyn turned her head toward him, as if she had heard it. Her brow furrowed delicately.

LORD ABBOTT HAD EMITTED a low growl after his declaration, and Gwen stiffened at the sound. It unsettled her more than she cared to admit. When he had chosen to sit beside her, she had allowed herself to believe, if only briefly, that he was drawn to her. That there might be a spark of genuine interest behind his gallant offer.

But that sound. That deep, reluctant utterance.

It did not speak of attraction. It spoke of duty.

Resolve returned to her like an old friend. Marrying Lord Abbott might simplify matters. It might even be advantageous from a certain point of view. But it would not be right.

Forcing a gentleman into marriage was beneath her. A moral failing she would not permit herself to commit.

She was not without options. Her father had the means to support her modest independence. A quiet life, perhaps in the country, with books and lectures and letters. She could disappear from society's eye and pursue her studies in peace.

"And I have informed Lord Abbott that I appreciate his offer, but it is not necessary."

Her father's grin faltered. It dropped from his face like overripe fruit tumbling from a sagging branch.

"Not necessary?"

Gwen nodded, firmly. She had hoped, naïvely, that her father might understand. That he might share her concerns about obligation and integrity. But the gleam in his eye earlier had revealed his excitement, his certainty that she had at last made a brilliant match.

It would not be easy to convince either man that this was a terrible idea. But she would try, with every ounce of strength she possessed.

"I have no wish to put Lord Abbott in that predicament," she said quietly. "I am certain he has far better marriage prospects than myself, and I do not wish to tie the gentleman down for something for which we are both responsible."

Beside her, Lord Abbott shifted. His shoulders flexed

slightly beneath his coat, as though some invisible weight pressed upon him.

"I assure your daughter," he said, voice rough with restraint, "that she is the very best of marriage prospects. It would not be a hardship in the least to announce our betrothal."

Gwen held her chin high. "And I wish to assure Lord Abbott that I am more than capable of taking care of myself. I free him to find a more suitable partner."

"I am perfectly capable of selecting a wife," he countered, his tone sharpening. "And I believe that Miss Smythe ought to have a greater appreciation of her worth as a prospect for such."

Across the room, her father turned his gaze from one to the other, bemusement creasing his brow. His head tilted slightly to one side, eyes narrowing as he absorbed the volleys being exchanged. It dawned on Gwen that they were, in effect, *sparring*—with him as the referee, neither of them willing to speak their full mind while he remained uncertain of the facts.

"Could one of you explain to me," he said, voice suddenly edged with steel, "what exactly unfolded on the terrace?"

Gwen's breath caught. Her father was slow to anger, but when he showed signs of growing vexed, it was wise to take heed.

"I thought Lord Abbott had informed you of what transpired?" she asked cautiously, voice softening in deference.

Lord Abbott shifted once more, and Gwen felt the firm line of his thigh brush against hers through the thin silk of her gown. A jolt of awareness shot through her. She stared rigidly ahead.

Good grief. He was the most handsome man she had

ever sat this close to. Which was precisely why she was addressing her father, rather than him, directly. To look at him, truly look at him, was simply too daunting a prospect.

"I simply laid out the broad strokes," Lord Abbott murmured.

"Well, now I wish to hear the specifics," Papa rejoined without hesitation. His voice was edged with suspicion, and the pleasant lines of his face had drawn taut with concern.

Lord Abbott cleared his throat and brought a hand to his mouth. "I encountered ... your daughter on the terrace and was overtaken by her beauty beneath the moonlight. The words of Manilius sprang forth, and I was caught utterly unaware when Miss Smythe responded in kind. Which was when I ... um ..." He coughed again, the sound more awkward than convincing.

Gwen turned her gaze to her father in time to see his features transform from wary to triumphant. His face broke into his customary grin, and he gave a knowing nod, as though some prophecy had at last come to fruition.

"You witnessed the perfection of my only daughter," he said, "and fell at her feet, defeated by her magnificence."

It was not a question. It was a proclamation.

And Gwen wanted to sink into the floor.

Her father's oft-repeated declaration, offered in jest a fortnight past, now hung in the air like smoke after a cannon blast. She had the absurd impulse to fan the words away, as though dispersing the remnants of some dangerous spell.

To her horror, Lord Abbott tilted his head in thought, and then a matching grin spread across his face.

"Quite so," he said.

They looked at one another with the *bonhomie* of shared

ideas, and Gwen was left feeling both outnumbered and mortified.

Papa turned to her with renewed purpose. "And then what happened?"

Gwen's legs bounced in agitation, and she kept her eyes firmly on the floor. "Lord Abbott approached me ... and then we ... um ... embraced."

"Embraced?"

"Well ... yes ... we ... uh ..."

She gestured helplessly, her arms flailing in a wide arc, as though sheer motion could substitute for words. Realizing how absurd she must look, she gave in to her fate.

"Kissed!" she burst out. "We kissed! And then the guests walked out and found me, his lips pressed to mine and his hands upon my buttocks!"

Her father burst out laughing.

Lord Abbott had turned a deep shade of crimson as she spoke, and Gwen herself was aflame with embarrassment. Yet, to her dismay, the gentleman beside her had the audacity to burst into corresponding laughter.

It was not what she needed at all.

The last thing she wished for was the forging of a genuine *camaraderie* between her father and this alarmingly attractive man, particularly when her every instinct was urging her to dissuade them both from the absurd notion of matrimony.

She made a faint sound of protest, though she could not help the involuntary shiver that coursed through her at the sound of Lord Abbott's husky laughter.

Egad, she thought. *He is a most enticing specimen of manhood.*

At intervals, she still half-believed this must be some elaborate dream. What other explanation could there be for a man such as he to speak so fervently of marriage, while insisting she was the prize?

Gwen, Gwen, the Spotted Giraffe, arguing against a proposal from one of the most eligible gentlemen in the *ton*. What would the girls from school say to that?

It was incomprehensible.

And beyond these walls, the ballroom surely hummed with scandalous speculation, eager anticipation, and whispered wagers. The entire world, it seemed, was awaiting an announcement.

Overwhelmed, Gwen dropped her head into her hands, fingers absently toying with strands of hair as she searched for some fragment of clarity amid the chaos unraveling in her mind.

Beside her, Lord Abbott fell silent, and she suspected—no, she *knew*—he had noticed the depth of her distress.

"Mr. Smythe," he said quietly, "would you permit me to speak with your daughter alone? We ... have much to settle between the two of us."

Her father, ever obliging in the face of such gallantry, responded with good cheer. His chair scraped lightly as he stood.

"I shall be on the terrace," he said, departing with a soft tread. The French doors clicked shut behind him, a gentle sound that nonetheless marked the room as now wholly theirs.

"Gwendolyn—"

"Gwen." She did not lift her head. "Only Papa addresses me as Gwendolyn."

There was a pause. Then, softer than before, "Gwen." He let the name linger. "It is lovely. A lovely name for a lovely woman."

She scowled at the rug. "There is no need to flatter me

now that you have seen me in the light. I am well aware of my appearance."

A warm hand appeared in her field of vision and gently took hold of hers. She allowed him to draw it down onto the settee between them, though she kept her head turned, braced in her other hand, eyes still fixed on the intricacies of the woven pattern beneath her slippers.

"I saw you in the entry hall," he said softly. "From the receiving line. I knew who you were when I met you on the terrace."

She stilled.

Then, slowly, Gwen dropped her hand and looked up at him.

He met her gaze squarely. There was no mockery in those eyes. Only sincerity, a quiet reverence that made her breath catch. Admiration, even.

She fidgeted beneath the weight of it, unsure what to do with such attention.

"Truly?" she asked.

"You put me in mind of a Botticelli masterpiece."

He reached forward, his fingers deft and gentle, and tucked a stray curl back into her coiffure. It was a strangely intimate gesture, more affecting than the passionate kisses they had exchanged in the moonlight.

She realized, with a jolt, that she must look rather a fright. Her hair ... her gown ...

She wanted to believe him. Every woman would wish to believe such words, especially when they were spoken in a voice that sounded like velvet and truth combined. If it were even the smallest bit true ...

"You have seen Botticelli firsthand?" she asked, voice hushed.

He nodded. "I could take you to Italy," he said. "A Grand Tour, if you desire it."

Gwen sucked in a breath, her eyes widening at the prospect of viewing great art. "I do not wish to force you into a union. The kiss was as much my fault as it was yours."

Lord Abbott's eyes raked over her face. "There is no force. I ... find I ... I find that I wish ..." He paused, rubbing a hand over his face as he searched for the right words. Gwen was fascinated. It was clear the gentleman was just as affected by this unexpected entanglement as she was. What would he say, once the words came to him? She waited, breath caught in her chest.

"Before this night, I had no desire to marry. But now that we are here together, I wish to do the right thing, and I find that there are no reservations creeping in the corners of my mind. This is what I wish to do. It would be an honor to make you my wife."

Lord Abbott's gaze found hers with the final declaration, and Gwen saw nothing but sincerity in the depths of his rich brown eyes. Compelled to speak, she parted her lips to voice the only thought that had pushed all others away, leaving behind a single, dazzling hope for the future.

"*If I could write the beauty of your eyes, And in fresh numbers number all your graces—*"

His gaze did not falter, even for a moment. His deep voice answered hers with perfect confidence.

"'*The age to come would say "This poet lies; Such heavenly touches ne'er touched earthly faces."*'"

Gwen shook her head slowly, utterly fascinated by his voice. By him.

She imagined marrying this man, discovering the intricacies of his nature, being cherished by him. She imagined babes with chocolate thatches of fine hair and bright brown eyes and books shared across armchairs, poetry whispered beneath covers, and fires crackling warm on Christmas Eve. She imagined moonlight and kisses, soft touches and sighs, strong hands and delighted shivers.

Gwen remembered the unwavering love shared between her father and mother, the joy that had filled their home upon Gareth's birth, and the quiet hopes she had buried deep within her own heart. And in that still moment, she knew she wanted to say yes.

"Are you certain?" she asked softly.

Lord Abbott's lips curved into a crooked, utterly disarming smile. "I am."

Gwen's thoughts churned with astonishing speed. The choice before her was stark. The certainty of social ruin ... or the unknown of a future with this man.

She had not met Lord Moreland personally, but his reputation preceded him. The Abbotts were considered an honorable family. Loyal, charitable, and admirably prudent with their considerable wealth. Lord Abbott's name had never been tainted with scandal, at least not to her knowledge. The only recent whispers involved his sister, who had evidently made a love match under somewhat hurried circumstances.

"I like to read," she said abruptly, testing him.

"So do I."

"You would not mind if I continued my studies?"

His grin widened. "I would encourage it. We shall debate the philosophers and quarrel over which of them proves most persuasive."

She paused. "And this ... this would be a real marriage? Not merely a matter of propriety?"

His gaze dropped to her lips, which she licked

nervously. A hint of amusement tugged at the corners of his mouth before he replied, voice low and warm. "It shall be a real marriage. Of that, you may be very certain."

Color bloomed across her cheeks. She glanced away, only to find herself inadvertently staring at the broad chest she had crushed herself against not long ago. The very one she had longed to touch with reckless hands beneath the cloak of moonlight.

And to her horror, her own hand rose now, as though independent of her mind, to trace the firm line of his wool coat. Beneath her fingertips, she could feel the rapid thrum of his heart matched only by the wild rhythm of her own.

Some part of her remembered that she had planned to remain steadfast. To convince her father and this gallant stranger that the notion of marriage was preposterous.

But another part, perhaps the truest part, was still the girl who had dreamed of love. Of finding a kindred spirit. Of building a life with someone who would value her mind as much as her heart.

Of curling into strong arms and whispering hopes into the night.

Of stepping boldly into a future her mother would have approved of.

She exhaled, long and slow. And gave her answer.

"Then we shall see where this path might lead."

Even as Lord Abbott's face lit up and he leaned forward to press a gentle kiss to her lips, Gwen's brow furrowed slightly.

A thought had surfaced, unbidden and troubling.

She did not recall his name on the guest list.

How had he come to be here this evening?

CHAPTER FIVE

"Quality is not an act, it is a habit."

Aristotle

AUGUST 14, 1821

Gwen opened one eye to find that morning had long since arrived. A thought, not yet formed, tickled the back of her mind. Something about the ball ...

She turned over, settling down again to return to sleep. The night had been long, and she was far too exhausted to rise just yet.

Her eyelids flew open.

The vague, niggling thought erupted into vivid memory.

"Stuff!"

Across the room, a blur of movement resolved into

Octavia Hanning, her lady's maid, who came bustling into view as if she had been standing vigil for the slightest sign of Gwen's waking.

"Is it true?"

Gwen fluttered her lashes, trying to shake free the cobwebs and catch up to Octavia's breathless urgency. "Is what true?"

"You are betrothed? To Lord Moreland's heir?"

Gwen groaned, pulling the coverlet over her head and burying her face in her pillow. Last night had not, as she had half-hoped, been a dream.

"Well? Are you to wed?" Octavia pressed, clearly too secure in her post after seven years to respect any notion of boundaries. The thin, sharp-featured woman in her early forties was a mix of dry wit and crusty pragmatism, entirely lacking deference when behind closed doors. Gwen would not have changed her for the world. Octavia was her stalwart. Practical, loyal, and entirely her own woman.

"If Lord Moreland does not raise an objection and forbid the match, then I suppose I am to wed."

"You let a gentleman put his hands on you?"

Gwen groaned again, burrowing deeper into her pillow.

"And he kissed you? On the lips?"

"Go away!" Gwen mumbled. She recalled now that her father had uncorked champagne in celebration after announcing the betrothal to their guests, who had then lingered well into the early hours.

Champagne.

That would account for the dull ache behind her eyes.

"I'm so impressed!"

Gwen frowned into her downy sanctuary, then slowly lifted her head to glare at her maid. "Impressed?"

"You landed your gentleman by compromising him!"

Gwen scowled, her disbelief sharpening. "I did not compromise him! He laid his hands on me!"

Octavia shook her head, a trifle too large for her reed-thin frame, not listening to a single word Gwen had uttered. "I knew you could do it. I told everyone belowstairs that Gwendolyn Smythe is not destined to be left on the shelf. Our mistress would see to it herself, she would. The right man would come along and notice her, and she'd wed, I told 'em."

Gwen pulled a face. There it was again. The right man. Had everyone in her household been awaiting the mysterious arrival of this mythical paragon?

"That is sentimental claptrap! What even is a right man?"

Octavia turned those round, watery blue eyes on her with exaggerated amazement, tilting her head as if Gwen were the simpleton. "The man who sees you for the original you are, of course. Lord Abbott is the one! Why else would he've followed you onto the terrace, if not to pursue you?"

Gwen gaped. The suggestion rocked her. Had he followed her? She had been well removed from the ballroom, beyond the gallery near her father's study. How would he have found her unless he had followed?

"That does not make sense," she murmured. "Why would Lord Abbott follow me?"

Octavia straightened her back, fists planted on her narrow hips. From Gwen's prone position, the maid looked like a colossus preparing for battle. "Because you're a beautiful young lady! An original. He recognized your worth."

"That is ridiculous," Gwen mumbled, pulling the coverlet over her head once more.

"No, it ain't! Those girls at school were repugnant little arses. You ought not pay them any heed."

"Not just schoolgirls. Married ladies of the *ton*, fully grown, who take every opportunity to remind me of my supposed deficiencies."

Octavia snorted with disdain. "More like married tarts of the *ton*. And what would they know? Their husbands all keep mistresses while they pretend nothing is amiss. The footmen told me what was going on in the little drawing room down the hall."

Gwen groaned. "So Lord Abbott will marry me and then discard me once he tires of being proper."

"Nay!" Octavia flung her arms. "This is different. Lord Abbott was so besotted, he trapped himself into marriage for a taste of your lips. That is love if I ever saw it."

"Dash it all!" Gwen cursed, clutching her pillow. "That is exactly what people will say. That it is a love match and then laugh like hyenas that *Gwen, Gwen the Spotted Giraffe*, snared a future viscount."

A long silence fell. Gwen peered out cautiously to find Octavia stewing.

"I wish you'd stop listening to those women," the maid finally muttered. "They are not experts on what a gentleman might want. They're only experts on repeating what their mothers taught them, because they have no minds of their own."

Gwen gave a bitter twist of her mouth. "They are experts. At getting married."

"Well, you're getting married!"

"Because of the scandal! Because Lord Abbott feels honor-bound to do the right thing. If not for that, I would still be a pitiable spinster."

"You're no spinster. You're a young woman of value, and your mama would be proud of you."

Gwen's jaw tightened. "She would not be proud that I have trapped a man into marriage."

Octavia sighed and pushed at Gwen's hip until she rolled slightly, making room on the bed before plopping down beside her. "Mrs. Smythe would understand. She would say that in a single magical moment, the right man found you. And fate took its course."

Gwen fell silent again, her thoughts turning inward, saddened and sobered by the ache that came whenever she thought of her absent mother.

Octavia Hanning had tended to the Smythe women for many years and was now practically a member of the family. Through Gwen's long, often lonely years, Octavia had stood faithfully at her side. Being a young woman of sharp intellect and scholarly bent had rendered Gwen something of an oddity to both the men and women of her class, but Octavia had always been her champion.

"I know not what happened," Gwen admitted, her voice wistful. "One moment I was simply wishing for someone with whom to share the glory of the heavens, and the next ... Lord Abbott was beside me. Then, before I understood what had passed, we embraced ... and half the ballroom stumbled upon us."

Octavia nodded sagely. "I think Lord Abbott is a good man."

Gwen blinked. "Why do you say that?"

"There is no gossip about him. He finished at Oxford, went on his Grand Tour, and since returning has caroused with his friends, as gentlemen do. But he's not visited any widows or courtesans, nor danced with any young ladies."

The vast and intricate network of belowstairs gossip never ceased to astonish Gwen. Octavia often knew more about noble families Gwen had barely encountered.

"And his family?"

"Lord and Lady Moreland have a spotless reputation. No paramours on either side, and all accounts say they are sincerely devoted to one another."

Gwen nodded thoughtfully, her thoughts turning to the viscount. How would Lord Moreland react upon learning his heir was to wed her?

"And what of his sister? The one who caused a stir in the scandal sheets?"

Octavia gave a grunt. "We're all a bit muddled over that. The Abbott servants don't like to talk about their household. Miss Abbott claimed she was with Lord Filminster on the night of the coronation—when he was nearly arrested, mind you—but there's been no whispers of improper conduct in any house she's visited. Not much known contact with Lord Filminster either, which makes the suddenness of it all ..." She waved her hands together in a lewd gesture, her meaning unmistakable. "They wed within days. And the servants at Ridley House? Tight as a drum. They'll say nothing."

Gwen reflected on this in silence. Either the servants were frightened into silence or the baron and his new wife inspired such loyalty that no gossip could escape.

It was a curious thing to imagine marrying into such a family, one she had never encountered. Lord Abbott himself was still a stranger. A breathtaking stranger with commanding lips, passionate eyes, and a scholar's mind, but a stranger all the same.

"Do you know," she asked softly, "why Lord Abbott was at the ball?"

Octavia shook her head, causing little tendrils of her mousy brown hair to escape the knot at her nape. "The footmen are amazed. Dennis said he might have seen Lord

Abbott and another gentleman enter with Lord and Lady Hays, but no one knows for certain. There has been no talk of Lord Abbott seeking a bride, so his presence at your father's ball is the subject of much speculation."

Gwen frowned, her brows drawing together as she sat upright against the pillows. "And this ball is not even part of the Season. Most families have already gone to their country seats for the summer since the coronation celebrations ended. Papa scheduled it now precisely to save on expenses."

Octavia clapped her hands together, her grin infectious and bright. "What does it matter how he came to be here? The end result is what counts. You're finally to wed. You'll be a beautiful bride, entering into a powerful family. And one of your little ones will inherit the viscountcy one day!"

Gwen's heart squeezed. A vision rose unbidden in her mind of a small boy with tousled chocolate curls and inquisitive brown eyes, clutching a book of Latin verse as he asked his mama to explain Manilius. A wave of tender yearning stole through her, curling around her spine and nestling somewhere deep in her chest.

Yes, marriage to Lord Abbott might have arisen from scandal, but if it led to children, to love and companionship, to sharing her thirst for knowledge, it could be a blessing in disguise.

She reminded herself of his promise. A real marriage, he had said. His gaze had not wavered when he made that vow. And Octavia's reports suggested that fidelity was a family trait amongst the Abbotts, which would be more than she had dared to hope for.

Gwen thought of a little boy with chocolate brown hair and bright eyes as she had done the night before, and a wave of yearning threaded through her veins to settle in the region of her heart. This might be a strange beginning to a marriage, but, if nothing else, her desire for children of her own would be fulfilled. Little ones she could teach the wonders of the ancient world to.

It was rather overwhelming to contemplate her sudden change in circumstances. The only issue that nagged at the edges of her consciousness was to mull over why Lord Abbott had been at the ball.

Why had he been on the terrace?

And, why in heaven had he kissed her when no eligible man before him had displayed any inclination to do the same?

There was no denying that Lord Abbott was an enigma.

"He is coming today," she finally said. "To negotiate the marriage settlements."

Octavia grinned, revealing a crooked smile. "It's a wonderful day. Your mama would be overjoyed that you finally found a handsome gentleman of your own."

Gwen thought about what her mama would say if she were here. She would have been impressed with Lord Abbott's knowledge of Manilius and Shakespeare, but she would have had questions about his presence at the Smythe ball.

Would Lord Abbott tell her the truth about his presence, and his appearance at her side under the pale light of the celestial bodies above, if she were to pose them to him?

She might be betrothed, but she knew not her distinguished groom.

It seemed unbearably rude to question him about his attendance at the ball after the monumental steps he was taking to protect her reputation in polite society.

What was she to do? Blatantly accuse him of illicitly entering their home as if he were unwelcome? He was certainly higher in stature than the Smythes, so it seemed wrong to inadvertently imply some sort of wrongdoing.

Gwen wished there was a way to get to the bottom of it. To understand why he had been at the ball, and what had made him say those romantic things in the study when he had persuaded her to proceed with the nuptials.

Octavia chose that moment to interrupt her musings with a blissful sigh. "Just think, I'm to attend a future viscountess!"

Gwen huffed in laughter, her friend's naked ambition pushing all concerns from her mind as she buried her head into Octavia's bony shoulder and thought about what it would be like to have access to the huge libraries of the Moreland estates.

He had promised her Italy.

Perhaps, if the stars remained aligned, she would see it all. Books, beauty, and a life begun under the pale watch of the moon.

"WHAT HAVE YOU DONE?"

Lady Moreland's wail pierced the refined stillness of the drawing room like a shriek on the battlefield. It was earsplitting. To be fair, Christiana Abbott had once again been called upon to endure the blows of scandal within her family. Only a month past, their daughter Lily had been compromised, entangled in whispers and scrutiny for providing a controversial alibi to her now-husband. And now, here stood Aidan, bearing tidings of a second impropriety. His own.

This was, indeed, a trying Season for the Countess of Moreland.

Hugh Abbott, the viscount himself, quickly rose from his high-backed armchair and went to her side. He perched on the damask-upholstered settee beside his wife and placed an arm, warm and steady, around her shoulders.

"Calm yourself, Christiana," he murmured, his voice low and soothing, the very embodiment of noble restraint. "It shall all work out."

Lady Moreland twisted toward him, her brocade shawl slipping from one shoulder. "What has befallen our children?" she moaned, her eyes wild and anguished. "Did I fail to raise them aright? Two scandals in one month!"

Then she buried her face in her delicate hands, the lace of her sleeves brushing against her flushed cheeks as she openly wept.

Aidan winced, his posture stiffening. Perhaps he should have spoken privately with his father first, rather than deliver his announcement to both parents simultaneously. It was an error of strategy that he now deeply regretted.

"I apologize, Mother," he said quietly. "I have taken steps to make the matter right."

Lady Moreland lifted her face, her chestnut-brown eyes glossy with tears, and gave another cry. "How?"

Aidan stood silent, struggling for words. He did not wish to upset her further. Words, after all, were the currency of poets and liars, neither of which seemed particularly helpful at the moment.

Lord Moreland cast his son a discerning glance before sighing, a sound weighted with long experience. It was clear he had pieced together what Aidan was yet to confess.

"Aidan has done the right thing," he declared gravely. "The honorable thing."

Lady Moreland blinked at her husband, confusion

chasing away some of the panic clouding her features. She turned her head toward him, brows knitted.

Lord Moreland laced his fingers together as he settled into the rhythm of explanation. "If all goes as expected," he said carefully, "Aidan shall soon provide another heir to the Moreland title."

Aidan blinked, thrown by his father's deft turn of phrase. Had he truly just recast the scandalous events of the previous night into a glowing family advancement?

Lady Moreland's expression softened, understanding stealing slowly across her tear-streaked face. "Aidan is to wed?" she breathed.

Lord Moreland gave a solemn nod, then reached up with his monogrammed handkerchief to gently blot the moisture from her cheeks. His actions, though simple, conveyed the grace of a marriage long tempered by shared burdens and unspoken understanding.

"And then," he added, smoothing the edge of the linen over her delicate temple, "he shall have babes. Sons and daughters. Our grandchildren."

Thoughts flitted across Lady Moreland's expressive face as she processed this newfound prospect of grandchildren. "I should have the servants visit the attics and bring down Aidan's and Lily's baby things," she announced, already rising to move toward the door.

Lord Moreland nodded in agreement, his tone calm but decisive. "An inventory should be taken immediately."

She swept from the room with revived purpose, her skirts rustling like wind across silk. Her departure left behind the faint scent of violets and the charged silence of two men confronting the fallout of family honor.

Father and son exchanged a weighted glance before Lord Moreland exhaled slowly, then turned his full attention to Aidan. "Your mother has suffered a great deal this past month. First Lily's reputation was sullied. Then certain acquaintances, the sort who pretend to be pillars of grace, quietly withdrew their invitations. And then Lily was nearly ..." He broke off, his hands fluttering mid-air, the conclusion unspoken but understood.

"I am deeply sorry for all of it," Aidan murmured, guilt threading through his voice. "I should have spoken to you first ... before Mother became involved."

Lord Moreland sighed once more and leaned back in his chair, stretching his long legs out before crossing one ankle over the other. His thoughtful gaze bore into Aidan with a quiet authority. "Then tell me, what were you doing at the Smythe ball? I was not aware you had any interest in making a match."

Aidan looked away, the fine carpet suddenly of immense interest. "I was ... searching," he mumbled.

A slow inhale came from the other side of the room. "Searching for what, precisely?"

"Evidence that Mr. Smythe may be responsible for the murder of Lord Filminster last month."

Aidan's voice dropped to a grim undertone, and he continued to study the toes of his riding boots. The only sound that followed was the faint ticking of the ormolu clock on the mantel, and then ... an audible groan from his father.

"Is that a genuine possibility?"

"It is," Aidan replied, lifting his eyes only briefly.

Lord Moreland cursed under his breath, a rare slip in composure that made Aidan flinch. "Deuce it. I do not know Smythe well, but he is a charming man with influence and friends aplenty. His elder brother, I am told, thinks highly of him."

Aidan thought of the letter he had uncovered. The one written by the baron, naming Smythe and expressing grave suspicion. The memory only cemented his growing certainty. Smythe was no genial host. He was a man hiding something dangerous.

"Miss Smythe is innocent in all this," he said firmly. "And considering my actions last night, it is now my duty to protect her ... both now and in the days to come."

Lord Moreland shook his head, slowly and with resignation. "And perhaps you can enlighten me on how you came to compromise a young lady of the *ton* in the first place. Your mother is not wrong. It is hardly the standard of conduct with which you were raised. The line between honor and indiscretion was never blurred in this household."

Aidan braced himself, lifting his chin. "I lost my head," he admitted, boldly meeting his father's eyes.

Lord Moreland studied him intently, his own sharp eyes assessing. The familial resemblance between them was unmistakable. Cut from the same cloth, yet Aidan bore his mother's warmer hues. For a fleeting second, he imagined a future son—bearing Gwen's flame-colored hair, her sapphire gaze—running through the halls of Moreland House.

"You do not usually lose your head over women," his father noted, more statement than question.

"I do not usually meet women like Gwen," Aidan replied quietly, with a conviction that silenced further inquiry.

Lord Moreland's features relaxed by the smallest degree, though his voice remained deliberate. "So this young woman has made an impression, then?"

Aidan immediately bobbed his head in assent. "She is Venus, with the mind of a scholar."

Lord Moreland tilted his head, clearly bemused. "And how exactly did you compromise her? I would appreciate the particulars, considering half of London will be nattering of it by breakfast."

Aidan swallowed. "I ... we ... I was embracing her ..." He paused, vividly recalling how Gwen had confessed the details the night before in near-identical fashion. "My hands were on her ... posterior. And we were ... kissing. Passionately."

He might as well have admitted to pinching a goose in the market square. It was mortifying, like a schoolboy caught licking icing from the pantry bowl rather than the actions of a man of five and twenty, university-educated and well-traveled.

Lord Moreland groaned and dragged his large hands over his dismayed face. "That is damning," he muttered, his voice muffled by his palms. "And out of character?"

The final word carried weight. A question, but also a challenge.

Aidan squirmed, shifting uncomfortably in his chair as he searched for the words to explain behavior so unlike his usual reserve. "I was overcome. She was radiant in the moonlight. And when I quoted Manilius, she responded in kind."

His father's brows lifted a fraction. "She sounds ... unusual."

Gwen was unusual. She was extraordinary. A blazing comet against the staid sky of *ton* femininity. "She is," Aidan said softly, the corners of his lips curving into an involuntary smile. His thoughts, as ever, trailed down paths of memory to her fascinated gaze, the feel of her pressed close in the night.

Lord Moreland leaned forward, fingers steepled. "And

her father may have murdered a peer to secure an inheritance?"

Aidan groaned and dropped his head back. "I know. What have I done?"

"I am not entirely certain," his father replied, his tone dry. "The one fact presently clear is that we have a marriage contract to negotiate. It would be best," he added, "if you did not uncover conclusive evidence of Mr. Smythe's guilt until after the wedding."

Aidan's head whipped up. "You would prefer I delay an arrest?"

"I would prefer not to deliver fresh trauma to your mother in one fell blow. She requires time to recover from Lily's ordeal." He waved a hand as though to banish further discussion on the point. "First the wedding. Then the arrest. Not both at once."

Aidan considered this, then nodded. "I can refrain from investigating Mr. Smythe until after the ceremony."

Lord Moreland inclined his head. "Good. It must be soon, of course. The scandal will already be racing through Mayfair."

"You support my decision?"

"The lady's circumstances do not signify," his father said quietly. "You must act with honor. You ruined an innocent woman, and that action carries consequences. You are my son, and I shall support you through them."

The words rang with the weight of legacy. Aidan, who had spent his life emulating his father's measured dignity and quiet strength, felt their significance to his very bones.

"I am sorry," he said, "to bring shame upon our family."

"You have always been a son to be proud of," Lord Moreland said, his voice softening. "I must believe this young woman is indeed remarkable, or you would not be in this position."

Aidan's expression lightened. "She is bewitching."

His father raked a hand through the thick dark hair they shared. He was already retreating into strategy. "Perhaps, after the wedding, your mother and I shall retire to the country. If an arrest is made, we would be wise to remove ourselves from town."

Aidan nodded. "And Gwen as well. I would not have her caught in the chaos."

His father's gaze sharpened. "Especially if Smythe proves to be more than he appears."

Aidan's expression sobered. Mr. Smythe's warmth and charm had not been helpful. If only the man were easier to loathe.

Instead, his reckless actions might one day shatter Gwen's heart, and he would bear the burden of helping to rebuild her spirit in the wake of a second scandal. One that would not be so easily mended with a marriage contract and declarations of devotion. The prospect chilled him. This next disgrace, should it occur, would be devastating and unrelenting.

The one saving grace was the name he bore. The title of Moreland carried weight. Enough, perhaps, to shield Gwen from the worst whispers that would follow.

"Smythe indicated he would be available this afternoon to negotiate the marriage settlements," Aidan said quietly. "I hoped you and I could attend together?"

Lord Moreland gave a single, brisk nod. "I shall cancel my appointments. It is imperative we forestall the scandal."

Aidan rotated his shoulders, attempting to ease the tightness gathering at the base of his neck. Less than a month had passed since his father had rearranged every engagement to ensure Lily's swift union with Filminster. Now, here he was again, asking the same indulgence of a man who had already borne more than his share of familial upheaval.

It weighed heavily on him. Who would have imagined that both he and Lily, devoted heirs of a distinguished line, would find themselves marrying under the shadow of public disgrace?

Nothing enraged Gwen more than witnessing the mistreatment of others. Thus she banged on the window, alerting the coachman that she wished to stop. Octavia, sitting on the bench opposite her, groaned loudly as the carriage drew to a halt.

"Please do not involve yourself!"

She glanced at her lady's maid, who sat next to the pile of books Gwen had only just purchased. "I cannot do that."

"London is filled with sad stories. You cannot shoulder the burdens of the world."

"But I can do something about this one."

The footman opened the door, lowering the steps so Gwen could disembark. She quickly climbed down, with Octavia mumbling rebukes as she followed Gwen out onto the street.

"This is a bad part of town. We shouldn't be stopping here."

"We have both a footman and a coachman to defend us if needed. Gird your loins and stir your stumps!"

A heavy sigh was the only answer, as Gwen strode back up the street.

A hulking halfpenny showman in a tan overcoat and a

battered, old three-pointed hat was operating his mechanical exhibition of puppets, squeaking in a ludicrously high voice as the role of Punch, she supposed, who must be moving across the tiny stage hidden from view.

"Sir, do you make it a habit to mistreat small creatures?"

The showman looked up, his broad face scowling at her interruption. A mother stood with three children, two of whom stood upon a bench and had their faces pressed to the little viewing holes to watch the show within the mechanical contrivance of the traveling tinker.

Behind his dull buckled shoes, tied to a piece of string at the opening of an alleyway, a small white and brown mongrel cowered in the shadows.

"What d'ye want?" grumbled the showman.

The two children looked up from their viewing holes to see what the interruption to their show was about.

"Your dog. I saw what you did." Gwen firmed her jaw in what she hoped was a menacing manner.

The tinker scowled again, narrowing his bloodshot eyes. "An' what do ye think ye saw?"

"You kicked him. Hard. In the ribs. See?" Gwen pointed at the shivering mongrel, who was hunched over as if wounded. The mother of the three children gasped, bending to peer around the wooden show cabinet.

The woman rose back up with a look of outrage. "Mister, is that true?"

"Wha' of it?" The defensive posturing of the scruffy reprobate did not unsettle Gwen at all. At least, not too much. She moved closer to glare at him, holding her breath lest she be overcome by his stench. He topped her by a few inches, but she refused to be intimidated.

"The dog is defenseless. There was no cause to kick him so."

"The cur were annoyin' me."

The mother gasped again. "Come. We are leaving, boys."

The two lads standing on the bench groaned. "Mama, we want to finish the show!"

"We shall find another amusement elsewhere. Come along."

The older daughter followed as their mother grabbed hold of her boys' hands and led them away. The girl looked back as they walked away, peeking at Gwen in something akin to awe.

"Cor! You be brave, miss. That man is huge!"

Gwen smiled in acknowledgment before returning her attention to the showman.

He had moved closer, towering over her in a menacing fashion. "Now, lookie here! See wha' ye done? That be me audience. Ye done lost me money."

A stockinged calf swept at the mongrel, which had come forward during the disturbance to sniff at Gwen's slippers. The dog whimpered, backing up to avoid the club-like appendage. Gwen noted that the little thing was gaunt. Clearly, the brute was not feeding his animal enough.

Gwen stared down at the dog who suffered at the feet of the bully who had him tied to a dirty string, and she could not walk away. Having confronted the man, and subsequently losing him business, Gwen knew precisely who would bear the brunt of his frustrations. She might have made matters worse for the poor mongrel.

Octavia shifted from foot to foot by her side. "Do not you do it, Gwendolyn Smythe. Do not you do it!" she muttered just loud enough for Gwen to hear.

The showman leaned closer, his fetid breath causing Gwen to bend away in disgust. "Wha's that?"

Gwen raised her head to stare him in the eye. "She asked how much for the pup?"

"Tarnation!" Octavia sounded peeved, probably contemplating the fact that the dog would be the cause of untold troubles once Gwen took him home.

But the mongrel, which must have had the blood of North Country Beagle coursing through its thready veins, was staring up at her with big brown eyes and floppy chestnut ears. All she could think of was how the filthy little animal needed her help.

The showman straightened up in surprise. "Me dog?"

"Aye, how much for the dog?"

He shook his head, his hair lank over his collar. "The dog's a pest, inna 'e? No good to ye."

"How much?" Gwen stared at him, unwavering in her resolve to remove the little pest as far from the tinker as she could take him.

He grunted, shrugging. "A shilling."

Gwen fumbled through her reticule, feeling about her coins until her fingers measured out one the size of a shilling. She yanked it out and presented it triumphantly.

The halfpenny showman took it from her with large blunt fingers. His long, grimy fingernails made her nauseous at the sight, but she released the shilling and took the string from his opposite hand.

He shook his head in dazed amazement. "The dog a cur, ain't 'e?"

Gwen raised herself to her full height, squaring her shoulders. "But now, sir, he is my cur."

With that, she turned and led the dog away. Octavia

groaned, catching up to her side and mumbling beneath her breath the entire length of their walk.

When they reached the carriage, Gwen leaned down to pick the dog up and place it inside, wondering whether her gloves would survive the contact with so much filth.

"Faugh! He reeks something fierce." Octavia's exclamation barely registered as Gwen fought back the impulse to gag, almost dizzy from the pungency of such a little animal. "He is a right skunk!"

"She. She is a right skunk. And a good wash will do her wonders." Gwen had checked when she had picked the animal up, an action that she was sure had cost her a favorite pair of gloves. Surely, such a depth of odor could not simply be washed away?

Octavia mumbled as she followed Gwen back into the interior of the carriage, quickly cranking the windows open to let in fresh air. "It better wash away, or that beast will be living in the stables."

Gwen looked down into the big brown eyes staring at her from the shadow of the bench. "She will be fine."

Octavia settled in next to the pile of books, shaking her head in perplexment. "I shall never understand why you are so quick to defend others, but not yourself, Gwendolyn Smythe."

Gwen stared back at the dog, whose snout was quivering with interest, sniffing the air of the carriage. How it did not gag on its own smell was a mystery. "I do not know. It is easier when it is not me."

"You have a fire in your belly, girl. You need to use it against your adversaries, or you shall never claim your rightful place in society."

Sighing, Gwen leaned back into the puffy squabs to catch a breath of fresh air from the open window before the impulse to cast up her accounts could best her. The little hound's stench had a life and will of its own, which permeated the entire carriage with its power. "I do not need the approval of others. I shall find my own way."

Octavia shook her large head again, her bulbous eyes sympathetic in the dim light. "We all need connections. You must allow your new betrothed a chance to bring you happiness and status within that high society. You deserve it more than anyone I know."

Gwen nodded, but she did not know what she was agreeing to. It was merely a signal she had heard what Octavia had to say. It still seemed an impossibility that she was to marry a man like Lord Abbott.

When she had learned this morning that Lord Abbott, his father, and their solicitor would be meeting with Papa in his study, Gwen had hurriedly made plans to depart their home for the day. She was not ready to meet Viscount Moreland after being caught with his heir and forcing a marriage.

For her cowardice, she had acquired a malodorous little dog to care for and had only postponed the inevitable meeting with Lord Abbott's presumably disappointed parents.

CHAPTER
SIX

"We make war that we may live in peace."

Aristotle

AUGUST 15, 1821

Aidan entered the club and made his way through a bank of tables and chairs toward the farthest corner, where Filminster and Trafford awaited. The space buzzed with masculine murmurs and the occasional sharp clink of crystal thunking down on wooden surfaces, a familiar din beneath the chandeliers' low gleam. Polished mahogany and aged leather infused the air with a subtle tang of wax and tobacco.

Several gentlemen stopped mid-conversation to follow him with their eyes. Whispers dogged his heels like a stray hound. He felt the weight of their scrutiny as surely as if he had been draped in velvet robes rather than his plain wool coat. Relief flickered through him as he approached the corner alcove, which was chosen, he noted with gratitude, for being too far from neighboring tables for their conversation to carry.

Dropping into a plump armchair, its arms creaking slightly with age as they took his weight, Aidan breathed deeply. The scent of pipe smoke and ink-stained newsprint mingled oddly in the back of his throat. Being the subject of gossip was a novel experience. Heretofore, he had lived a faultless life, guided by duty and honor. Now, he could only hope that Gwen was not suffering too acutely in the aftermath of their indiscretion two nights past.

Across from him, Trafford scowled and leaned forward, thrusting a folded news sheet across the table. The paper was faintly smudged, its corners softened by prior hands. Aidan glanced down, scanning the headline. It chronicled the uproar caused by their embrace. His memory supplied the precise weight of Gwen in his arms, the softness of her form pressed against his. A flicker of heat stirred at the recollection. She had fit against him with startling ease, her height nearly matching his, making it effortless to claim her lips.

"Have you lost your mind, Little Breeches?"

Gone was Trafford's usual nonchalance. Filminster lifted a hand, palm out, to stay his friend's temper.

"It appears that matters have gotten out of hand." His brother-in-law's tone was measured, though his brow quirked with curiosity. "Or did you uncover something that cleared Smythe of murder before …" He allowed his brows to rise with suggestive flair.

"Before you stuck your tongue down his daughter's throat in a marvelous display of discretion and judgment,

Little Breeches?" Trafford's voice sharpened, his shoulders taut beneath the fine stitching of his jacket. The ivory buttons at his cuffs glinted in the lamplight like polished accusations.

"Why are you angry?" Aidan asked, not from petulance but genuine puzzlement. Trafford's pique surprised him.

"This one and his wife are in danger"—Trafford gestured at Filminster with a curt flick of his gloved fingers—"and you were meant to be tactful about investigating the man. Instead, you drew unwarranted attention not only to yourself, but to me. Aunty Gertrude sent a note to my father yesterday to inform him that I was at the ball, and that my companion has ruined an innocent. The whole family is in an uproar."

Filminster coughed into his fist, a gleam of amusement in his eye. "To be fair, Trafford, you did complain that you were bored."

Trafford scowled. "I create my own entertainment. Dragging Father into it is not entertaining."

Aidan's brother-in-law allowed himself a small smile, which Aidan found reassuring. Perhaps life at Ridley House was beginning to right itself ... if only they could apprehend the murderer. That, more than anything, was the key to ensuring Lily's future safety.

"I think Smythe might be our man." Aidan reached into his inner coat pocket and withdrew a page, carefully folded. He placed it on the table in front of Filminster.

The other man ran a hand through his dark curls before lifting the sheet. His gaze scanned the contents with growing focus.

"It is a list of assets that Smythe has sold. All within the past two months, if you check the dates. He appears to be in some financial distress, which would certainly provide motive for protecting his inheritance."

Filminster ran a gloved finger down the list, the vellum page crackling faintly as he turned it. He whistled low under his breath and looked up at Trafford. "This is a small fortune. Smythe must be spending a great deal of blunt to need this."

Trafford frowned, drawing the list toward him to scan it more closely. His eyes flicked from line to line, the sunlight from a tall window glinting off the signet ring on his right hand. "I have been occupied with our other suspects, but I have heard no mention of gambling or mistresses in connection with Smythe. No whispers or murmurs from the clubs or gaming hells that might explain his need for funds."

Filminster leaned forward again, fingertips brushing the creases in the paper. "Could he be involved in a land purchase? That might explain the need for liquid capital."

Aidan considered the question, absently adjusting his cravat. "There was no mention of such during our parley yesterday. Miss Smythe's dowry does not amount to much, so my father made generous concessions in the interest of expediency. I shall have to raise the matter with Smythe the next time we meet. It would be useful to learn if he has a legitimate reason for this sort of divestiture of assets."

Filminster nodded thoughtfully. "Your sister is astonished by the news. She tells me it is quite unlike you to be caught in such a compromising manner."

Aidan straightened in his chair, the faint creak of the leather underscoring his discomfort. "Gwen is ... special."

"So special that you are willing to risk marrying into a family under investigation for murder?"

Aidan dropped his gaze to the table's polished surface,

tracing the dark grain with his eyes. He could not explain what had happened in the moonlight. He only knew that his desire to protect the young woman, to shield her from the vicious scrutiny of the *beau monde* and spare her from potential ruin, had become imperative since they were discovered.

"If Smythe is our man, Gwen will need protection. Whatever comes of this, she is innocent. She does not deserve to face the world alone if her father is arrested."

Trafford interjected then, his voice steady. It was a welcome distraction. He gestured toward the list with a flick of his fingers. "I am looking into the other men listed here, but none of them display a tangible motive such as this. Smythe's behavior—selling off property, artwork, even family jewels—certainly suggests that he is concealing something significant."

Aidan nodded. "I spoke with my father about it. He agreed the number of transactions was suspicious. He observed that it could be an effort to cover staggering debts or to finance a major acquisition. Filminster, perhaps you might discreetly inquire whether any such purchase has been recorded or rumored, while Trafford continues his investigations into the others?"

"I have already eliminated one of these men." Trafford withdrew a small leather-bound notebook from his coat and opened it, flipping to a marked page. He cast a cautious glance about the room to confirm no club employees lingered nearby, then returned his attention to the notes. "Miller, along with his elder brother who holds the title, was present at a soirée that lasted well into the morning hours following the coronation. The household staff confirmed their presence. Both brothers were reportedly so deep in their cups that they could scarcely stand, let alone slip away to commit murder. Their carriage was not summoned until dawn, and the dinner was held far too distant from Ridley House to have allowed for a clandestine excursion by foot."

Filminster inclined his head in acknowledgment. "My runner, Briggs, confirmed that Miller is independently wealthy. No financial motive. That is one name we may remove from suspicion."

Trafford withdrew a pencil from the inner pocket of his waistcoat and neatly scored through a name on the list, the soft rasp of graphite faint beneath the low hum of conversation around them. Four names remained. Aidan stared down at them, yet it was Smythe's—first on the page, written in his own precise hand—that held his focus like a hook in the mind.

"The more I think about the baron's letter, the more convinced I am that Smythe is the man we seek," he said, his voice low. "His older brother is a baron, which means your uncle likely sat with him or near him at the coronation. That would have been the baron's primary opportunity to speak with anyone before his murder. Smythe's finances are in disarray, and my father confirms that the baron, his brother, is deeply fond of him. Just as the letter implied."

Filminster shook his head, his gaze thoughtful, his features touched with pity. "God help you, if that is the case, Aidan. I cannot imagine what it would be to deliver such a blow to Lily. Your bride will be devastated if her father is tried and hanged. More so if her husband is the accuser. I do not envy the position you are in."

Aidan's expression shuttered. His voice, when it came, was subdued. "Lily must be protected, no matter how difficult it might be. And I will take care of Gwen, if that comes to pass."

"I understand. But …" Filminster hesitated, then pressed on gently, "I hope for your sake, and hers, that we uncover another suspect."

"I concur. It is quite a pickle you have put yourself in, Little Breeches." Trafford's languid tone had returned, his earlier irritation now gone. He was once more the picture of repose, his legs stretched comfortably beneath the polished oak table. "Your bride is going to despise you if you do this."

Aidan did not like that thought. The notion of Gwen's hate—her warmth turned to coldness, her mouth drawn tight with betrayal—sat like a stone in his gut. What he wanted was her warm body nestled beside him, the press of her mouth beneath his, the glorious words of poets on her lips. He wanted to hear Manilius and Shakespeare spoken in her melodic voice, to spar with her over Aristotle's writings by the drawing room fire. Love, intelligence, and honor … for the rest of their days.

"I will work it out," he said, but an undercurrent of doubt threaded his words.

He closed his eyes, drew in a breath scented faintly with old paper and the oil of polished wood, and reached inward.

I must work it out.

"I will work it out." This time his voice held confidence. Finality.

Filminster looked down, visibly relieved not to press further. He and Aidan were hardly confidants, their bond forged not through familiarity, but mutual concern for Lily's safety. They had met through circumstance, not affinity, and though civility bound them, trust was only slowly earned.

Still, Aidan regretted the solitude of his situation. Having only recently returned from the Grand Tour, he had no close allies in London. There was no one with whom to confess the impossible knot he found himself ensnared.

Filminster rubbed a hand across his jaw, his cuff rustling against the wool of his sleeve as he sought something useful to offer. "Perhaps we will find another viable suspect. Maybe Smythe has a reasonable explanation for the funds he is acquiring."

That would be the best possible outcome. Yet Aidan could not shake the weight in his gut. Something about Smythe's actions rang of evasion, of desperation disguised as dignity. He did not allow himself much hope. The deeper the investigation, the clearer it became that the path led to the very doorstep of the woman he was coming to cherish.

He would marry Gwen before the matter advanced further. It was imperative. With the banns read and the vows exchanged, she and her younger brother would be under his protection, no matter how muddled the waters became thereafter.

Gwen and Octavia stepped into the modiste's salon owned by Signora Ricci, the soft chime of the bell above the door announcing their entrance like a whisper of expectation. The air inside was delicately perfumed with rose water and starch, threaded with the subtle spice of imported silks. Gwen held a folded sheet of thick cream-laid paper, her father's neat script listing everything she must acquire to reflect her new rank.

She was to be married.

Once she took her vows with Lord Abbott, she would no longer be the mere niece of a baron, navigating society's edges. Nay, she would ascend to become the wife of a future viscount, one tied to a family flush with influence and ancient silver. The thought quickened her breath. The scale of it loomed like the Tower itself. Daunting, cold, and inescapable.

But Signora Ricci was her secret talisman. Her hidden weapon of self-assurance.

Years ago, after a particularly mortifying ball and too many cutting remarks from snide schoolmates, Gwen had prowled Mayfair for a modiste who could dress her long limbs and boyish figure with elegance. She had found Ricci tucked into a quiet corner near Hanover Square, an Italian widow with a flair for flattery and a talent for architectural draping. That first gown, soft mulberry silk with a daring Grecian fall, had been nothing short of a rebirth.

"Ah, *la signorina* returns!" the modiste called from behind a half-drawn curtain, her thick Italian accent as warm as hot chocolate. "Come, we make the swan ready for her coronation, *sì*?"

Ricci had always dismissed the cruel whispers of English debutantes, those who called Gwen a giraffe behind her back and mocked her want of curves. According to the signora, Gwen would be hailed as a rare Venetian opal on the Continent. Gwen knew it was salesmanship, but in those days, it had been salvation.

While Gwen unbuttoned her gloves at the display near the front window, Octavia was already elbow-deep in bolts of fabric, fingering the textures with the scrutiny of a jeweler evaluating pearls. She murmured disapproval at most selections, frowning at garish taffetas and favoring the finer muslins and crisp lawn cottons for morning gowns.

The bell over the door rang again, sharp and unwelcoming.

Gwen glanced over her shoulder, and her stomach tightened in dread, a visceral pull as unmistakable as nausea. Entering with her usual coterie of whispers and expensive perfume was Millicent "Milly" Jameson, now Lady Tuttle of West Essex.

Her nemesis.

Milly's gaze landed on Gwen with surgical precision. Her narrow eyes gleamed with satisfaction as her mouth curved in a sneer sharpened by memory.

"Well, well. Gwen, Gwen ..."

She let the name dangle in the air like a noose. *Gwen, Gwen, the Spotted Giraffe.* The old insult echoed in Gwen's ears, as vivid as ink upon white muslin.

Gwen stood straighter, her spine stiffening like a ramrod, though no answer came to her lips. Always, with Milly, she was caught defenseless, ensnared by the echo of long-past humiliations that still clung to her skin like soot.

"Milly ..." she managed, her voice a croak that tasted of old shame.

Milly's painted lips parted in mock innocence. "Is it true, Gwen-Gwen? Are you to join our ranks as a viscountess?"

Gwen swallowed hard, her throat dry. Words, usually her allies, abandoned her the instant she locked eyes with the past. With her.

It was always like this with the old schoolgirls, the original guard of her torment. Their memory had claws. Though a decade might have passed, the echo of their laughter was sharp and fresh as if carved into her skin only yesterday.

Those two years at Miss Hedgerow's Academy for Young Ladies had been a daily gauntlet. The other girls had despised her from the first. Her awkward height, her reserve, her grief for a mother lost to illness, and her head forever buried in Greek or philosophy rather than court gossip. They had given her a name, the Spotted Giraffe, a reference to the freckles that marred her skin and her gangly figure, and they had wielded it like a cudgel. Her father, distracted by his own mourning and by the demands of his estate, had only intervened once it was too late. He had withdrawn her at last, but by then, her confidence was rubble.

Books had been her only solace. They never mocked or sneered. They listened. They made her feel clever. Safe.

Society, on the other hand, was a minefield laced with traps like Milly.

As Gwen floundered, Octavia appeared at her side like an avenging angel in stout woollen attire. She stepped slightly ahead, her broad shoulders forming a bulwark of protection.

"That is correct," Octavia said in a firm tone. "Miss Smythe is betrothed to Lord Abbott."

Milly's gaze did not shift to acknowledge the servant. Her cold eyes swept over Gwen like a critic inspecting a flawed painting. She was the picture of high-society perfection, clothed in a seafoam pelisse embroidered in pale ivory thread. At least six inches shorter than Gwen, she had the full figure that fashion idealized. Generous bosom, nipped waist, glossy golden curls, a porcelain complexion without freckle or flaw. Her nose was sculpted and narrow, her lips a perfect rosebud. It was well-known she had received several offers her first Season and had married a viscount twice her age with a healthy estate and a voice in Parliament. She had not let Gwen forget it.

Milly arched a finely plucked brow, voice silky. "Lord Abbott is quite the catch. Although I had not heard he was blind."

The barb landed. Gwen felt the heat rise along her throat, and her vision narrowed at the edges. She barely registered the low sound of displeasure at her side.

Ouch!

Gwen winced, whipping her head toward Octavia, only to find her companion smiling sweetly at a bolt of champagne silk, her eyes bright with mischief. The lady's maid tilted her head just so, an unmistakable signal.

Stand up. Push back.

Gwen cleared her throat. Her fingers tightened on the glove she still held in her left hand.

"Lord Abbott and I are to wed," she said, her voice steadier than she felt.

Another rumbling growl from her side, more insistent now. Octavia's version of a battle drum.

Gwen lifted her chin. "He is ... quite taken with me."

Milly's laughter rang out through the salon, brittle and theatrical. It jarred with the gentle rustling of fabrics and the murmur of shop girls in the back rooms. The sound cracked open the vault Gwen had tried to seal. Memories of awkward dancing lessons, the smell of chalk, and girls sniggering behind gloved hands. The ache of wanting her mother. The guilt of troubling her grieving father.

"Is he?"

Octavia squared her shoulders, inhaling sharply through her nose as if preparing to launch a volley at the polished predator before them. Her stance was protective, coiled energy beneath plain muslin and a modest fichu. But before she could speak, Gwen felt herself detach. For a breathless instant, it was as though she rose above her body, observing the scene as one might a diorama in a shop window.

And from that vantage point, something shifted.

The fear, the remembered taunts, the years of silent endurance all looked smaller from a distance. Faded. Like ink washed thin by time.

She was no longer that girl.

Lord Abbott had seen her. Truly seen her. He had drawn her into his arms and kissed her with conviction beneath moonlight softened by spring haze. He had whispered poetry, tender and sensual, and called her Botticelli's Venus. He had sought her company with purpose, with intention. No man as admired as he was would do such things unless he wished to.

He had chosen her.

"He is," Gwen said.

The words were crisp and clean as snapped linen. Unapologetic.

She had given him ample opportunities to turn away. Yet he had remained, pursuing her with sincerity and something tender that lived beneath the surface of his charm.

From the corner of her eye, she caught the swift flick of Octavia's glance. Surprised, then fiercely proud.

Milly blinked. The reaction was faint, but it betrayed her surprise. That Gwen had answered with conviction seemed to upend her expectations. Her expression reassembled itself into something patronizing.

"Certainly, dear. An heir must ensure the continuation of the line."

Broodmare, is it?

The inference stung. But Gwen did not flinch.

And why should she? Lord Abbott had never sought a wife. He had not paraded about Almack's courting likely matches. He had admitted, with all the bluntness of a man caught unawares, that marriage had not entered his thoughts until her. It was not obligation that had led him to her door.

"Certainly," Gwen replied smoothly, her voice like silk stretched taut. "That is his duty."

She spoke with the serenity of someone holding a winning hand.

Milly's eyes narrowed, her lips twitching. She pressed a manicured hand to her curls, smoothing an imaginary flyaway as she delivered her next barb. "Do not be alarmed when he grows bored and seeks the attention of more ... lovely ladies of the *ton*. I, myself, was hailed as a diamond of the first water."

The smugness was almost luminous. She tucked a curl behind her ear in a practiced gesture of self-congratulation, clearly imagining that Gwen would shrink beneath the comparison.

But she did not.

Gwen felt a strange, exhilarating lightness take root in her chest. Not giggling light, but the clarity that comes when shame slides away and the truth is allowed room to breathe.

Octavia's head jerked forward in warning, her lips parting to deliver what would no doubt be a colorful retort. Her crooked teeth flashed like a wolfhound's. But Gwen lifted a hand slightly, enough to still her.

She had this.

"I heard your Lord Tuttle is continuing his line," Gwen

said, her tone airy and pleasant. "His mistress in Cheapside is said to be increasing, I believe?"

Milly drew back a fraction, her upper lip twitching in a gesture that could have passed for a sneer, or perhaps, in that moment, a suppressed hiss. It was well known, even if never spoken aloud, that men of the peerage often kept mistresses. As Octavia had pragmatically noted the day before, such arrangements were common knowledge but never openly acknowledged, especially not in the midst of a modiste's elegant shop.

"I am merely thankful," Gwen said lightly, "that my betrothed is young ... and besotted with me."

She lifted a hand to her hair—those long, flame-kissed tresses that had earned her more ridicule than admiration in her youth—and twined a curl between her fingers with new appreciation. The world had always insisted her coloring was unfashionable. But in the soft moonlight, beneath Lord Abbott's gaze, she had felt radiant.

He had compared her to Botticelli's *Birth of Venus*, not mockingly, but as though it had risen spontaneously from within his soul. She was tall and willowy, certainly, and her hair did echo that legendary goddess's vivid hue. But more than that, she remembered how he had looked at her. Like she was art come to life.

And his interest had been no act. She had felt the truth of it, undeniable and arresting.

She was not some practical acquisition chosen for lineage or coin. She was a woman wanted. Passionately, irreversibly.

"Which is why," she added with a subtle smile, "we shall enjoy our travels to Italy once we are married."

Lawks. The thought had tumbled from her lips without due caution.

A flush of heat rose beneath her collar as she registered what she had just revealed. Was she overstepping? Had she claimed too much? She had only meant to speak her hope aloud, to stake a small claim in the bright future that now shimmered within reach.

But for the first time, Gwen felt what it was to own her circumstance, to believe in the sincerity of Lord Abbott's intentions and the wild possibility that something resembling her parents' great love might be blooming anew.

To believe that she could be cherished.

To imagine children whose eyes lit when they looked upon their parents. Secure, adored, proud.

Milly gave a dismissive huff. "We shall see."

It was a weak parry. A final flick of the foil with no strength behind it.

Gwen smiled, radiant and firm. "We will."

Octavia's eyes glistened with pride, her entire posture bouncing with barely concealed triumph. Her mistress, at long last, was standing her ground.

Gwen caught the expression and made a subtle face in return, as though to say, *Good heavens, did I truly say all that aloud?*

Still, the thrill of striking back instead of fleeing sent a fizzing energy through her limbs. *Lawks,* she thought again, half-amused, half-alarmed. *I hope I have not overstepped.*

She did not wish to be one of those girls who grew vain at the first taste of triumph, only to have her pride crumble with the next social blow. But Lord Abbott had seemed sincere, and everything Octavia had relayed about his family spoke of kindness and honor.

Perhaps ... just perhaps ... this truly was her time.

CHAPTER SEVEN

"In all things of nature there is something of the marvelous."

Aristotle

AUGUST 17, 1821

Gwen stared at her reflection in the glass, anxiously adjusting the folds of her gown while Buttercup whined and circled her slippers. The pup, newly scrubbed and brushed by a diligent groom in the mews, was scarcely recognizable from the bedraggled creature she had adopted.

Fortunately, Buttercup had revealed herself to be an amiable shadow, content to trail Gwen from room to room and gaze up at her with doleful brown eyes and a twitching snout, as if awaiting instructions only Gwen could give.

"What if they do not like me?" she asked in a whisper.

Octavia snorted, twisting a final curl into place atop Gwen's head with efficient fingers. "What is there not to like? You're a delight."

Gwen's mouth tugged sideways. "Not according to anyone I know."

"Oh, posh. The girls from school were envious, and the boys ... foolish to a man. Anyone with an ounce of sense finds you charming."

"But Lady Astley looked ready to faint when we were found on the terrace."

"Lady Astley is an embittered old bat," Octavia said, releasing a breath through her nose. A few wispy tendrils escaped from the nape of her neck, betraying her haste. "She would have reacted the same if you had been caught reading sermons aloud. Her household staff tells stories that would curl your hair faster than any iron."

Despite herself, Gwen smiled. But the tension returned almost at once. She resumed rhythmically clasping and releasing her hands, until—

"Stop that." Octavia gave her knuckles a quick tap. "You will crease your gown before the dinner even begins."

Startled, Gwen glanced down and saw the wrinkled patch she had created. With a wince, she tried to smooth the delicate silk, though her fingers trembled. The dinner had dominated her thoughts, looming like a performance for which she had not rehearsed nearly enough.

She was to meet his parents.

The butterflies in her stomach launched into a fresh frenzy, and she pressed a hand to her middle, feeling slightly unwell. What must they think of her? What had they heard about the evening on the terrace?

Aidan.

She mouthed his name silently, still unable to believe she was to marry so esteemed and handsome a gentleman.

Her gaze drifted to the nearby table, where *Debrett's Peerage* lay open, spine cracked from repeated consultation. With familiar fingers, she turned to the entry for the Viscount of Moreland once more, though she could have recited the text from memory by now.

The Abbott family boasted a long and illustrious line of titled ancestors, while Gwen's own lineage felt painfully unremarkable by comparison. Her father was the third son of a minor baron, only set to inherit because his eldest brother had no heirs and the middle brother had passed away two decades earlier.

And her mama? A scholar's daughter with no ties to society or even the gentry. Respectable, yes, but entirely unsuited to the ballrooms of Mayfair.

What must they think of Lord Aidan Abbott's offer of marriage to insignificant Gwendolyn Smythe?

Gwen, Gwen the Spotted Giraffe.

The cruel schoolyard chant rose unbidden in her mind, and the bravado she had summoned at the modiste's shop when facing down Milly dissolved in a flash. Tentative confidence was no match for the thought of meeting the Morelands—a distinguished and wealthy family with ancestral estates and discerning expectations.

What if they stared as Lady Astley had done? What if their astonishment turned to dismay?

What if they found her entirely unworthy?

What if they simply did not like her?

"Right, you are ready," Octavia announced, stepping back with a satisfied nod.

Gwen glanced up to see her reflection in the long mirror, now crowned with a carefully arranged fall of red curls. The rest of her thick hair had been coaxed into an intricate chignon, worthy of any duchess's daughter.

She tilted her head. Then tried the opposite side. Bit her lip and squinted.

For a brief, shimmering moment, she caught a resemblance to the figure Aidan had once compared her to. Venus, as painted by Botticelli.

But the likeness flickered and collapsed as swiftly as it had come, and the butterflies in her stomach staged a fresh revolt.

"The Morelands will be here soon."

"They will hate me."

Octavia pursed her lips, unimpressed. Without ceremony, she seized Gwen's arm and hauled her upright. The maid barely reached Gwen's chin, a fact that only sharpened her awareness of her own too-tall, too-angular frame.

With resolute determination, Octavia shepherded her out of the bedchamber, pausing only to close the door behind them and leave Buttercup safely inside. The soft sound of the dog's whine echoed down the hall as they marched toward the stairs.

Halfway down, Octavia was forced to release her. There was no graceful way to descend in tandem given their height disparity.

Gwen glanced behind her. Just a few steps back. She could run. Duck into the music room. Lock the door and claim a sudden megrim.

Surely, they would understand?

But then she imagined their first impression. That she had fled the dinner like a frightened debutante in a sentimental tale. No, far better to face them with at least a shred of dignity.

Even if every instinct urged retreat.

They reached the ground floor and turned toward the small drawing room. Gwen entered and halted in the center, absorbing the quiet elegance. The silk wallpaper, the restrained scent of lavender from the hearth rug, the ticking of the clock in the corner.

"Shall I bring you some tea while you wait?" Octavia asked.

"That will not be necessary. Papa will join me shortly." Gwen began to pace, agitated energy leaking through every step.

"You'll wear a hole in the rug," Octavia observed dryly, her eyes drifting to Gwen's feet—those too-large, undeniably unfashionable feet that never allowed her to glide, only stride.

Gwen stopped pacing, teeth sinking into her lower lip. "They must hate me already! Their celebrated heir ... forced to wed a spotted ginger! Just imagine what their grandchildren will look like!"

Octavia drew herself up to her full, if modest, height, placing both hands on her hips with the authority of a general inspecting troops. Her tone rang with indignation.

"Gwendolyn Smythe, you are a treasure. The Morelands are fortunate indeed to welcome you into their ranks."

Gwen's mouth fell open in horror, because standing just beyond her father in the doorway, perfectly framed by the arch, was an elegant woman whose presence silenced the room.

She had the same chocolate-brown eyes as Aidan, and the sheen of her silk gown, woven in subtle, harmonious hues, spoke of refinement and assured taste. Though her appearance was youthful, a delicate scattering of silver near her temples betrayed her identity.

Behind her stood a tall gentleman whose square jaw

and salt-and-pepper hair bore an unmistakable resemblance to Lord Aidan Abbott. His lips twitched, betraying the effort it took not to laugh.

Octavia, catching a glimpse of the doorway's reflection in the glass, spun about and clapped a hand over her mouth. Her eyes locked with Lady Moreland's. Too late.

She dipped into a deep curtsy, but faltered, clearly mortified. "Milady!"

"And who might you be?" Lady Moreland asked with a calm coolness that demanded precision.

"Mrs. Hanning, milady. I am lady's maid to Miss Smythe." Octavia's voice trembled despite her effort to sound composed.

Lady Moreland raised a brow, arch and elegant. She advanced a few steps and surveyed the flustered woman. "Indeed. Is it customary in your service to address your mistress by her Christian name?"

A small strangled sound escaped Octavia, drawing Gwen from her frozen state.

"Mrs. Hanning served my mother when I was a child," Gwen said quickly, forcing her voice steady. "We are ... rather close."

Even as she spoke, she realized the room had filled. Her father stood beside Lord Moreland and Aidan, all three men witnesses to the brief interrogation. Octavia, glancing back at Gwen with a look of despair, seemed unable to summon another word.

To Gwen's alarm, Lady Moreland now turned her discerning gaze upon her. Gwen fought the urge to shrink beneath it, willing herself to maintain composure. But her stomach was in knots, and the longing to disappear remained acute.

"Miss Gwendolyn Smythe, I presume?"

Gwen inclined her head in silent confirmation, her throat tight.

To her astonishment, Lady Moreland swept forward and took her gently by the arms in an embrace.

"Your lady's maid is not wrong, Gwendolyn," she said warmly. "We are most fortunate to welcome a young woman of such grace and accomplishment into our family."

She leaned in and pressed a soft kiss to Gwen's cheek.

Gwen's eyes widened. She flicked a glance toward Aidan—Lord Abbott—seeking explanation. He merely smiled and offered a faint shrug, as though his mother's unpredictability was nothing new.

"We shall welcome your babes as if they are our own," Lady Moreland declared.

Gwen blinked, uncertain she had heard correctly. "Babes?"

"Our grandchildren, of course," the viscountess said with the ease of a woman who made plans with serene efficiency. "Have you considered names yet? I would be pleased to suggest a number of estimable options from the Abbott line ... very distinguished forebears."

Her mouth parted in amazement. Surely, this could not be real. Gwen half expected to wake with a start and find it was still the evening before the dinner, her dreams having conjured this strange introduction.

This was not how one met the parents of one's betrothed. Was it?

Lord Moreland stepped forward and took her hand with a warm, practiced bow as his wife moved aside. "A pleasure, Miss Gwendolyn. Lady Moreland is, as you can see, quite delighted by the notion of welcoming a new generation of Abbotts. But before we get ahead of ourselves, I believe we have a wedding to discuss, my dear."

The last was addressed to his wife, who gave a light, dismissive wave as though such details were rather beneath her, mere ceremony, when grandchildren were the true prize.

Gwen discreetly pinched the fabric of her skirt against her leg. Just to be sure. Nothing changed. Perhaps she had dreamt the pinch?

Across the room, her father was positively glowing, his blue eyes bright with amusement and pride. Clearly, the mention of heirs had met with his enthusiastic approval. Gwen, on the other hand, was barely holding herself together.

Still, she managed a curtsy, awkward but passable. "Thank you, Lord Moreland."

Then, at last, she turned to face her betrothed.

Lord Abbott.

Aidan.

He bowed with practiced ease, a glint of warmth in his expression. "Good evening, Gwen. You are ravishing tonight."

His gaze swept over her, appreciative but gentle. And just like that, the tension in her chest lessened. For a moment, all her frantic thoughts were suspended, replaced by the quiet, haunting memory of moonlight and shared words.

"Lord Abbott," she replied softly, the name catching on her breath.

It was odd to think this was only their second meeting. They had shared more in a single evening—conversation, vulnerability, a promise—than she had with any gentleman in her life. And now, here she was, standing before his parents, while the topic of future progeny had already been raised.

Just a week ago, she had resigned herself to spinsterhood. Now she was stumbling through a formal introduction and grappling with subjects that she had never raised outside the privacy of her own thoughts.

"I think it is acceptable," he murmured, "to address me as Aidan?"

His brown eyes gleamed in the lamplight. Mischievous, daring, and a touch too handsome for her peace of mind.

Aidan.

She had whispered that name into the quiet of her bedchamber since finding it in *Debrett's*. She had said it beneath her breath, mouthing it like a secret.

Lady Gwendolyn Abbott.

That had played on repeat in her thoughts as well. She liked the sound of it.

Lord and Lady Abbott.

Too late, Gwen realized she had been staring at him for far too long. Their families stood in observation, and she was woolgathering like a schoolgirl in church.

"Aidan," she blurted, flushing as she withdrew her hand.

The entire scene still felt too polished, too charmed, to be genuine. A handsome and eligible heir had offered for her. His parents were receiving her with open arms. And apparently, a curated list of names for their future grandchildren. Her father looked like a cat who had not only cornered the cream but had spied the cheese tray as well.

Something, surely, was about to go wrong.

Although she had attended countless social gatherings, Gwen had no idea what to do next. She stood awkwardly, unsure of her role in the unfolding tableau.

Which was when Providence intervened, disguised in the form of Jenson, the butler, appeared in the doorway.

"Dinner is served."

Aidan stepped forward and offered his arm. Steady, well-formed, and thoroughly male. Gwen blinked down at it, momentarily startled, before slipping her hand into the crook of his elbow with tentative grace.

She could feel the strength beneath the fabric, the solid warmth of him at her side. It would have been far too easy to lean in, to sigh with appreciation.

Fortunately, good manners, and the presence of his entire family, restrained her from such an indelicate display.

∽

AIDAN FOUND himself once more entranced by his Venus. Gwen's presence had a way of quieting the clamor in his mind, even now as her hand rested lightly on his arm, sending a faint ripple of warmth up through his sleeve.

He had scarcely registered the strange exchange between his mother and Gwen's maid, his thoughts temporarily diverted by the gentle pressure of her fingers. But the momentary reverie faded as he glanced along the hallway and noticed something unsettling.

Missing paintings.

Here and there, along the walls, pale rectangles marked where portraits or landscapes had once hung. Their absence was stark. Faded wallpaper framed the ghosts of what had recently adorned the corridor.

It was yet more evidence of Mr. Smythe's liquidation efforts. Aidan had already noted signs of financial strain, but this … this was far more extensive than the short list he had compiled over the past fortnight. Smythe had been parting with family possessions far longer than Aidan had suspected.

As they entered the dining room, Aidan's mood dimmed. He wanted this evening to belong to Gwen, to celebrate their impending marriage, to allow himself a moment of calm. But as his eyes swept the shelves along one wall, he saw that the display was sparse. Fewer *objets d'art* than any well-appointed home ought to contain.

What should have been there was not.

He took a steadying breath.

His father had asked him to delay any further investigation until after the wedding, only days away now. But each omission, each silent space, frayed his patience. The dead baron, the persisting threat to his sister. None of it had been resolved.

Lily with the bold voice and unguarded heart. She deserved far better than a distracted brother playing at betrothal while danger loomed.

Their parents moved to their seats, and he accompanied Gwen around to the far side of the table. He drew out her chair and helped her to sit, catching the shimmer of lamplight on her hair before taking his own place beside her.

He must set these thoughts aside ... at least for now.

Filminster and Trafford had warned him that the path ahead would be treacherous, to be both a faithful fiancé and a vigilant protector. The weight of that dual responsibility pressed down on him as he exhaled in a quiet puff of breath.

Gwen's head turned toward him at once, eyes flickering with concern. He managed a small smile for her benefit, willing himself to be present.

Beneath the table, he reached for her hand.

Her fingers met his with a shy stillness. When he

gently traced his thumb over her knuckles, she did not pull away. Instead, her hand curled softly into his, the quiet gesture anchoring him more firmly than any spoken vow.

For a moment, they remained thus, hands joined beneath the linen-draped table, a private connection beneath the polite hum of conversation.

The footmen entered, setting out the first course as his mother launched into a cheerful recitation of distinguished Abbott ancestors. Mr. Smythe responded with his own modest offerings from the Smythe family history.

Aidan glanced at Gwen. She was biting her lip as she lifted her spoon, clearly doing her utmost to remain composed.

"Chestnut?" he asked gently.

She nodded. "It is Papa's favorite."

"And yours?"

"I do not much care for soup," she admitted.

"What do you care for?"

She looked over at him, the barest smile forming at the corners of her mouth. "Fruit. Oranges, especially."

Aidan suppressed a low breath in his throat, remembering the faint taste of citrus on her lips during their moonlit kiss. The recollection sent a flush of heat through him, sharp and unexpected. He had never known such an immediate and visceral fascination with a woman, not like this. Not the pull of her presence. The memory of her fragrant hair, the way she had looked up at him in surprise and wonder. It lingered.

And soon, they would be married.

The thought stirred something perilous, and he forced his attention back to the moment. Still, the idea of a quiet stroll on the terrace after dinner, where he might steal another kiss and taste her sweetness once more—was hard to resist.

Keeping his voice low, so their parents would not overhear, he leaned slightly toward her. "Was that the scent I breathed that night?"

Gwen flushed instantly, color blooming from her neckline to her cheekbones, momentarily dimming her freckles.

"There is bergamot in my soap," she murmured.

Aidan inhaled again, savoring the memory and the subtle fragrance now clinging to her skin. "The moon shines bright. In such a night as this. When the sweet wind did gently kiss the trees and they did make no noise ... in such a night ..."

She nearly choked on a spoonful of soup, coughing behind her napkin and darting him a reproachful look. Her gaze flicked nervously toward their parents to ensure they hadn't overheard.

"Shhh," she hissed under her breath.

Aidan's grin widened. "Not for a moment, sweet Venus."

He was no practiced flirt. Yet with Gwen, poetry sprang unbidden to his lips, along with musings far less poetic. He pictured her hair unbound, her fingers twined with his, the warmth of her hand in his. He thought of what it meant to be husband and wife in the truest sense.

With effort, he shook off the vision and grounded himself once more at the table, focusing on the quiet clink of silver and the murmured conversation around him.

"We used to travel north during the summer," Mr. Smythe was saying, his voice calm, pleasant. "But alas, this year we shall remain in London."

The comment jarred Aidan from his woolgathering.

There had been a bill of sale for a Yorkshire property

among the documents he had reviewed. And now, with Smythe seated before him, this was his chance to learn something.

"Father and I were just discussing the purchase of new property to add to our portfolio. Do you have any suggestions, Mr. Smythe?" Aidan watched the other man carefully as he posed his question. It would be heaven-sent if the man admitted he was purchasing something, thus disproving that he was desperate for funds and canceling him as a suspect from their list.

Smythe hesitated, his eyebrows coming together for just a second before responding. "No, I am afraid not. It has been some time since I dealt with any land purchases."

Aidan's heart sank.

And yet he pressed forward, still hoping for a clue.

"Do you intend any significant investments in the near future?"

The question was jarring, causing his father to throw him a cautionary glance. Aidan kept a straight face, but he knew Hugh Abbott was well aware that he was fishing for information.

Frederick Smythe sobered for several seconds, and Aidan silently willed him to admit to something, anything, that would explain the mounting bills of sale. Then, at last, Gwen's father smiled his familiar easy grin.

"What could I possibly purchase? A gentleman has no need of anything but property!"

"Indeed!" Aidan's mother agreed at once. "Owning land is the ultimate investment. There is no need of any other."

Smythe tilted his head, his eyes dropping, just briefly, but enough for Aidan to recognize the slip. Then the gentleman let out a booming laugh and banged the table with his hand.

"Land is the best investment."

Next to him, Gwen lowered her head and stared at her bowl of soup. And Aidan knew.

He knew something was amiss and that Gwen might know it, too.

A new dread stirred in his chest. He had never considered that she might be entangled in her father's affairs. It was one thing to investigate Frederick Smythe. It was another entirely to suspect that the woman he had kissed beneath the moonlight, whom he was bound to marry, might carry secrets of her own.

Curses.

His breath tightened. How could he possibly reconcile his vow to protect Lily with his promise to cherish Gwen?

Lord Moreland chose that moment to shift the conversation, his eyes flicking in subtle warning. "How is Lord Weston? I know him well from Lords, but I have not seen him since the coronation."

Smythe grimaced faintly. "My brother is well, but he was called away. Our family home caught fire, you see. He was needed to attend to it."

Aidan's parents expressed their dismay in unison.

"Was anyone harmed?"

"Did the house survive?"

Smythe nodded. "The staff are all well. They managed to save most of the contents, but the west wing was lost."

Aidan's interest was piqued as the conversation turned to the disaster that had befallen the Smythe family. Could this be why Gwen's father needed funds?

But no, that did not make sense. The bills of sale demonstrated that Smythe had been selling off possessions for a minimum of the past two months, and news of the fire must have reached his brother after the coronation if Aidan's own father had met him there.

Aidan felt the deep bite of disappointment. There was still no bona fide reason that might remove Smythe from their list of suspects for the killing of Lord Filminster. How much simpler his future would be if he could clear the man of the crime. The path forward would be far less tangled, especially with Lily's safety hanging in the balance.

After dinner, they adjourned to a small drawing room. The atmosphere was warm, fragrant with lemon oil and beeswax, and Aidan invited Gwen to the terrace. One of the privileges of being betrothed was the allowance of certain concessions, such as walking alone. Many couples took advantage of this liberty in anticipation of their vows.

But for Aidan, this brief stroll offered more than escape. He longed for a reprieve from the burden of secrets and suspicion, from the ache of watching Lily face danger, and perhaps, too, to see whether Gwen might be a balm against the relentless unease of the past weeks.

Gwen nodded with composure, rising to link her arm with his. Her fingers rested lightly in the crook of his elbow, her perfume a gentle combination of citrus and soap. They passed through the French doors into the early twilight, the last rays of sunlight casting a golden hue across the terrace stones.

Despite his yearning to forget all that troubled him, Aidan's thoughts pressed forward.

"Why is it you are not leaving London this year?"

His companion set her jaw with quiet resolve, her gaze fixed on the horizon. A soft glow illuminated the curve of her cheek as she placed her hands upon the stone banister. "My father found the need to sell the property," she replied, her tone edged with pride and defensiveness. "He did not wish to disclose it, because land ownership is the mark of a true gentleman."

"Why?" he asked gently.

She shook her head, curls catching the fading light. "He has a plan, but he has not discussed it with me. He merely informed me that it was necessary to sell."

Aidan drew a breath, the tension easing from his shoulders. Relief swelled within him, pure and unfiltered. Gwen had spoken with transparency. She knew no more than what she had shared, and he believed her. Whatever Mr. Smythe was involved in—debts, desperation, or worse—it did not touch Gwen's hands. And soon, she would be under Aidan's protection, secured from the ruinous reach of scandal.

He turned slightly to study her profile, lit from behind by the amber remnants of the day.

"Tell me something of yourself," he said quietly.

Gwen tilted her head in question, and Aidan absorbed the sight of her fiery red hair glowing in the last glimmers of dusk. He could look at her forever. "Such as?"

"What do you do with your day?"

Her blue eyes found his, a flicker of defiance igniting their depths. "My mother was a scholar of the ancient world, like her father before her. I study in the library ... and I have published papers."

"Truly?"

"Yes, under a pseudonym, of course."

Aidan smiled. "Of course."

"As my mother did before me."

"I should like to read them."

"Truly?"

He nodded, warmed by her surprise. "Truly."

"You do not mind that I ... engage in such pursuits?"

"If it leads to reciting Manilius in the moonlight, I am wholly in favor of it. Imagine what you will teach our children."

The sun had fully disappeared now, and the first stars blinked into existence overhead. She groaned. "Your mother is obsessed!"

He chuckled softly. "My father chose to make our ... situation ... palatable by commenting on the benefits of our union. My mother has been distressed lately, but the notion of grandchildren has quite lifted her spirits."

There was a long pause, broken only by the soft rustle of leaves in the evening breeze. Then Gwen spoke again, her voice more subdued. "Then, I suppose I am happy to be of service in some small way."

Aidan turned toward her, the moonlight catching the glint of copper in her hair. "You are of the greatest service, Venus."

He reached for her gently, cradling her against him with quiet reverence. His fingers lightly traced the curve of her cheek, and for a moment, he simply breathed in her presence. Oranges and something warmer, like a sun-drenched memory. When his lips met hers, it was but a whisper of contact, tentative and reverent.

She sighed, and he deepened the kiss, slow and exploring, their breath mingling in the growing dark. The intensity of her response was more than he had hoped for, yet perfectly attuned to his own racing heart. He drew her closer, savoring the warmth of her form pressed against his, each point of contact seeming a vow.

His hand moved to the small of her back, anchoring her as though he might lose her to the shadows if he let go. Aidan was overwhelmed by the gravity of what he felt. She was not merely a diversion. She was becoming essential.

Pulling back slightly, he found her eyes wide and shimmering in the moonlight. Her lips were parted, breath soft against the night air, and he longed to kiss her again, but restrained himself.

Brushing his thumb across her cheek, he murmured, "From her fair and unpolluted flesh, may violets spring."

She gazed at him as though he had woven starlight with his words, and he swallowed hard. He wanted this woman. Not only for tonight. For all his days.

Whatever the coming days held—danger, scandal, the truth about her father—he prayed he would still deserve the look in her eyes when it was done.

CHAPTER
EIGHT

"Youth is easily deceived because it is quick to hope."

Aristotle

~

AUGUST 18, 1821

Gwen awoke with a hollow pang of guilt to find Buttercup perched beside her on the coverlet, eyes unblinking and reproachful, as though the little creature had been appointed her moral sentinel.

"Do not look at me so."

Buttercup's slender snout twitched, and she let out a quiet whine from deep in her throat before hopping down and scurrying out the door, claws clicking against the floorboards. Perhaps she needed to visit the necessary, Gwen mused, though her hasty exit felt pointed, as if in censure.

Flopping onto her back with a sigh, Gwen stared at the

canopy above her head and let the weight of the previous evening descend upon her shoulders. Had she been wrong to tell Aidan about the Yorkshire estate?

Would it wound her father's pride to know she had revealed such a truth? He had always been fastidious about his reputation. Yet Aidan had asked her a direct question, and evasion had never been her strength. The truth had slipped from her lips before she had fully registered the implications. Still, what good would deceit have done? He would learn of it in time.

Life amongst the *ton* was exhausting. So many rules. So many unspoken expectations. And always the looming specter of scandal. It was absurd to her that the sale of one's property could invite whispers of disgrace. The land had been her father's to sell. Why must that choice imply failure?

Yet in society's eyes, ownership meant everything. Her father had once possessed holdings that gave them standing, however modest. With only the London estate remaining, he now barely met the definition of "landed." And in the rigid arithmetic of the *beau monde*, that changed everything.

Her marriage to Aidan would resolve much of this. It was a stroke of fortune, an unexpected turn in a Season that had begun with minimal expectations. Had the sale of the Yorkshire estate become widely known, she might have found herself entirely unmarriageable. Their family's connections were acceptable but not the most impressive, their resources limited, and her dowry modest.

She rolled to her side, propping her head on her hand, and stared toward the window where light filtered past the drapery in pale stripes. Why was Papa doing this? She had suspicions, but he had kept his reasoning to himself.

"Do not concern yourself, Gwendolyn. I know what I am doing."

Gwen turned over as the swish of drawn curtains filled the room with pale morning light. Octavia, ever punctual, had opened the drapes to let the day in. She hoped Aidan meant everything he had implied last night, but what could she do now but trust him? For years, her father had reassured her that the right man would appear. Against all probability, he had been proved correct.

"Word of your wedding is out," Octavia announced briskly.

Gwen looked up at her lady's maid, whose cap sat slightly askew from this angle, making her appear as though her head teetered precariously atop her shoulders. With a sigh, Gwen pushed herself upright to rest against the headboard, the coverlet pooling around her waist.

"Apparently, it's a love match," Octavia continued, moving to plump the pillows at the foot of the bed.

Gwen gave a soft huff of laughter. "That is a bit rich. We only just met the night of the …" She waved a hand, unwilling to summon the memory aloud.

"I have it on good authority that Lady Astley is telling everyone that Lord Abbott is smitten with your red hair."

Gwen frowned, unsettled. "Does he have a history of chasing women with red hair?"

Octavia shook her head. "He has no reputation whatever in regard to women. Lord Abbott returned from his Grand Tour a couple of months ago, and until the ball, his name had not been linked with anyone."

Seeing Gwen's skeptical expression, Octavia raised her brows. "I checked again. No history of redheads. No history at all."

Gwen looked down, twisting her fingers in her lap. "Do you think ... that he is genuinely enthralled with me?"

Octavia bent to give her a quick, heartfelt embrace. "I do."

"Would it be so," Gwen whispered. "Imagine if we might be faithful partners and have many children together. Gareth would be an uncle, our family would grow, and Papa would have grandchildren. We have all been so lonely since Mama ..." Her voice caught, tears welling. "I could teach them ..."

Octavia straightened, her tone gentle. "Just as Mrs. Smythe once did."

Gwen swiped the tears from her lashes and nodded. "Just so."

"It's well deserved, you hear?" Octavia's voice took on a firm note. "All these Seasons, I knew you were a catch. We were just waiting for the—"

"Right man." They said it together, eyes meeting in shared amusement before laughter bubbled up between them.

"Mr. Smythe said he would appear," Octavia went on. "The master said there'd be a gentleman who was overcome by your magnificence and the perfection of your mind and would fall at your feet ... and he was right."

"Papa is an eternal optimist."

Octavia grinned, revealing her crooked teeth in a smile that Gwen had loved since childhood. "What's the alternative, Gwendolyn Smythe?"

Gwen made a face, tapping her chin. "To become an embittered old bat?"

A shout of laughter burst forth. "Precisely! The alternative is to be Lady Astley."

"Who is now telling everyone that it is my red hair that

attracted the gentleman to my side? Only last year she was whispering to her friends that my red hair was a curse and the reason I would never wed."

"Hah! Not so private, from what I hear."

She twisted the edge of the coverlet between her fingers, reluctant to admit the secret blooming within her heart, but needing, desperately, to voice it aloud. "I ... like him, Octavia. I truly do. I want this to succeed. He is handsome and kind and clever, and I never dreamed I would find such a match."

A bony hand emerged from the folds of Octavia's work dress and tapped her gently on the thigh. Gwen shifted further back, making room as the older woman perched on the edge of the mattress with the ease of long familiarity.

"Those girls at school muddled your head," Octavia said with quiet authority. "You were always meant to make a fine match with a wonderful man, but they convinced you that you were ugly. Do you know why they did it?"

Gwen shook her head, miserable at the awful recollections.

"They envied you," Octavia said, matter-of-fact. "You sailed through your lessons. No matter what you turned your mind to—Ancient Greek, needlework, music—you excelled. Your cleverness unsettled them. So they banded together to make nothing of you. It was cruel and meaningless, because you were the sort who would have helped them shine, too, if they'd only asked."

Gwen blinked hard. "But ... Mama was a revered beauty. I have been mocked for nearly ten years."

"And now," Octavia said softly, "a gentleman has seen what I see. A true original."

In her heart of hearts, Gwen wanted to believe it. To believe in moonlight and magic. In the notion that a decent, intelligent man had not only noticed her, but desired her. That she need not choose between a joyless match or a solitary future. Her parents had demonstrated a love built on companionship, of homes filled with books and children, and laughter around the hearth.

Gwen heaved a long, shuddering breath. "I must make this work. This is my chance to build a family."

"That's the spirit, Gwendolyn Smythe!" Octavia said with a proud little nod, eyes gleaming.

～

AIDAN STARED at the note in his hand, suspended in that uneasy space between hope and dread. The cryptic contents gave him no indication of which sentiment to favor.

There has been a development - Filminster

BLAST HIS BROTHER-IN-LAW for these cryptic notes. Would it have been so difficult to clarify what sort of development? Something that vindicated Frederick Smythe? Or something that condemned him? Or perhaps something entirely unrelated, which would only entangle matters still further?

Rolling his shoulders and stretching his neck from side to side, Aidan tried to dispel the tension burrowed in his spine. He resolved to finish his breakfast while the servants prepared his mount. He had not slept well, and sustenance would help combat the fatigue that clung to him like damp wool.

He gestured to Thomas, their head footman, and made his request quietly before returning his attention to his plate. Eggs and ham. Simple fare, but welcome. The past days had been a series of interruptions and investigations, each more aggravating than the last. Best to take advantage of the opportunity to eat while it presented itself. The note, after all, had not indicated urgency.

Once fortified, Aidan departed the Abbott townhouse and rode to Ridley House. He dismounted with efficiency and knocked, waiting with the tense patience of a man prepared for almost anything.

The door opened to reveal Michaels, the Ridley butler. It was the same man who had saved Aidan's sister from a desperate servant, an act of bravery not soon forgotten. Aidan had thanked him on the day of the incident, yet Michaels's notoriously curt demeanor made it difficult to discern whether his gratitude had been well received. Aidan still found himself uncertain how to conduct himself around the man.

Members of the *ton* were not, as a rule, expected to engage closely with household staff, especially in homes not their own. But the Abbotts had always been somewhat unorthodox in that respect. A familial warmth had developed between their household and their long-serving retainers, an intimacy born not of indulgence but of mutual respect.

Still, this was not his home. And Michaels was not his servant.

But what if the man in question had saved your sister's life?

"Michaels," Aidan said, inclining his head in a brief nod.

The butler stood stiffly, his expression unreadable, eyes steady and unblinking.

Aidan clenched his jaw but kept his tone civil. "Is Lord Filminster at home?"

Michaels gave a curt nod. Stepping aside, he allowed Aidan entry into the front hall. After closing the door, the butler turned and led the way to Lord Filminster's study, his tread so heavy and measured it echoed down the corridor like the march of a regiment.

Aidan followed, shaking his head slightly at the enigmatic servant. Lily had mentioned that Michaels had been offered retirement in gratitude for his heroism, but had chosen instead to remain in service. It was difficult to imagine that the man found any joy in his duties, yet Aidan supposed there must be some private satisfaction in maintaining his post. Michaels's demeanor was, to Aidan's thinking, rather like that of a sphinx, unreadable and faintly disapproving.

Still, the man had once saved Lily's life, and that merited forbearance. As long as Michaels wished to remain, Aidan would endure their awkward interactions without complaint.

And truth be told, he mused, *Michaels's continued presence might prove fortuitous, given that the true killer remained at large. A man who had demonstrated such courage might be needed again before all was done.*

Upon being shown into Filminster's study, Aidan discovered Trafford already present, draped carelessly in an armchair. The man remained, in Aidan's estimation, something of a puffed-up fool with his parade of embroidered coats, theatrical waistcoats, and an encyclopedic collection of legwear. Still, even Aidan had to admit that Trafford had proved a surprisingly useful ally in their ongoing investigation. The fellow was persistent, and loyal—two traits that were not to be discounted.

With a nod, Aidan sank into a faded armchair and stretched his legs before addressing his brother-in-law, who sat behind a large mahogany desk with an air of collected gravity.

"Well, Ridley, are you going to brief Little Breeches here or not?" Trafford asked, his tone lazy and amused.

Aidan squashed the irritation that flared. Despite his best efforts, the retort slipped out. "It is Filminster, not Ridley."

Trafford arched a brow, his head cocked toward Aidan. "Is he not Brendan Ridley, my old chum from around Town?"

Aidan's tone cooled. "Is he not now the Baron of Filminster? Lord Filminster? Otherwise known to his peers as … Filminster?"

Trafford waved a languid hand. "Tempers are short and patience is frayed. I shall allow your comments to pass without rebuke."

Aidan exhaled sharply. It was not untrue. His patience was indeed fraying. The urgency of ending the danger to Lily gnawed at his composure. And there was Gwen, his Gwen, who now lived in the periphery of every waking moment and every dream.

Last night had been a torment of restless images. Her eyes catching the starlight, her breath warm against his cheek, the press of her hand in his. In his sleep, those memories had stolen past his defenses, weaving a tapestry of longing and what-ifs. He had awoken unsettled, caught between longing and regret, his heart hammering with equal parts want and restraint.

Perhaps it had been a mistake to take her onto the

terrace. But it had not felt like one. Not in that moment. Not with her gaze holding his. Not with her presence stilling the chaos within him.

He drew in a breath and tried to push the memory aside.

"I apologize," he said at last, eyes still on the desk. "You have known Filminster for years, Trafford. Address him as you wish."

Trafford smirked. "I shall, Little Breeches."

Aidan curled his fingers into a fist, his knuckles whitening. The ongoing taunt was not worthy of acknowledgment. Trafford might never relinquish it if he suspected how very aggravating it truly was. This was Aidan's own fault for engaging. He ought to have allowed Filminster to respond instead of letting himself be baited.

"Did something happen?" he asked, redirecting his attention to his sister's husband, who, as it turned out, had been paying not a whit of attention to the exchange.

Filminster was staring down at the rug, a rich swirl of colors that seemed to hold his entire focus. Aidan recognized the expression. He had worn it often enough himself in recent weeks, when the outside world dimmed beneath the weight of a single, relentless question.

How do I unmask the killer and resolve this muddle before Lily is hurt again?

Trafford cleared his throat with exaggerated purpose, and Filminster blinked, returning to the present.

"What happened?" Aidan prompted again when the silence stretched.

Filminster folded his hands atop the desk. "The runner, Briggs, has had men stationed discreetly on the street outside. He reported that someone has been watching the house. At his suggestion, we reduced the visibility of our guards, hoping to draw the watchers out. One of them broke into the library last evening. He escaped before the Johns could seize him."

Aidan surged to his feet, the chair creaking behind him. "How long has the house been under surveillance? Why was I not informed?"

Filminster met his gaze, his voice calm but his eyes shadowed. "There was no reason to cause you undue concern."

A tide of fear rose, sweeping over Aidan in a wave that blurred reason. *Lily.* The thought of her in danger yet again turned his voice sharp as he began to pace. "Why do you not simply take Lily to Somerset? Remove her from this peril?"

Filminster exhaled, the sound weary. "Briggs believes it is safer to remain here. At Ridley House, we have guards, footmen, and familiarity with our surroundings. On the road, we would be exposed, vulnerable in carriages."

"But they are not after her!" Aidan snapped. "They want the letter. They are searching for evidence, not launching an assault."

"If the killer suspects we have the letter," Filminster replied evenly, "he might send men to intercept us. Out on the turnpikes, we would be open to ambush with little means of defense."

Aidan raked a hand through his hair. "But the proof we need may lie in Filminster! We could solve this. We could end this."

"It is not so simple," Filminster said, more gently now. "My uncle kept exhaustive records. Attics full of papers, journals, and accounts. It would take weeks, perhaps months, to locate what we seek. I can entrust such a task only to myself, and perhaps one or two of Briggs's most trusted men. I will not risk Lily's safety for a journey that may yield nothing."

Aidan's frustration boiled over as he turned again, pacing the worn rug. Every day they remained in Town, Lily was at risk.

"Then remove with Lily to my parents' home," he said, his tone edged with iron resolve.

Trafford rose and rolled his shoulders with a languid stretch. "It will not help, Little Breeches. Here, Filminster has guards, and there is Michaels and the household besides. Your parents, as I understand, will be taking the majority of their servants to the country after the wedding. It is better for Ridley and his wife to remain here."

"We need to solve this!" Aidan's voice tightened with frustration. "Lily cannot remain in Ridley House indefinitely."

"Today is Saturday," Trafford replied with maddening calm. "Which means you are to wed in precisely one week. Lord and Lady Moreland depart the week after, so you will be free to pursue further inquiries. Briggs continues to investigate Smythe's sales, but nothing new has yet come to light."

Aidan raked his hand through his hair. "How? How am I to find out anything? I collect my bride Saturday morning and then reside with my parents whilst our own house is prepared."

Filminster, who had remained silent, now interjected. "Perhaps you could persuade Smythe to host you in his own home for a time? Say that your parents' townhouse requires urgent repair, and you thought it best ... for Miss Smythe's comfort ... that you remain under her father's roof until your new residence is ready?"

Aidan rubbed a hand across his face. The suggestion

had merit. His father had given instructions to ready one of their London properties, but that process would take several weeks yet. To claim the house required urgent work would not be too far from truth.

"It is a strange request," he mused. "But I could call upon Smythe and propose the idea. I shall suggest we marry in his home if I am to carry off this fiction. It will not do for him to visit ours."

"That may indeed be for the best," Filminster said, hesitating only briefly. "I know it is a great deal to ask, but I would be grateful. Smythe remains the only one on our list with any substantive hints of duplicity. He could be the one."

Aidan's heart sank, a familiar ache settling in his chest. He raised a hand to knead it, hoping futilely to press back the dread that curled there. He had hoped fervently one of the other men under investigation might prove guilty. Anyone but Smythe. Anyone but Gwen's father.

Filminster must have noticed his disquiet. "We are continuing to investigate the others. But if Smythe killed my uncle, he must answer for it."

"I know," Aidan replied hoarsely. "Lily's safety is at risk, so I do not need reminding that I must reveal the truth if he is guilty."

Filminster stepped closer, placing a hand on Aidan's shoulder with a touch that was awkward but sincere. "I regret that you are in this position ... Aidan."

Aidan nodded and, clearing his throat, made a quiet effort at reciprocation. "Thank you ... Brendan."

Trafford, never one to let sincerity linger too long, smirked as he resumed his sprawl in the armchair. "It is heartwarming to witness family closeness."

Aidan shut his eyes, the corners tightening with frustration. *Trust the fop to ruin the moment.* "Get lost, Trafford."

Brendan laughed, the earlier tension melting from his features. For an instant, Aidan glimpsed the man his brother-in-law might be under normal circumstances, a man more inclined to levity than duty. "You are one of us now, Aidan. Only Trafford's nearest and dearest tell him to get lost."

Aidan shook his head with dry disdain. "If the day ever dawns that Trafford and I are counted friends, you are to take me out back and put a musket ball through my head. It will mean I have descended into some grotesque parody of existence."

Trafford pulled a face, feigning injury. "Careful, Little Breeches. You may wound my delicate sensibilities."

"Do you possess any?" Aidan shot back without missing a beat.

The fool shrugged. "On occasion."

Aidan snorted, the sound half amused and half appalled. As much as Trafford vexed him, he had to concede, grudgingly, that the man had a peculiar talent for breaking through his darker moods. Perhaps, in certain moments, and under exceedingly specific circumstances, the other heir did serve some purpose.

He exhaled, the flicker of humor sliding from his features. How had it come to this? He was searching for a murderer, guarding his sister, and shielding the woman he was soon to marry from potential scandal. All at once. The weight of it pressed heavily upon his shoulders.

Next week, he would wed Gwen. And everything—every tangled, precarious thread—would become more complicated still.

CHAPTER NINE

"Hope is a waking dream."

Aristotle

AUGUST 25, 1821

Buttercup, Octavia, and Gwen stood in the entrance hall of the Smythe residence, quietly observing as footmen carried Lord Abbott's trunks up the stairs and into the bedchamber adjacent to hers. Aidan's valet, a gaunt figure with impeccable attire and a voice pitched with the precision of a court musician, directed the activity with fluttering fingers and a sharp eye.

The whole situation felt most peculiar. Her father had informed her, quite matter-of-factly, that she and Aidan would reside in the family home until their new household was ready for occupation. And so it was settled.

Gwen was not aware of any precedent for a peer of Aidan's standing to install himself, post-nuptials, in the home of a gentleman several rungs lower on the social ladder. Yet given that Lord and Lady Moreland were soon to retire to the country, it seemed the most practical arrangement.

"What do you suppose is in Lord Abbott's trunks?" Octavia asked, tilting her head as another heavily laden servant passed by. "There are so many of them."

Gwen inhaled through her nose, considering, before replying with a confident air. "Books. The extra trunks contain his books."

Octavia's brow lifted in mild surprise.

"He has just returned from the Continent," Gwen elaborated. "He quotes Marcus Manilius and Shakespeare with the kind of fluency one could not feign. He must read constantly."

A slow smile spread across Octavia's face. "He does not look like a scholar."

She lifted her hands to sketch the breadth of Aidan's shoulders and the tapering line to his hips, before finishing with a conspicuous cupping motion that drew Gwen's breath to a sudden halt.

"Octavia!" The word was a gasp of protest, though its force was blunted by long-standing familiarity.

The lady's maid merely shrugged, wholly unrepentant. "I know you've noticed, Gwendolyn Smythe."

Buttercup whined at their feet, her pink tongue lolling in canine approval of Octavia's indelicate insinuation.

Gwen blushed fiercely. The telltale heat began at her décolletage and surged up her throat to her cheeks, a fiery tide that left no doubt of her mortification. She said nothing. There was no need. Octavia would draw her own conclusions from that alone.

The maid gave her a sidelong glance. "I thought as much. Just think ... tonight is your wedding night. You shall have the opportunity to behold, first-hand ..." She repeated the cupping motion with exaggerated flair, her meaning all too clear.

Gwen exhaled, a flustered puff escaping her lips. The very notion of Aidan entering her bedchamber made her limbs go oddly weightless. Of course she had imagined their first private kiss, removing his coat, touching his shoulders ... Her blush deepened. *Enough!* It would hardly do to faint in the hallway from the weight of her own imagination.

Mercifully, Octavia shifted course. "Did you ever learn why the wedding was delayed until now?"

Grateful for the change in topic, Gwen seized it. "It was to allow for his cousin to return from Somerset. Lord Moreland insisted that the scandal had settled enough, now that the wedding was announced, to send for his niece and her family. Apparently, she grew up with Lord Abbott and his sister."

Octavia tilted her head in thought, then her eyes widened. "Do you mean the Countess of Saunton?"

"I believe so. Lady Sophia Balfour."

Octavia let out a choking sound. "And is Lord Saunton accompanying her?"

Gwen turned from the hall, brows raised. "Yes, why?"

"Do you know who Lord Saunton is?"

"No, not particularly."

"His father was Lord Satan. Infamous for seducing the staff and ruining reputations. The younger Saunton was said to be the same ... until he married a girl he scarcely knew. Last year, he acknowledged a child born out of wedlock by a maid. The boy lives with them now."

This information jarred against the image Gwen had formed of the Abbott family. Dignified, respectable, above reproach.

"Why would such a family permit that match?" she wondered aloud. Then her eyes widened. "Ought we warn the maids downstairs to be cautious?"

Octavia raised a hand to nibble absently at her thumbnail, the tension written plainly across her broad, expressive face. But then, with a sharp breath, she dropped her hand and straightened her spine. "I have not heard anything recent," she said briskly, "but I shall inform the housekeeper. Cook will know if there is any risk in serving him."

"Perhaps the maids ought to remain out of sight until his departure," Gwen suggested, her brow furrowed. "The footmen can manage the main rooms for the time being."

Octavia gave a swift nod and darted off, skirts fluttering like a startled flock of starlings. Her hurried step and bobbing head only added to the impression, an image Gwen often observed in the Smythe gardens when birds took sudden flight. Her maid's unease was unmistakable.

Buttercup watched the retreating woman with her characteristic squint, the slight baring of her teeth suggesting commentary on the hazards that awaited unguarded women. Gwen, observing her, could not disagree. Their own meeting had arisen under such danger.

Yet, despite all warnings, Gwen could not help but feel a flicker of intrigue. What must it be like to encounter such a man? A notorious rake, reputed to have seduced staff and cast shame upon his family name. He was hardly the sort of gentleman her father would welcome into their circle. Still, if there was no threat to the women belowstairs, she could not deny a faint thrill at the prospect of observing such a man with her own eyes.

What astonished her most was that Lady Sophia Balfour, Aidan's cousin, had welcomed her husband's illegitimate child into their home. Had she done so willingly? Or had duty compelled her? Was she privately humiliated, or had affection somehow triumphed over pride?

The connection to the Abbott family confounded her. Octavia had spoken of them in terms that implied discreet propriety. This, however, complicated the portrait.

Turning back toward her chamber, Gwen nudged Buttercup inside with a gentle foot, offering a quick scratch behind the ears before shutting the door. The little dog trotted to the hearth as Gwen moved to the mirror.

Her wedding gown awaited.

Signora Ricci had crafted it in a rich shade of azure, and now it clung to Gwen's figure with soft precision. The silk was luxurious yet delicate, as though spun from seafoam, and Gwen had selected the color with a very particular inspiration in mind, *The Birth of Venus*. Aidan's admiring words had lingered with her, and this hue, like morning mist above a calm ocean, had seemed apt.

She had taken a risk with the contrast. Red hair and green-blue silk made a striking combination, and she hoped, perhaps too eagerly, that he had meant what he said. That he did, in fact, find her beautiful.

Nerves fluttered low in her belly, not with dread but with the sweet tremble of uncertainty. Should she descend to greet the arriving guests on her own? Or wait for Octavia's return?

But then she recalled the strained exchange between her lady's maid and Lady Moreland. It was entirely possible that Octavia, still cowed by the dowager's commanding presence, would find reason to remain out of sight.

Gwen sighed, shoulders squaring before the mirror.

Alone it is.

Squaring her shoulders, Gwen summoned what confidence she possessed, assuring herself she had judged Aidan's preferences correctly. Despite her habitual skepticism, a number of hopes had quietly taken root in her heart. Her father's enduring optimism had proved contagious, and Gwen prayed, fervently, that she would not come to rue the decision to allow herself to dream.

After so many years spent skirting the outer edges of the *beau monde*, enduring its condescension with dignity, she now dared to imagine a future filled with companionship, respect, and perhaps even affection. If fortune were kind, she might come to count herself among those rare few who married well in both title and temperament.

As she prepared to leave her room, she turned to Buttercup and whispered, "Sorry, girl. This is not the time to follow me."

The little dog whined, her haunches wiggling against the floor in dismay. Yet she did not attempt to move from her place near the mirror, clearly electing to await Gwen's return with canine resolve.

Gwen smiled and closed the door gently behind her.

Descending the staircase, she paused before the small drawing room, the very room where she had once endured her first meeting with Aidan's parents, and stepped inside to find that their guests had already arrived.

Aidan moved toward her at once. With a graceful bow, he extended his arm.

He was sartorial perfection, his navy coat molded to his shoulders, the rich wool catching the morning light. Gwen accepted his arm, and his voice, low and warm, curled through her like a silken ribbon.

"You are ravishing this morning, Miss Smythe."

A thrill danced down her spine. She smiled demurely and turned her gaze to the gathering, surprised to find the company more numerous than expected.

By the window stood a man of striking stature, towering well above six feet. With his blond hair and storm-gray eyes, he bore the look of a Norse marauder. Something about his countenance was familiar, though she could not recall ever having been introduced.

Beside him stood a young woman of elegant bearing, her dark chestnut curls styled high atop her head in an intricate arrangement that suggested wealth, taste, and a modiste with a deft hand.

Aidan led her toward the pair with unmistakable deference, which all but confirmed her suspicion that the imposing gentleman held the highest rank among them.

Coming to a halt, Aidan spoke. "Miss Smythe, I have the honor of presenting His Grace, the Duke of Halmesbury."

Gwen's brows lifted in surprise. Indeed, she had recognized him.

The duke offered a courtly bow, his baritone voice resonant. "The pleasure is mine, Miss Smythe. Felicitations upon your wedding."

Gwen dipped into a curtsy, murmuring a polite response as her gaze flicked, ever so discreetly, around the room to discern who else she might be obliged to greet this morning. Her father stood near the fireplace, bouncing lightly on the balls of his feet, his ever-present grin fixed in place. Clearly, he was near to bursting with pride over the distinguished connections Aidan had brought into their modest family.

Aidan turned next to the lady beside the duke. "Your Grace, may I present Miss Smythe."

Gwen swiftly curtsied again, belatedly realizing that this was the Duchess of Halmesbury. The duchess was a tall woman, though still several inches shy of Gwen's height, and visibly with child. A soft roundness marked her growing figure, and her brandy-colored eyes gleamed warmly as she smiled.

"Miss Smythe," she said graciously, "welcome to the family."

"F-family?" Gwen echoed, startled, her wide eyes darting to Aidan. But it was the duchess who answered.

"My brother, Lord Filminster, is married to Lord Abbott's sister. His Grace and I returned to Town upon hearing of the nuptials."

"Oh." It was a woefully inadequate reply, but Gwen's mind had stalled, still reeling from the revelation. *Why had Octavia failed to mention this?* The connection to Halmesbury, one of the few dukes in the kingdom, was certainly the sort of intelligence a lady's maid ought to impart.

Before she could dwell on it further, Aidan continued the introductions. Gwen turned next to meet Lord and Lady Saunton. Despite Octavia's scandalous tidings about Lord Saunton's early reputation, Gwen found him courteous and unexpectedly entertaining. His emerald-green eyes twinkled with amusement, and he seemed wholly captivated by his wife.

Lady Saunton was a poised young woman with soft reddish-blonde curls and a gentle confidence that Gwen admired immediately. Her manner bespoke intelligence and a quiet strength, and her hand remained securely linked with her husband's throughout their conversation.

Their dialogue was briefly interrupted when Lady

Saunton's skirts stirred, and from behind them emerged a small boy with sable-dark hair and eyes to match his father's. He blinked solemnly up at Gwen.

"Hallo," he greeted her without ceremony.

Taken aback, Gwen inclined her head. "How do you do?"

"Are you Cousin Aidan's new wife?"

Lady Saunton laughed lightly. "Not quite yet, Ethan."

The boy's brow furrowed. "Does she play chess, Mama?"

"I am not certain," Lady Saunton replied. "Perhaps you ought to inquire."

Ethan regarded Gwen with a contemplative expression, his earlier boldness giving way to a hint of shyness. "Do you play chess?" he asked at last.

"I do."

"After you marry, will you play with me?"

Gwen smiled, charmed by the lad's earnestness. "We must enjoy the wedding breakfast first."

"And then we can play?"

She nodded. "Then we can play."

"Good."

Ethan vanished behind the Countess of Saunton's skirts once more, the tails of his little green coat the last glimpse Gwen caught of him. She remained momentarily bemused. That Lady Saunton should show such easy affection toward the boy, whom Gwen presumed must be the very child Octavia had whispered about, spoke volumes. There was no hint of discord between the trio. Rather, they appeared much like any loving family.

Next, Gwen was presented to the local vicar, a round-faced man with a bald crown and long white side-whiskers that gave him the look of a kindly cherub.

"I appreciate your presence this morning, Vicar," Gwen said, dipping into a respectful curtsy.

"Not at all, Miss Smythe," he replied jovially. "Lord Moreland's generous donation to our parish ensured my attendance. We are quite grateful."

Aidan moved on with the introductions, presenting Lord Filminster, who bore the same dark chestnut hair and brandy-colored eyes as the Duchess of Halmesbury, clearly her brother. He bowed politely and offered a reserved smile, but unlike the others, there was a certain guardedness in his manner. Gwen returned the gesture with demure courtesy, sensing he was not one inclined to idle chatter.

The formality began to ease as Aidan introduced those closest to him.

"And this is my sister, Lady Filminster."

A petite young woman stepped forward with an eager smile. Her hair was a shade richer than Aidan's, and her eyes sparkled with warmth. She seized Gwen's hands without hesitation.

"Please call me Lily! We are to be sisters, are we not? Oh, I adore weddings. They always make one think of the future and possibilities and babes. Imagine! Another scandalous match, barely a month after my own ruin. What an extraordinary turn life has taken!"

Gwen blinked, startled by the torrent of cheerful words.

"Aidan tells me you love to read," Lily continued, undeterred. "I have recently developed an interest in French military strategy. Do you have a favorite subject?"

Still reeling slightly, Gwen hesitated before answering. "I favor the Ancient Greeks. Aristotle. Homer."

A soft, appreciative sound escaped Aidan, and Gwen caught the flicker of admiration in his gaze.

"Oh, that is rather beyond my abilities," Lily said with a

good-natured laugh. "Aidan and Sophia are the scholars of the family. I must resort to a dictionary when studying French! But Greek ... how fascinating!"

Then, quite suddenly, her expression turned thoughtful. She glanced over at her father, something unreadable passing across her features, before turning back to Gwen.

"Welcome to the family," she said quietly. "Whatever the future brings, I am truly delighted to call you sister."

Then the young woman enveloped her in a hasty, somewhat clumsy embrace before stepping back with a bright smile. Gwen found herself momentarily winded by the exchange. Lady Filminster might have been no larger than a schoolgirl, but her energy could easily fill a ballroom. Her personality was certainly far grander than her diminutive frame.

At last, Aidan led Gwen toward his parents, and she was surprised to see that they had been joined by an elderly servant. The woman, clearly advanced in years, was dressed in a simple maid's uniform. Wisps of white hair framed her wrinkled face like a downy halo, and her mobcap drooped sideways in quiet rebellion.

Lady Moreland greeted Gwen graciously, then turned to adjust the slipping cap with motherly precision. Aidan brought Gwen to a halt in front of the maid without offering explanation.

Leaning down with theatrical volume, Lady Moreland shrieked into the woman's ear, "THIS IS MASTER AIDAN'S BRIDE!"

Gwen startled slightly at the outburst, blinking as the old maid turned her faded eyes toward her and smiled. With a somewhat wobbly curtsy, the woman offered her silent blessing.

"This is my father's nursemaid," Aidan explained

gently. "Nancy helped raise us all. She was Lily's companion for many years, and my parents thought she might enjoy attending the ceremony."

Gwen felt a sudden, unexpected surge of kinship. The Abbotts, for all their grandeur, seemed to value the same things her own family held dear. Loyalty, longevity, and the quiet dignity of lifelong service.

Lady Moreland must have perceived her thoughts. "Where is that curious lady's maid of yours?" she asked, a note of inquiry rather than criticism in her voice. "Does she not wish to witness your vows?"

Gwen smiled, the warmth in her expression unfeigned. It seemed she and Octavia had misjudged Lady Moreland's opinions upon their first encounter. "I shall ring for her at once."

"Yes, my dear. We ought not keep the vicar waiting. I am certain he has other duties to attend."

Octavia was summoned, and Gwen stood quietly for a moment, taking in the gathering around her. So many new relations. So many titles. And yet ... they had all proven more welcoming than she had dared hope. Even Lord Filminster, who remained somewhat reserved, had been polite.

Perhaps, just perhaps, this would all turn out better than she had ever imagined.

Aidan cast her a glance, his eyes lingering, and Gwen felt her heart skip. There was something in his gaze, an expression of admiration mingled with promise, that made her wonder whether tonight might mark not merely the start of a marriage, but the awakening of something far deeper.

Despite the caution she had worn like armor for so

many years, Gwen found herself daring, truly daring, to believe in her father's vision of the future.

Perhaps ... this would become the love match she had once dreamed of.

~

WHILE THEY TOOK THEIR VOWS, Aidan felt both bliss and remorse. The sacred weight of the moment pressed upon him, binding him to Gwen not only in duty, but in a tender, growing affection. It had been quite a surprise when he had learned that the duke and duchess had returned, along with his cousin Sophia and her husband, the Earl of Saunton.

The linked families had all met yesterday, except for his own parents. Lord Moreland had not wished to involve Lady Moreland in the discussion. Aidan agreed that there was no reason to distress his mother when they did not yet know the truth about the baron's murder.

It had soon become clear that their arrival was not merely to celebrate the wedding. It was a deliberate and thoughtful show of support for his bride in the event that Smythe was accused of murdering Brendan's father. Apparently, his brother-in-law had apprised them of the investigation in confidence. That the matter still lingered unresolved cast a faint shadow over today's ceremony.

The duchess had commiserated over the complexity of the situation, pointing out that she understood the troubles that a father could visit upon his daughter. Aidan had not known that she had had a troubled relationship with the late baron, but he was aware that Brendan Ridley and the late Lord Filminster had been estranged. The news sheets had reported the scandal with relish.

There had been a lengthy discussion with all parties present at Ridley House, where the murder had taken place a month before. The somber setting had offered a rather grisly reminder of why Aidan was in this strange position to begin with, straddling the line between loyalty and suspicion, affection and obligation.

Nevertheless, as he gazed down at Gwen in her soft blue-green dress—modest and elegant, with tiny pearl buttons at the wrists and lace detailing at the collar—he could not bring himself to regret this wedding. She had accepted him with quiet strength, and he could only be thankful that Lord Trafford was not in attendance to remind him of his shortcomings or to forewarn of the future strife that would surely arise if Smythe turned out to be the culprit.

Today was a complicated union of interests, but at this moment, Aidan was mostly anxious about what would happen this evening when he joined his bride in the marriage bed. In the house of a man who might be a murderer.

Frederick Smythe was clearly exuberant about the connections who had visited his home this morning, grinning and rubbing his hands together in greedy, childlike joy. Aidan supposed any man would be overjoyed to scale the ladder of high society so abruptly, but there was an element of naked ambition to Smythe's behavior that was difficult to stomach. The man's delight was too unchecked, too eager, as if he viewed his daughter not as a treasure, but as a coin well spent.

Unfortunately, despite Aidan watching Smythe closely during the introductions, the man had displayed no telling reaction to meeting Lily and Filminster, which Aidan had hoped he might, given the circumstances. His composure had been infuriatingly bland.

"Wilt thou have this woman to thy wedded wife, to live together after God's ordinance in the holy estate of Matrimony? Wilt thou love her, comfort her, honor, and keep her, in sickness and in health; and, forsaking all other, keep thee only unto her, so long as ye both shall live?" intoned the vicar.

On the one hand, Aidan wished they could resolve the murder in order to ensure Lily's safety. On the other hand, it was with a sense of dread that he considered informing Gwen of such terrible news. It was obvious she was close to her father. He imagined if he were to discover that his own father had murdered a man ... such a revelation would be utterly devastating. All he could do was resolve to remain at her side and be a good husband and partner, no matter what might come to light.

"I will," Aidan stated, his voice firm and confident, echoing with the certainty of his vow.

And then, he could no longer think about the future, for it had quietly arrived and stood hand in hand with him. His thoughts, unbidden, drifted to this very night, not with fear, but with the awe of what lay ahead. A shared life, a shared bed, a bond that would grow more intimate with each passing day.

"Wilt thou have this man to thy wedded husband, to live together after God's ordinance in the holy estate of Matrimony? Wilt thou obey him and serve him, love, honor, and keep him, in sickness and in health; and, forsaking all other, keep thee only unto him, so long as ye both shall live?"

He watched Gwen, who hesitated for the briefest moment, then responded in a shy voice, "I will."

Aidan was captivated by her radiance in the morning light streaming through the great fan-arched windows. Her golden-red lashes cast delicate shadows upon her cheeks, and he prayed in silence that Trafford would uncover a different suspect. If the worst were true, the blow would surely fracture her. He wished to spare her that pain.

He wanted his bride to experience a long and happy life, to know joy without fear or shadow. But as his eyes flickered over to Frederick Smythe, he could not help but notice the almost ravenous gleam in the man's eye. Smythe's delight at forming ties with nobility bordered on the unseemly. It lent credence to the suspicion that desperation might have driven him to dark choices, especially if the baron had posed a threat to his aspirations.

The vicar at length concluded the service. When it was over, Gwen looked up at Aidan, her blue eyes aglow like twin lanterns on a misty night. He smiled down at her. "We are wed."

She swallowed hard, her lips parting slightly as she whispered, "We are wed."

Her words, so simple yet profound, landed within him like a seal pressed into warm wax. Aidan's thoughts returned once more to their wedding night, not with impatience, but with a deep and solemn curiosity. He was no longer a bachelor, but a husband. Would she be shy? Would she feel safe with him? He ached to be worthy of her trust.

They linked arms, and together led the wedding party from the drawing room toward the wedding breakfast, their footsteps quiet, but full of the tremulous hope of something just begun.

Gwen picked at her breakfast, scarcely able to believe that she was finally married. Tonight, her groom would come to her chamber, and they would begin their quest for children, a thought that sent a shiver of delight and apprehension down her spine. She pressed her fingers lightly to the rim of her teacup, trying to anchor herself in the moment.

Aidan was resplendent. Tall, confident, and youthful, he laughed as he debated with his sister on his other side, the sunlight catching the burnished waves of his hair. There was something steadying in his presence, a quiet confidence that had soothed her these past days.

You barely know him.

The whisper of her consciousness was an unwelcome disquiet, threading through the peace she strove to maintain.

I will learn about him, the braver part of her replied, swift and sure.

You do not know what kind of husband he will be. What if he is cruel?

She shut her eyes for a brief second, attempting to quell the wave of unease washing over her. She was simply nervous, was she not? It was only natural. Aidan had proved himself a thoughtful suitor, generous in manner and considerate in speech. If he bore any hidden motives, surely he would not have agreed to dwell in her father's household where every glance might be observed by her parent. His family had greeted her with warmth, their regard sincere. Even Lord Saunton, whose reputation lingered on the edges of scandal, had treated her with kindness.

"Are you done eating?" A childish voice interrupted her thoughts.

Gwen looked up to find little Ethan gazing at her with large hopeful eyes from a few seats down the table. His hair curled at the nape of his neck, and his expression was so earnest it tugged at something deep within her.

Lady Saunton smiled at Gwen in apology. "Hush, Ethan. Allow Lady Abbott to finish her meal in peace. She will not forget her promise to play."

"Why do I call him Cousin Aidan, but I must call her Lady Abbott?" Ethan pointed a diminutive finger at Gwen and her groom, the question delivered with guileless candor.

"It is up to Lady Abbott to decide how she wishes to be addressed. We only just met her this morning."

Gwen laughed. The lad was lively and charming, not at all what she had expected when Octavia had explained the Sauntons' situation. "Cousin Gwen would be acceptable to me," she offered warmly.

Ethan beamed. "Are you finished eating yet, Cousin Gwen?"

She looked down at her plate and determined that her appetite had made a quiet exit. "Shall we play in the library?"

Ethan clapped his hands in delight. "Yes!"

He scrambled out of his chair, running around the table to wait for Gwen with the exuberance only a child could muster.

Aidan leaned closer, speaking in a low voice near her ear. "You are part of the family now. Ethan will expect a game in all future encounters."

His voice curled through her, warm and steady, like the brush of velvet gloves across her skin. Gwen nodded, acknowledging both the words and the quiet thrill they brought. "I do not mind."

Once she had risen, she took hold of Ethan's tiny hand, and together, they walked to the library, his fingers tucked trustingly into her palm. Gwen contemplated what it would be like to have a little one of her own to care for, so lively and bright, and then realized in mild disbelief that it had become a genuine possibility.

Huzzah! I am married!

The thought rang in her chest with soft wonder.

Several hours later, their party of guests began to depart. Gwen and Aidan stood with her father in the front hall, bidding them farewell as the carriages rolled away from the house. His sister and her husband were the last to leave, Lily chattering in a nervous manner before embracing Gwen with an awkward sincerity that Gwen found endearing.

Once the door closed, the three of them stood in silence until her father announced that he would be in his study and excused himself, leaving them alone.

Gwen remained motionless, watching Aidan with pensive anticipation. Would he kiss her now that they were alone? Would he draw near and claim this new bond between them?

Aidan blew out a breath, then turned to smile at her, though it seemed somewhat uncertain around the edges. "I ... have a meeting at my club ... and I shall return later."

Disappointment rose like mist from the floor, cool and sudden. She had expected something different. His voice, though calm, carried the ring of evasion, as though he needed to flee.

Was he unhappy about their marriage, tied as it was to scandal and suspicion? He had seemed committed, even eager. But now he appeared desperate to be away, and her heart gave a quiet thud of concern.

"Um ... I shall see that the servants have unpacked your things and ... await your return."

Aidan nodded, not quite meeting her gaze, then bowed. The gesture was polite, respectful, but painfully formal. It did not suit the intimacy of the day they had just shared. Without further word, he turned and slipped out the front door with unexpected haste.

How was he to reach his club? There had been no carriage waiting. Would he catch a hackney?

Gwen held her arms stiffly at her sides and shook out her hands, an effort to dispel the anxious tension building within her. Was her groom regretting their vows? She had not thought so earlier. But now? Now she did not know what to believe. And it was far too late to change course.

AIDAN HAD WALKED several miles through London streets, attempting to clear his thoughts. It had not worked. His mind circled like a restless horse, unable to outrun the anxiety coiled in his chest. He could not stop thinking about this evening, about what was expected of him as a husband.

The mechanics were no mystery. But that knowledge did little to ease his turmoil.

Seated alone at a back table in his club, Aidan stared down at the untouched brandy he had ordered. Around him, the murmur of deep conversation and the clink of fine crystal glasses filled the air, mingling with the rich scent of cigars and polished wood. Other gentlemen indulged in

French spirits and jocular debate, but Aidan remained apart.

Like the rest of the Abbotts, he did not drink spirits, an enduring habit formed out of respect for his cousin Sophia and the vow she had made long ago. On occasion, he would order a brandy to avoid distressing the club's servers, who hovered uncertainly when he remained unserved.

He considered the glass now. Perhaps one swallow would soothe him and settle his nerves?

Not that tonight's duties were unwelcome. Quite the opposite. He had imagined Gwen—dreamed of her, truthfully—since that night on the terrace when her eyes had met his. But imagination was a far cry from reality, and Gwen was an innocent. She deserved more than awkward uncertainty or the ill-timed clumsiness of a man overthinking every step.

What if he disappointed her?

"Little Breeches."

Aidan grunted under his breath. Of course. He had managed to find the one club in London where he might stumble across Lord Trafford.

Looking up, Aidan set his jaw and forced a passable smile, though irritation thrummed beneath it.

Trafford approached with his usual theatrical flair, dressed in a bronze jacquard coat so bright it threatened to dazzle the chandeliers. Beneath it, an ebony waistcoat was embroidered in a pattern that seemed to shimmer whenever he moved.

Aidan could not help noting, grimly, that whatever allowance the Earl of Stirling granted his son was clearly too generous, if one judged by the foppish excess of his attire.

The other heir dropped into the chair opposite,

sweeping a practiced hand through the deliberately tousled curls at the crown of his head. Aidan rolled his eyes. Nothing screamed affectation like Trafford's two-toned hair, wheat-hued on top and a darker brown beneath. The result of artifice, no doubt, and a valet far too eager to indulge in chemical experimentation.

"I thought you wed today," Trafford remarked.

"I did," Aidan answered curtly.

"Then why are you here?"

Aidan rolled his shoulders and forced himself back into the chair with a show of ease he did not feel. "No reason."

"Is the whole ..." Trafford gestured vaguely in the air, as if conjuring smoke.

"No." The muddle with Gwen's father—and the knowledge that, now her future was secured, Aidan must return to his investigation into Smythe—weighed heavily upon his conscience. But today, that was not what troubled him most.

"Are you well, Little Breeches?"

Aidan snorted. Only Trafford could offer sympathy and insult in the same breath.

"What are you doing here?"

The other heir dropped his gaze, his usual levity dimmed. "I ... cannot be at home right now. There are ... issues."

Aidan tilted his head, examining the shadows under Trafford's eyes. The man was clearly unsettled.

"Are you staying at the club?"

A brief nod was the only response.

Aidan did not welcome the prick of sympathy that stirred within him, slow and persistent, like the kindling of a hearth fire. It appeared they both bore burdens unspoken.

Trafford gave his head a little shake, as if tossing away

unwelcome thoughts, then leaned forward on the table. "But what of you, Little Breeches? You appear melancholy, and your bride awaits."

Aidan cleared his throat, dropping his gaze to the polished floorboards. "I think you know, considering your charming little sobriquet for me."

A pause followed, filled only by the low hum of the room. A hand entered his peripheral vision and plucked up his drink. The quiet clink of glass against teeth came next, followed by a deliberate swallow. Then ...

"It is true, then?"

Aidan nodded, heat rising to his cheeks.

"You have never ...?" Trafford left the question dangling, incomplete.

Another reluctant nod.

Trafford exhaled slowly. "I suspected. There was never any gossip about women. Some whispered that perhaps you ... well, never mind that. I have seen the way you look at Lady Abbott ... it leaves little doubt. But why have you never pursued ...?"

By Jupiter, this is an uncomfortable subject.

Aidan had spent so long abroad that he had few confidants left in England, and he never imagined that the first person he would confide in about this would be Trafford. Yet, oddly, there was something pacifying in speaking the truth aloud to someone who, for all his polish and pretension, had seen more of the world than most.

"I believe that such an act should be shared between people who care for one another," he said, his voice quiet but firm. "I never met a woman I wished to offer that part of myself to ... until Gwen."

Trafford stared at him for a few moments before huffing a laugh. "A man with standards. I shall order another drink so I may toast that which Diogenes only dreamed of. I have found an honest man."

Aidan groaned. "I am deceiving my bride, so not as honest as I would wish."

"That aside, I think it is rather endearing, Little Breeches. You come from a good family and you possess morals. There is nothing in that to be ashamed of."

"I am not ashamed. Unless"—Aidan leaned forward, his hands curling into fists on the table—"you decide to share this conversation, in which case I will be forced to defend my honor in a most vigorous manner."

Trafford's lips quirked into a smile. "This conversation remains our secret. I am, however, profoundly impressed with my own talents in the field of deduction. When I first inquired after you, the notion crossed my mind briefly, but I dismissed it as too unlikely. It appears I am quite the investigator."

"Splendid," Aidan muttered. "Find a murderer other than Smythe, then. It would spare Gwen a great deal of pain if someone else could be shown to have had a motive."

"I am working on it. Ridley is rather dear to me, old chap."

Aidan rolled his shoulders again, the tension never fully leaving them. "I suppose I should go home and ..." He made a vague gesture, the very act of articulation too mortifying to attempt.

"There is a book in my rooms that might assist you."

Before Aidan could protest, Trafford sprang from his chair and disappeared down the corridor. Within minutes, he returned, dropped into his seat once more, and placed a small leather-bound volume on the table between them.

Aidan picked it up, frowning at the strange symbols

stamped on the cover. "I am quite the scholar, Trafford, but even I do not read Sanskrit."

Trafford shook his head in mock despair. Leaning over, he opened the book and flipped a few pages. "There are illustrations, Little Breeches."

Aidan drew the book closer. The moment his gaze landed on the images, his breath caught and his collar felt suddenly too tight. The artistic renderings, though elaborate, left little to the imagination.

"Is this legal?"

"The activities? More or less. The book itself? Probably not."

"I understand the general ... framework," Aidan said stiffly. "I do not need these." He pushed the book back across the table.

Trafford snickered and slid it right back. "You might find there are more ... interpretations of the task than you assumed. Trust me, and pay attention to the visuals."

Aidan sighed and tucked the volume into his coat. He would hire a hackney and explore the illustrations somewhere far more private.

"Now," Trafford said with relish, "I shall impart some of my personal wisdom on the subject."

"Please do not."

"You wish to know what I know, Little Breeches. And believe me, Gwendolyn Abbott will be a very happy woman if you listen carefully."

Aidan shoulders slumped, surveying his options. Return home with vague notions, return to the Abbott townhouse and pester his father for counsel, or remain here and endure Trafford's unsolicited lecture.

"Dash it, just make it painless."

Trafford tsked like a disappointed tutor. "Do you want painless or effective?"

Aidan dropped his head into his hands, utterly mortified to be receiving matrimonial advice from the most ostentatious peacock in London. "Effective, I suppose."

That was all the encouragement Trafford required. With the enthusiasm of a man presenting a military strategy, he launched into a tactful, if spirited, dissertation on how best to proceed with one's duties as a newlywed husband, complete with occasional euphemisms and far too much confidence.

CHAPTER TEN

"Love is composed of a single soul inhabiting two bodies."

Aristotle

Gwen was not sure what to do. Her new husband had left hours ago, and still he had not returned. It was nearing the hour to prepare for dinner, yet she had imagined something quite different for this evening. She had envisioned they might retire early. That she would wear her azure gown, selected carefully for this very moment.

Now she stood rooted in indecision.

Should she change for dinner? Or remain in her wedding gown, a hopeful symbol turned strange with every passing minute?

They were frivolous thoughts, and she knew it. Yet they served to distract her from the quiet panic that had been building in the pit of her stomach ever since Aidan had departed with such haste. The more time passed, the more certain she became that he regretted marrying her. And that notion, so sharp and bitter, was especially painful now that she had met his family and had begun to feel the warmth of belonging.

She had thoroughly enjoyed the afternoon with little Ethan and the others. Most of her social life had been spent in the company of those much older. Younger women had often regarded her with clipped politeness or subtle malice, and the younger gentlemen had shown such cool indifference that meaningful conversation had been a rarity.

Today had been different.

Among his family, clever engaging people of various temperaments, Gwen had found a tentative hope for the future. It felt as though a door had quietly opened to a life she had not dared to imagine, one filled with laughter, with conversation, with true companionship. She had anticipated invitations and letters, outings and dinners. She had even allowed herself to look forward to a new chapter with Aidan, with tentative joy.

Gwen closed her wardrobe. She had been standing before it for several minutes without making any decision at all.

"He hates being married to me," she murmured.

"Nonsense!" Octavia's reply was swift, but a note of hesitation in her voice betrayed her doubt. "He ... just had ... something important to do. Someone important to see."

At Octavia's feet, Buttercup gave a low whine, as if lending her small agreement. The dog's soft brown eyes fixed on Gwen with canine intensity, as though she too shared in the collective concern.

"On our wedding day?" Gwen asked, her voice barely a whisper.

Octavia turned away, clearly at a loss for words. Buttercup remained seated, ever watchful, her gaze unwavering as Gwen moved about the room in restless fits, picking up gloves, then placing them down, smoothing a hem that did not need smoothing.

Buttercup tilted her head, her silent companionship both comforting and a little accusing.

"Should I change for dinner?" Gwen asked aloud, to no one in particular.

Octavia stepped forward, her voice gentle now. "Perhaps I should bring up a tray?"

Gwen nodded silently. Her father had already declared that he would not be available for dinner, which meant she would be left to eat alone at the vast dining table, an image far from appealing, especially when her thoughts would dwell only on Aidan's continued absence.

After Octavia departed, Gwen wandered toward the window and sank into the indigo wingback armchair, her mother's old favorite. Picking up her well-worn copy of *The Odyssey*, she attempted to immerse herself in Homer's epic. But after reading the same line thrice without comprehension, she tossed the book gently onto the side table.

Buttercup, ever loyal, padded after her and settled heavily upon Gwen's slippered feet, her warm weight a silent encouragement to calm herself.

Have I made a mistake?

The thought was as unwelcome as it was disheartening. It seemed too soon, entirely too soon, for such doubts to take root. She had hoped to float in blissful contentment for at least a few days before reality and uncertainty crept in.

Drumming her fingers against the plush armrest, Gwen stared out at the garden, its hedges pruned into gentle curves, the lawn sloping toward the silver ribbon of the

Thames glimmering in the evening light. Her father's only remaining property, yes, but still a jewel. An oasis amid the hum of London life. She would miss this place once she and Aidan established their new household.

The indigo chair, though, that she would take with her. It bore memories of afternoons spent beside her mother, of laughter and shared stories. It brought her peace, and she would not leave it behind.

Mama would tell me to buck up and take action.

But how?

She did not even know where Aidan had gone. And she could hardly go dashing about Town in search of him. Noblewomen did not storm gentlemen's clubs. At least, not as a rule.

Although ...

She was married now. That came with freedoms, did it not? Even Milly, dreadful as she had been, had shown no hesitation in bending the rules.

Perhaps it was time she did the same.

Gently slipping her feet from beneath the still-resting Buttercup, Gwen stood, her expression firming with resolve. She had spent years seeking solace in libraries and books, withdrawing from the callous treatment she had endured in her youth. But this ... this was her life now. Her marriage. Her chance to build something new.

She strode toward the door, her decision made. She would wait no longer. Aidan needed to face her, and if he had any regrets, well, he could nurse them later. After he had done his duty and shown her the courtesy she deserved.

Whipping open the door, she let out a startled shriek.

Aidan stood on the other side, hand raised as if to knock.

He was in a state of partial disarray. Barefoot on the polished wood, his buckskin breeches slightly dusted from travel. His coat was on, but no waistcoat or stockings, and the column of his throat was bare, his shirt undone.

Clapping a hand to her chest, Gwen stared at him, her heart galloping behind her ribs.

"Where have you been?" The question burst from her lips before she could compose her thoughts.

Aidan held her gaze, his voice low, steady, and sincere. "Thinking about you."

Her brows drew together. It was tempting to believe his words, to let her heart be soothed by them, but what did they truly mean?

"What does that mean ... that you were thinking of me?" she asked, her voice barely above a whisper.

Aidan drew in a deep breath, as though steadying himself. "I was considering the honor of joining you in your bed."

The air seemed to thin, caught somewhere between her chest and throat. His eyes drifted to her lips, framed by dark lashes, and when he spoke again, his voice had deepened into something velvety and slow, like a fine claret warmed with honey.

"'O Helena, goddess, nymph, perfect, divine! To what, my love, shall I compare thine eyne? Thy lips, those kissing cherries, tempting grow!'"

Startled, Gwen felt a warm jolt run through her, not from the words alone, though they were exquisite, but from the fact that they were directed at her. Her!

Then, from the region near her ankles, came a low growl.

Both she and Aidan glanced downward.

"You have a dog," he said with an air of surprise.

"Buttercup," she replied. "I rescued her from a halfpenny showman last week after I saw him kick her in the ribs."

His brows lifted slightly. He studied the small bristling creature with amusement and something bordering on admiration. "She has thoughts about me entering your room."

It was true. Buttercup's hackles were raised, her eyes narrowed, her growl now a steady hum of displeasure.

"I think she wishes to protect you."

Gwen smiled, warmed by the little dog's fierce loyalty. "I am afraid you must leave now, girl." She stooped to gently gather the pup and swept her out into the hall, closing the door behind her.

When she rose and turned back, Aidan's eyes were fixed on her.

Her breath caught as she saw the intensity in his gaze, something tender and yet powerful. The recitation of Shakespeare had sent a fluttering warmth through her, but it was the way he looked at her now, as though she were both mystery and miracle, that stole her breath entirely.

Her pulse quickened, her skin tingling beneath his gaze. She licked her lips nervously, instinctively and noted the way his eyes flickered in response, as though that small gesture had unmoored something within him.

He stepped closer.

Not with force, but with solemnity. His hand rose and lightly rested at her waist, his touch tentative, seeking permission.

There was a long silence between them. One filled not with words, but the rhythm of shared breath.

"I have never wanted to rush something so badly," he whispered. "And never wanted to get it so right."

Her throat tightened with emotion. She could not quite speak, so she merely nodded.

Aidan reached behind him, his fingers fumbling briefly before the door closed with a quiet click. He did not move closer, not yet. Instead, he searched her face, as if to memorize it, every freckle and curve etched into his mind like a treasured line of verse.

When he did lower his head, it was slow. Intentional.

Their lips met gently. No blaze, no devouring, only the soft, shivering wonder of a first kiss as husband and wife. It was a vow made tangible.

There was no need for more. Not yet. The fire could wait.

A sudden growl caused them both to still and glance about.

Buttercup, ever vigilant, had apparently re-entered the room before the door had been fully shut. A silly oversight, Gwen supposed, but one that brought the moment to an abrupt halt.

Aidan huffed, not without amusement, and moved to the door. Gwen quickly bent down, gathering the bristling dog into her arms and guiding her firmly across the threshold. Buttercup gave one last pointed glance before Gwen's hand slipped back into the room, and Aidan closed the door with a soft finality, a small click signaling their temporary solitude.

A sharp, indignant bark rang out, followed by the sound of tiny paws scampering off, likely toward the kitchens, where sympathy could be found in the form of leftover beef.

Gwen stood, her cheeks warm with both fondness and anticipation. She turned back toward Aidan, who watched her with quiet intensity.

Her hands rose, not with haste but with wonder, to the

lapels of his coat. She longed to place her palms against his chest, out of the need to feel something true and real and steady beneath her fingertips. The coat shifted slightly beneath her grasp.

"Citrus," he murmured softly, as though just now registering her scent.

His lips brushed her cheek, warm and searching. She tilted her head slightly, savoring the intimacy of the moment. When his mouth found the curve of her jaw and then the edge of her ear, she shivered, not from desire alone, but from the raw sweetness of being seen and wanted.

Her breath caught.

"Faith," she whispered, overwhelmed by the strange, luminous newness of it all.

The coat slipped from his shoulders with a soft whisper of wool. She placed her hands upon the fine linen of his shirt, the warmth of him steady beneath her fingertips.

Aidan leaned in once more, his hand rising to cradle the back of her head with infinite care. When his lips met hers again, there was no urgency. Only a deep, unfolding tenderness. It was not a kiss of hunger, but of commitment. Of beginnings.

He drew her closer, with the gentle assurance of a husband finally home.

∽

Gwen lay nestled in the crook of Aidan's arm, her head resting against the warm, steady rise of his chest. Each beat of his heart echoed in her ear, a soft and wondrous rhythm that seemed to speak of promise. His fingers trailed absently through the strands of her hair, drawing light spirals as though trying to memorize its feel.

They had shared one moment of intimate union that night, Aidan insisting with gentle conviction that there must be restraint for her first time. There had been no urgency, only intention. He had treated the occasion as sacred.

Eventually, he rose to retrieve the dinner tray left just outside their door. Gwen watched him cross the room with a dawning sense of awe and belonging, her eyes following the strong lines of his back, the measured grace in his stride. This man was her husband, bound to her in name, in deed, in heart.

They were married.

For all her days, she would have this man by her side.

When he returned, he slipped beneath the counterpane and propped himself on an elbow beside her, offering her slices of pear and clusters of grapes from the tray. Between bites, he quoted lines of poetry—odes to beauty, to awe, to affection—pulling from memory the verses of great poets as if he had memorized them solely for her ears.

Gwen listened, mesmerized. Aidan was clever, tender, and thoroughly romantic. She had never known such attentions, such open admiration from a gentleman before. Several times throughout the ensuing hours, she fought the urge to pinch herself for fear this dreamlike moment might vanish. But the thought of waking to her old life was too dreadful to entertain, and so she let the dream linger.

She wanted this life ... with him.

She longed to be his confidante, to hear his verses whispered in that rich, steady voice. She wanted to forge a partnership rooted in trust, in shared burdens and joys alike. To exchange secrets in the dark and find peace in each other's arms. Their kisses—tender, exploratory, full of wonder—had already deepened her longing to remain enfolded in his embrace.

As sleep crept upon her slowly, like the settling hush of twilight after a golden dusk, she edged closer to him, pressing her cheek to his side and wrapping an arm around his waist.

Just as the veil of slumber claimed her, she murmured the truth that had danced in her chest since the moment he had appeared at her door.

"I love you," she whispered and fell into sleep.

CHAPTER
ELEVEN

"The law is reason, free from passion."

Aristotle

AUGUST 26, 1821

With the coming of dawn, pale light filtered through the curtains and touched the edge of the coverlet in a hush of gold. Aidan opened his eyes to find Gwen still nestled in his arms, her breath warm and slow against his chest. For a moment, he allowed himself the luxury of stillness. The phantasy that the world beyond this chamber was untroubled, that Lily was safe, the baron yet lived, and Smythe was above suspicion.

But such wishes were only illusions.

And yet, without those harsh realities, he might never have crossed paths with Gwen. The very thought caused a small involuntary thrum in his chest. He looked down at her, brushed a lock of hair from her cheek, and smiled softly.

He had not known how incomplete he had been until he met her.

So be it. If this was the burden fate had placed upon him, he would bear it. He would uncover the truth, no matter how grim, and cling to Gwen with all his strength.

Her sleeping face was serene, her features softened by dreams. He thought of the words she had whispered to him the night before. Simple, heartfelt, and unguarded. Words that echoed still.

He bent low and pressed a gentle kiss to her brow.

"I will endeavor to be worthy of your love," he murmured. "I promise this to you, Gwen Abbott."

With care, he eased her onto the pillow, watching as she murmured faintly in her sleep before settling once more into stillness. He rose, gathered his garments from where they lay scattered, and dressed with quiet precision. As he fastened the last button, his gaze lingered on two bare patches upon the wall, ghostly rectangles where once artwork had hung. More possessions sacrificed, no doubt, to the family's silent descent.

Crossing the room on soft footfalls, he opened the door with care.

In the corridor beyond, Buttercup waited with teeth bared and a growl rumbling low in her throat. Aidan smiled faintly.

"Go on, Buttercup," he said quietly. "She is just inside."

The dog wasted no time. She darted into the room and bounded onto the bed, landing where Aidan had lain. With a small huff, she curled beside Gwen, her head settling on her paws, protective and content.

Aidan pulled the door closed behind him, only to be met with an unexpected creak.

He turned, startled, to find Mr. Smythe rounding the corner from the stairwell. The older man jerked slightly, tucking a small notebook into his pocket with far too much haste, then schooled his features into their usual broad, unbothered grin.

"Mr. Smythe?" Aidan said, tone mild.

"Aidan, my boy," Smythe replied cheerfully. "A fine morning, indeed. I have already been up to see the sunrise. Glorious light today!"

Aidan returned a measured smile, but inwardly, unease coiled in his gut. Smythe wore the same attire from the day before. His cravat loosened, his coat creased at the elbows. The man had not risen early. He had only just returned.

There had been no mention of any engagements after the wedding. No plausible explanation for where he might have gone.

It was a stark reminder of why Aidan had maneuvered his way into this household. His vow to Gwen must be matched by vigilance. He had come not just to wed, but to uncover truths.

Smythe passed him without pause, vanishing into his own chamber. Aidan stood in the hall, frustration prickling at the base of his neck.

Had he not spent the previous day indulging Trafford's vulgar instruction or aimlessly wandering his clubs, he might have shadowed Smythe. But instead, he had surrendered those hours to avoiding Gwen, and now they were lost.

He would have to do better.

Drawing a breath, Aidan turned and strode away, his thoughts heavy. Whatever sweetness had been born in the night was now tempered by reality. Gwen slumbered unaware. But outside the door, the hunt resumed, and Lily depended on him to see it through.

Gwen stirred beneath the covers, her limbs stretching languorously as the memories of the night before wrapped around her like a warm shawl. It had been a night beyond her imagining. Poetry whispered against her ear, tender embraces, the brush of his lips along her brow. Romance had spilled into every moment.

She turned over, expecting to find her husband still near. But the bed was empty, save for the soft, rhythmic breathing of Buttercup, who lay curled at the foot of the bed, her long ears sprawled across the coverlet in a state of blissful abandon. Gwen smiled faintly at the sight.

And then the recollection struck.

She sat up abruptly, clutching the sheet to her chest, a flush creeping up her neck.

Had she told Aidan she loved him?

The thought drifted back like a intangible wisp of smoke. She could not remember deciding to say the words. Perhaps she had dreamed it, some half-conscious imagining whispered into the dark as sleep claimed her.

But ... had he drawn her closer in reply?

Her breath caught. If she had spoken aloud ... if he had heard ...!

Zounds.

What a disaster.

It was too soon. Far too soon.

She threw off the covers and rang for Octavia, panic

driving her as she hurried to the washbasin, splashing water on her face in a bid to shake sense back into her.

Buttercup raised her head briefly, one sleepy eye opening in mild curiosity, then dropped it again as though Gwen's crisis were nothing of consequence.

Why, why would she say such a thing? They barely knew one another!

If she had uttered those words, what must he think? That she was a featherbrained chit with no understanding of love or consequence? Gwen began to count on her fingers, her mind racing.

Once for the moonlight encounter. Once for the offer of marriage. Then ... two, three ... four meetings before last night?

Their wedding night made five.

Ye gods.

He must think her bird-witted. Utterly ridiculous. A child playing at love.

A sharp knock at the door interrupted Gwen's frantic pacing, and she called for Octavia to enter, her voice breathless with urgency. As the maid stepped inside, Gwen gestured wildly at the wardrobe while hastily sponging her face and arms at the washbasin.

"I must find my husband!"

Octavia's brows drew together in mild confusion, but she offered no comment. With quiet efficiency, she pulled a soft morning gown from the press, followed by a clean shift and a pair of stockings. Her hands paused only briefly as she stooped to gather Gwen's stays from the carpet, her expression neutral, as though such disarray were of no consequence.

Heat flared in Gwen's cheeks. She turned her back,

grateful for Octavia's discretion. What explanation was required in such circumstances?

She slipped into the stockings and shifted the linen over her head, lifting her arms as the fabric settled over her shoulders. Octavia moved to assist with the stays, tugging the laces firmly while Gwen fidgeted under her hands, heart pounding with nerves rather than the constriction of whalebone.

It seemed an age before the final fastenings were secured. As soon as her gown was buttoned, Gwen darted from the room, hair tumbling loose over her shoulders in defiance of convention. She offered no explanation for her flight, simply raced down the corridor, her slippers striking the polished floor with unladylike speed.

Behind her, Buttercup leapt from the bed and gave chase, ears flapping, her little paws a percussion of loyalty echoing down the hall.

Gwen descended to the breakfast room in a flurry, glancing wildly through open doors before halting at the threshold.

There he was.

Aidan sat at the table, a plate of eggs and ham before him. Yet he was not eating. His gaze was fixed upon the garden beyond the window, his fork hovering in midair, forgotten.

"Aidan?"

No reply.

She stepped farther into the room, her voice a little louder. "Aidan?"

He startled, his focus snapping back to her.

"Good morning," he said at last, placing the fork down and lifting his coffee in greeting.

Gwen hesitated, her fingers knotting together. Something was not quite right.

"How are you this morning?"

There was a pause. He did not answer at first, and when he did, it was absentminded. "Hmm?"

She repeated herself, softer now. "How are you this morning?"

A faint smile lifted his mouth, but it lacked affection. "Quite well. And you?"

His words were polite, but his eyes remained distant, his thoughts adrift elsewhere.

Gwen clenched her fists beneath the linen tablecloth, her stomach fluttering with unease. Something had shifted. He was no longer the same man who had held her so tenderly the night before, and she feared she had ruined everything with the rashness of her words.

Panic flared. They had shared an evening so perfectly aligned with her dreams. Warmth, understanding, the quiet thrill of belonging. And she had sullied it with sentiment spoken too soon. Why had she not simply allowed their new marriage the time to bloom naturally?

Determined to bridge the distance, she stepped forward and took the chair beside him. Buttercup followed, her body folding beneath the table as she nestled against Gwen's feet with loyal warmth. A footman appeared with a small plate of strawberries, and orange segments and set it silently before her.

Gwen stared at it. Her appetite had deserted her.

Should she mention her ill-timed confession? Or pretend it had never happened?

"Shall we do something together today?" she asked softly, the effort at lightness strained by the tension tightening her chest.

Aidan hesitated before answering, his voice distant. "I am afraid that will not do today. I ... have plans."

Gwen used her fork to nudge a single strawberry across the plate. He seemed entirely unlike the man who had come to her so willingly, so openly, under the starlight. Now he was all courtesy and reserve. She searched her mind in vain for some way to bring back the ease of that earlier connection.

"Oh."

"I might not be here for dinner," he added, glancing toward the window. "There are matters I must attend to."

Desperation bloomed within her. Buttercup stirred, shifting uneasily as if in quiet sympathy. Gwen leaned in slightly, lowering her voice so the servant could not hear.

"Will you ... will you come to my room tonight?"

She held her breath. *Please. Please, say yes.*

"We shall see what time I return."

The hope within her withered. Aidan stood and left the breakfast room, his footsteps receding, the absence of warmth in his parting weighing more heavily than silence.

Gwen remained seated, the cut fruit untouched before her. Her thoughts whirled. She had spoken too soon, offered her heart without provocation, and now he was pulling away.

Beneath the table, Buttercup whined softly, as though understanding her mistress's despair.

Aidan had been kind. Attentive. She had been too eager, too exposed. Too much.

And now she feared she had frightened him.

∼

AIDAN'S FINGERS brushed against the folded letter nestled in his coat pocket. As ever, Filminster's words were cloaked in ambiguity. Careful, no doubt, to avoid revealing too much should the message fall into the wrong hands. Yet Aidan discerned the intent with clarity.

It was time.

Whatever Smythe was entangled in, the moment had come to act and to uncover the truth for himself.

It happened again. I have doubled the guards.
- Filminster

Ridley House remained under watch, and word had reached him that another attempt had been made to force entry into his sister's home. The only comfort was that capable men had been stationed there, ready to prevent any harm from reaching her.

Aidan strode toward the library, thoughts turning over with increasing urgency. Upstairs, Smythe was presumably at rest after a night spent out, his absence only solidifying Aidan's growing suspicion.

Perhaps I should search his study once more?

The notion felt futile, but desperation made even a fruitless endeavor seem worth attempting. And still, a stronger thought pressed. He must follow Smythe himself. If the man slipped out again that afternoon, Aidan intended to know precisely where he went ... and with whom.

There were few choices. He might first call at Ridley House to obtain the particulars of the latest disturbance and still return in time to observe Smythe should he venture forth on further errands.

Better that than wear a path into the library carpet while Smythe slept peacefully above.

His mind settled, Aidan turned for the hall to give instructions for his mount.

But as he reached the entry, he found the butler in quiet discussion with two liveried workmen. Together, they were engaged in the delicate removal of the grand painting that hung above the primary staircase.

A sweeping landscape met his gaze. English ladies in elaborate gowns and towering hats adorned with lace and ruffles, their powdered hair lending them an ethereal glow as they strolled through what appeared to be St. James's Park. Small dogs cavorted at their feet, and the entire scene was captured with the fluid elegance of a master's hand.

It was not only beautiful. It was valuable. Possibly even a Gainsborough.

Aidan's brow furrowed. "What is this, Jenson?"

The butler, a slim man in his fifties with iron-gray hair and the composed demeanor befitting a long-standing servant, glanced over his shoulder at Aidan before returning his focus to the task at hand. Together, he and two workmen carefully eased the weighty, gilded frame to the ground with slow coordination.

Ordinarily, such proceedings would not be questioned by another gentleman, particularly not one outside the household. But Aidan was heir to a viscount, and few in service would dare withhold the truth from a man of his standing.

"Mr. Smythe has sold the painting, my lord," Jenson said with careful formality. "These men have come to collect it."

Aidan drew a hand through his hair, restraining the urge to curse aloud. His jaw tightened.

Again.

Each passing hour made the matter more evident. The

continued liquidation of valuables, the timing of the murder, the persistent surveillance of Ridley House. All pointed to a man ensnared in desperate schemes.

It reeked of concealment. A killer needing coin to bury evidence, to silence witnesses, to stay one step ahead of ruin. Funds had been spent. Hired watchers, a treacherous footman now dead, and the cache of hidden currency found among his belongings.

The ongoing liquidation of assets coincided with both the murder and the recent attempts to breach Ridley House. Both reeked of desperation. A killer who needed to hide evidence of his dastardly deeds and obtain funds for some mysterious reason. Covering up the murder of a peer would cost coin. There were men being paid to watch Ridley House, and the now-deceased footman who had attacked Lily weeks earlier had hidden quite a stash in his things.

Most of Gwen's dowry had been forfeited in light of the scandal, the Abbotts providing for her and their future progeny in the marriage contracts. Something Smythe had insisted on, and his own father had acquiesced to. Yet another indication that Smythe was obsessed with obtaining funds for some undisclosed reason.

As a result, Smythe had not been in a position to deny Aidan access to his residence because his contribution to Gwen's future had been practically non-existent.

Smythe's perfidy was on full display, and it was imperative that Aidan prove it and end this threat. If anything happened to Lily or her husband, the guilt would be too much to bear.

CHAPTER TWELVE

"At his best, man is the noblest of all animals; separated from law and justice he is the worst."

Aristotle

Gwen paced the length of the library, her steps rhythmic and increasingly forceful, as though she meant to wear a groove into the floorboards. Once, a fine Aubusson rug had muffled her footfalls, but her father had removed it the previous month, another vanishing luxury in a home slowly being stripped of its former treasures.

Her footfalls echoed, firm against the bare wood.

She was suspended in a peculiar limbo. Married, yet still living beneath her father's roof. A new life had begun in name only, delayed by circumstance. The house, once so familiar, was shedding its character, one possession at a time. Surely, when she and Aidan moved into their own residence, everything would feel different. Better. More theirs.

Stomp, stomp, stomp.

Patter, patter, patter.

Buttercup followed closely, her paws clicking along behind Gwen in a faithful mimicry of the pace, as though imagining it a sort of delightful chase.

But there would be no move for several weeks yet, and Gwen's mind refused to be stilled. She had made a mistake, spoken too freely, and now she feared their union had begun upon shaky ground. Aidan had been distant that morning, and she was certain he regretted her too-earnest words.

There must be something she could do to restore the easy joy they had shared the night before.

She pivoted toward the towering bookcases, then turned again.

Stomp, stomp, stomp.

Patter, patter, patter.

She made for the delicate library table she favored for correspondence, her every step echoing like thunder in her ears. In her mind's eye, she saw herself not as a young lady but as a herd of elephants crashing through the underbrush, her thoughts too chaotic, her heart too full.

"Lady Moreland is here."

Gwen stumbled to a halt, one foot slipping slightly on the smooth floor. "What?"

Octavia repeated the announcement, unfazed. "Lady Moreland is here."

Gwen shot her maid a wide-eyed glare, but Octavia simply raised her hands in surrender, as though to say, "What would you have me do about a viscountess calling unannounced?"

With a heavy exhale, Gwen weighed her choices. Truly, there was little to do but fret about Aidan's absence. Perhaps a visit might prove a welcome distraction. Perhaps Lady Moreland, with her poise and experience, might offer some wisdom. Perhaps, indeed, Gwen had no real choice but to receive her new mother-in-law.

Why, then, was she still standing there?

"Where is she?"

Octavia lifted a brow as if she had been asked whether the sun still rose in the east. "In the drawing room, of course."

"Bring a tea tray?"

The maid nodded and clapped her hands softly. "Come, Buttercup."

The dog obediently trotted after her, tail swaying, the pair disappearing down the hall in efficient tandem for the hope of nibbles.

Gwen drew a fortifying breath, smoothed her hair, then her gown, and ensured her composure was intact before leaving the library. Pausing in the hallway before one of the last remaining gilt-framed mirrors, one that had thus far escaped her father's determined culling, she checked her reflection. Satisfied she appeared presentable, she made her way to the drawing room.

Lady Moreland stood near the fireplace, her attention elsewhere, seemingly absorbed in her own reflections. She was, as always, the very model of taste. Her gown of Carmelite silk paired with a sash of Egyptian brown, the tones perfectly suited her complexion and bearing. Gwen admired the older woman's innate elegance. She wore fashion like second skin, always dignified and never ostentatious.

It was odd to see her woolgathering.

"Lady Moreland?" Gwen ventured gently.

The viscountess startled, then turned, a soft smile blooming on her striking features. "Gwen, please. Call me Mama Abbott. We are family, dear."

"I have ordered a tea tray, Mama Abbott."

"Then I suppose we shall sit and talk."

Gwen returned the smile, albeit with a thread of uncertainty. She crossed to a chair opposite and sat.

"I am not entirely certain why I am here," her mother-in-law confessed.

Gwen blinked. It was as though her own unspoken thought had been plucked from the air.

"I suppose it is that Lord Moreland and I are preparing to leave for the country, and I have found myself thinking about you and Aidan."

Gwen nodded, recalling that they were to retire from Town now that the wedding was concluded.

"Perhaps when I return to London, you will have good news for me." Lady Moreland made a faint, almost unconscious gesture toward her own midsection.

Gwen's cheeks flushed with sudden heat. She looked down, uncertain how to respond.

"It is just that ... since Lily's attack, I have begun to feel that our family is keeping secrets from me. And I cannot stop wondering what lies ahead."

Gwen sat straighter. Surely she had misheard.

"Lily's attack?"

Lady Moreland, who had been absently smoothing her skirts, looked up with a shadowed expression. "Last month. She was set upon by a footman ... one who had been involved in the baron's murder. She uncovered something and ... well, he tried to silence her."

Gwen surreptitiously pinched herself on the leg. Just to

be certain that she was awake, and this was not some strange bad dream. The creeping suspicion that she was asleep was a common manifestation since her first meeting with Aidan, it would seem.

"The baron's murder ..." Gwen sifted through her memories. "You mean the late Lord Filminster, who was found dead last month?"

Lady Moreland nodded. "That is correct. One of the footmen was hired by the killer, and Lily figured it out, so he attacked her. If it were not for the butler, she could have been killed."

Gwen gasped. "I have heard nothing of it."

Her mother-in-law dabbed at her eyes with her forefinger. "It was all rather shocking, but only the family knows of it. It is only right you be aware because you are family now, dear."

Gwen nodded in awe. "Thank you."

"It is a frightening prospect, to think of losing a child. I find myself thinking of you this morning. I wanted to assure myself ... that you would take care of my boy. He has carried such a burden of guilt since Lily was ruined. He feels he should have been with her that night, you see."

Gwen did not see. She had no clue what her mother-in-law was speaking of. Aidan was burdened with guilt over Lily's ruin? Was that why he had offered to marry Gwen when they had been discovered together on the terrace?

"Which night?"

"The night of the coronation, when Lord Filminster was murdered. Lily stepped forward as an alibi to Brendan Ridley, stating she had spent the night with him. She did not, of course. Lily is a young lady and would never do such a thing, but she said it because Ridley's paramour would not come forward. Lily ruined herself to prevent his arrest."

Gwen's eyes nearly popped out of her head. What bizarre intrigue was this?

She had been vaguely aware of the murder, and the ensuing scandal with Lily and her husband when Lily had informed the coroner that she and the new Lord Filminster had spent the night together. Apparently, that had been a lie.

Did that mean that Lily's husband, Gwen's new brother-in-law, could have murdered his father?

But no, Lady Moreland had implied that there had been a legitimate alibi who would not risk her reputation, so Lily had taken it upon herself to step forward. Gwen took a moment to marvel at the young woman's courage.

What, if anything, did that have to do with her and Aidan?

"It is very odd that Aidan managed to ruin a woman so soon after Lily's scandal. I am still at a loss why this happened to both my children. Do you think I raised them correctly?"

Lady Moreland was staring at her with brimming eyes. Eyes that reminded her of Aidan. Gwen's heart twinged in sympathy to see her mother-in-law so troubled. "Of course! Aidan is a perfect gentleman. What happened between us was an aberration. We were overcome by the majesty of the moon, and such exquisite poetry ... so now we are married. He did right by me."

"I am glad it is you, my dear. You seem resilient. Intelligent. You are a good match for my boy. When I first learned of this, I did not know what to think, but after meeting you, my mind has been at ease. At least ... regarding your suitability for my scholarly son."

Musing over the revelations, Gwen stood to move around the table and place herself on the settee next to

Lady Moreland. "Lily and Aidan are honorable people. Lily stepped forward to help Lord Filminster, and Aidan did not hesitate in offering for me. Your children are a credit to you, La—Mama Abbott. You raised them to stand by what they know in their hearts to be right, and they did so. The fact that their scandals were so close in time is ... a coincidence."

"You think so?"

"I do."

It was not altogether true. Gwen wondered whether Aidan's proposal was because he did not want to see a young woman ruined as Lily had been. Perhaps his resolve to marry her had not been so much about their mutual attraction, but merely his conscience driving his actions. He certainly was in a strange and distant mood now that their wedding night was over.

Yet ... their wedding night had been sublime. Something from a gothic novel or a poem by Lord Byron. Surely he must entertain feelings for her if he could spend so many hours in her company? It had been like they were marooned on a remote island, the only people left in the world. The way he had spoken to her had implied a deep regard.

One thing was certain. There were secrets to Aidan that he was not disclosing. His sister had been engaged in a scandal just a few weeks earlier, and this was the first she knew that he had blamed himself for what had happened.

And one more thing was certain. Gwen had been so absorbed by her own issues, her own needs and wants, that it had not struck her to think what Aidan might need.

Learning he was shouldering guilt over his sister made her realize her own selfishness over the past two weeks. What of her husband's needs?

He had stepped in to save her from scandal when he could have walked away. His family had been generous in negotiating financial terms because her father did not have the funds for a large dowry.

Instead of moping around, she needed to forge a true connection with Aidan. To become his partner and assist him with his burdens. They were to traverse life together, so she must stop feeling sorry for herself and demand her place at his side.

"You are a good girl, Gwen. My son and my future grandchildren are fortunate to have a woman like you to steer their lives."

Gwen was touched. When she first met Lady Moreland, she had thought the viscountess would be like the other mamas of the *ton*, dismissive of Gwen and her appearance. But from their first meeting, she had been warm and welcoming, embarrassing her and Aidan with talk of babes.

"You are a good mama, Mama Abbott. Watching over your children."

Lady Moreland sighed. "I do wish they would not keep secrets from me. They think I cannot handle the truth, and I confess it has been a trying time, especially after Sophia's troubles last year. I will allow them their privacy for now, but it does not prevent me from visiting you to secure your promise that you will take care of Aidan while we are gone from Town. He is a true gentleman, but he needs you. He attempts to carry his burdens without assistance, but do not allow him to do so."

Gwen took hold of Lady Moreland's hand and squeezed. "I promise to assist him."

Lady Moreland nodded. "Then I shall leave you to it. I hope to hear news of a prospective grandchild soon."

Gwen smiled, not precisely sure what came next, but determined to figure it out somehow. She must convince Aidan to talk to her about his problems.

Upon arriving at Ridley House, Aidan was greeted by utter chaos. Servants bustled through the hall, trunks hoisted, instructions shouted across the floors. The air was thick with tension.

Michaels caught sight of him but did not stop, only nodding toward the staircase before striding off to handle yet another unseen emergency.

A sharp bolt of dread struck Aidan, spurring him up the stairs two at a time. He raced to the drawing room, breath caught in his throat, and burst through the doors, only to find Lily in her husband's arms.

"Lily!"

Her delicate face rose from Filminster's chest. "Aidan, please do not panic."

But her words did nothing to quell the rising alarm within him.

"What is happening?" he demanded.

Filminster stepped back, his manner calm but grave. "There was another attempt to breach Ridley House."

"I know. Your letter said as much." Aidan gestured wildly to the tumult outside the room. "Why are the servants packing?"

Lily turned away, moving to the window that overlooked the street. "We have decided it is no longer safe to remain here," she said quietly. "I went to the library early this morning to fetch a book before breakfast. It was still rather dark ... I was in there for several minutes before I noticed a draught. When I looked toward the window ..."

She swallowed.

"I saw a man climbing in. I screamed."

Aidan's stomach twisted. Her voice was hoarse, and he flinched at the realization.

"You screamed yourself hoarse," he murmured. "Did he … did he harm you?"

His sister—his small, fierce Lily, who had already endured more than most—shook her head. "No. He fled the moment I cried out."

Aidan strode forward and gathered her into a fierce embrace. "I am so sorry, Lily."

She leaned into him for a moment, then pulled back to look up at him with tired eyes. "It is not your fault, Aidan. You must not carry this."

"How can I not?"

Her pale features were calm, but the weight of recent weeks showed in every line.

"I am happy. I love Brendan. This is the work of a madman … whoever murdered the baron. He is to blame, not you."

Aidan nodded slowly. "If anything happened to you …"

He did not finish.

"What now?" he asked instead. "Are you finally leaving for Somerset?"

Lily shook her head. "Briggs fears the roads are too exposed. Whoever is behind this is growing bolder."

Filminster cleared his throat. "We have been invited to stay with the duke and my sister at their London home. They have taken precautions. Guards have been hired, and our own servants and the Johns will remain here to defend Ridley House."

Aidan frowned. "The Johns?"

Lily offered a faint smile. "They are all named John. At least, that is what Brendan claims."

Aidan gave a soft exhale. "Thank God. You must be protected at all costs."

"Agreed."

Aidan let Lily go and raked a hand through his hair. His boots clicked sharply on the polished floor as he paced, the carved trim of the mantel glinting with morning light streaming through the tall, uncovered windows.

"Surely at this point," he said, voice taut with urgency, "if the killer is becoming so bold, we should report what we know to the authorities? Then he will lose interest in Ridley House once his secret is out."

Filminster sighed. "I have thought of that. That we might end his interest in us by disclosing the matter to the Home Secretary. But the perpetrator still believes that there remains a chance he can conceal his deeds ... that the baron's letter remains hidden. Which means we can still lure him out, draw him into the open. If we act too soon, he will vanish."

Lily crossed to the window and rested her hands lightly against the sill, the thin muslin of her sleeve catching the pale daylight. "I agree," she said, her voice unmistakably hoarse from her earlier fright. "So long as he believes the letter is in Ridley House and that we do not know why the baron was killed, we retain an advantage. A formal investigation would force his hand. He would flee, and we would never find him if he escapes England's reach."

Aidan watched her closely. The drawn lines around her eyes, the set of her jaw. Signs of weariness, yes, but also steel. "But what if he suspects that you and Filminster have already found the letter?"

She turned her head, her gaze steady. "I do not know. But he must still believe his inheritance can be secured. That hope keeps him within reach."

He stared at his sister. This pale, resolute woman bore little resemblance to the carefree girl he remembered, and he felt an unexpected swell of admiration.

"When did you become so clever?"

"I am not a girl anymore, Aidan Abbott. While you were away, I grew up. I improved my French. I read books on military strategy. Much happened in the past few years."

It was true. His return to England had revealed a family transformed. Cousins married to reformed rakes, sisters ruined for honor's sake. The women of his family had proven themselves to be as tenacious as they were courageous.

The thought of Gwen flickered through his mind, bringing a shift of warmth to his chest. She was observant, capable, certainly bright, but would she prove as resilient as Lily if she were forced to confront harsh truths about her own father?

"Faugh! What a tangled web this is!"

At that, Lily and Filminster both laughed. Short, startled sounds of amusement edged with strain. Aidan joined them, the absurdity of it all rising briefly to the surface like bubbles rising in a glass. Spies, secrets, murder, and hidden letters. It was all beginning to resemble a bad pantomime.

CHAPTER THIRTEEN

"Whoever is delighted in solitude is either a wild beast or a god."

Aristotle

~

When Aidan hurried back to the Smythe home, riding his mount around to the mews in the back, he found that a carriage was being prepared. As he had hoped, Smythe was on his way out. This might be the opportunity he needed to learn more about what Smythe had been doing.

Waving off the groom, Aidan turned to ride back out.

Finding a discreet position out on the main road passing the front of the house, he waited. Anticipation sang through his veins that finally he could take some sort of action. Where was Smythe heading to?

What if he is merely visiting his clubs?

Aidan hoped not. The frustration of not doing anything

to move this investigation forward was driving him quietly mad.

Valor snorted, pawing the earth with a heavy hoof.

"Easy." Aidan stroked the gelding's withers, composing himself to reduce his internal tension. It would not do to distress the beast with his own calamity when he needed to remain hidden.

Soon Smythe hurried from the front door, dressed in a dark and disheveled overcoat and his blue eyes flashing in the sunlight.

Aidan frowned, noticing for the first time that the black carriage had no markings. There was no reason to expect them because Smythe did not currently possess a rank, but along with the skirted coat he wore, it was practically impossible to recognize who was being driven.

Scanning the driver and footman, Aidan realized that they were not dressed in their usual livery. They, too, were *incognito*.

What fresh intrigue was this?

Aidan's spirits lifted, the thrill of the chase racing through his body. Finally, he had something to pursue. A tangible clue. He knew in his very bones that Smythe was on the move, ready to engage in some sort of dubious activity. This was not to be a routine errand to his solicitor or man of business. Smythe was hiding his identity to pursue his dark ends.

As the carriage drew off, Aidan carefully tightened his calf. Valor immediately broke into a trot, and they kept pace with the carriage as it moved down quiet streets. After a while they joined Strand Street, which was bustling with carriages, mounted riders, and pedestrians going about their business. St. James's Park was well behind them, and Aidan was careful to keep Smythe's carriage in sight, noting that they were heading east as the traffic grew more congested.

Turning off Fleet Street, Aidan followed the carriage which turned onto Thames Street, near the river, and the carriage kept heading west. Smythe appeared to be heading toward the London Docks, but who knew if they would just keep moving west beyond that point?

The closer they came to the docks, the more difficult it grew for Aidan to keep the carriage in sight. Merchants and dock workers mingled in congregation on the roadside, while wagons piled high with crates and barrels clogged the streets. Aidan pressed his mount forward, and just as he turned a corner, another rider came flying through a gap in the traffic.

Valor was startled by the sudden motion and proximity, rearing up and bellowing out a loud whinny. Aidan was caught off guard, attempting to keep Smythe's carriage in view, and next he knew, he had been bucked from Valor's back. As the earth flew toward him, Aidan hit the road with a roll, barely missing the large wheels of a passing wagon.

Bruised and shaken, he sprang to his feet and grabbed hold of the panicking Valor's reins, quickly tugging the gelding's head down and walking him back several steps to disengage his hindquarters. Valor acquiesced, panting in quieting agitation but relaxing his panicked stance.

Once his horse was secured, Aidan threw a glance over his shoulder and cursed loudly. Several passersby flinched and tossed him glances of reproval, but he paid them no mind.

Smythe's carriage was gone.

Leading Valor, Aidan limped to the side of the busy street and discovered his buckskins were torn above one knee. Inspecting his coat, he found several tears. Feeling about carefully, he perceived that he had badly bruised his upper arm and shoulder, but it seemed he had not broken anything. What he *had* done was lose his quarry and nearly gotten himself killed.

Disappointment burned through him, as hot as the passion he had shared with his bride the night before. Brushing the dirt off his clothes and swiping at his face, Aidan seethed with a fury he had never experienced before as he spat out the dust in his mouth.

Once he had fully caught his breath, he remounted Valor, who was now calm. They made their way gingerly down the street as Aidan searched for the vanished carriage.

People, horses, and vehicles were milling in every direction and he knew it was a pointless task, but he spent the next hour riding the cross streets and searching for Smythe, even dismounting to peer into the dim interiors of shops and taverns.

Eventually he gave in and turned Valor's head to return home.

He had failed. They knew nothing new about what Smythe was up to. All he had achieved was to acquire himself numerous abrasions and wreck his favorite breeches. Meanwhile Lily had been chased out of her new home by a thug, and he would need to hide these bruises from Gwen to avoid questions.

The low growl he emitted was drowned by the sounds of the street, but he did not give a damn if someone overheard him. This entire matter was out of hand. The best he could hope for was that Smythe would return to the vicinity, which meant that Aidan would have to follow him again.

It took some time to reach the Smythe home where

Aidan left Valor with a groom in the mews. Ordinarily he would have taken the time to rub the gelding down, but during the ride home, his muscles had made their protests known along with the contusions on his knee, upper arm, and shoulder, which had hit the street first and taken the brunt of his weight. He wanted to get out of his ruined clothes and bathe away the nameless grime that had become embedded under his fingernails.

Crossing the back garden, he entered the house and prayed he would not encounter Gwen. Once he was in his room, he would summon his valet and get some assistance to clean up. Perhaps his man had some sort of ointment to alleviate the accumulating pains. Climbing the steps to the next floor, Aidan kneaded his neck, which he must have wrenched in the fall.

Blazes! I could have been killed.

Aidan was thankful he had had enough presence of mind to drop into a roll as he had. Fortunately, because of the traffic, he and Valor had been traveling at a slower speed, or he might not have avoided tragedy—it did not pay to be distracted when riding.

Finally reaching his room, Aidan slipped in. He rang the bell, which he hoped would result in his valet showing up. Then he proceeded to tug the clothes off his body impatiently. Once he was undressed, he walked over to the mirror by the wardrobe to inspect his leg, arm, and shoulder. Livid bruises were already discoloring his skin in dramatic hues, in testimony to just how dangerous the fall had been.

Aidan rubbed his hands over his cheek, which was thankfully unmarred except for the grime that came off under his fingertips.

As he had suspected, he would need to avoid Gwen

catching sight of these. He did not wish to lie to her any more than necessary because he had their future marriage to consider. It would be better if she did not know.

The thought of his bride, now that he had not the distraction of Smythe to worry about until the man reappeared, had Aidan shiver with hot memories of their night together.

He was afraid the concerns weighing down on him this morning had made him act in an aloof manner when they had last seen each other at the breakfast table.

It was time for him to make amends to her once he was bathed and dressed once more, for he suspected it would be many hours before Smythe made a reappearance.

GWEN SAT IN THE LIBRARY, bent over her notebook as a shaft of sunlight slanted across the desk, illuminating the faded grain of the tabletop. She was translating Propertius, the Latin poet her mother had once hoped to work on before illness stole the chance.

Since her own health scare, Gwen had taken up the project with quiet determination. Life, she had realized, could change in an instant. Dreams deferred might never return.

Pursuing them while she had her health and youth had become a matter of urgency. It was the same reasoning that had led her to implore her father to take in a foundling. Now, a child of her own might be within reach, if only she could reclaim her husband's attentions.

That was why, when Aidan returned home, she would no longer wait in silence. It was time to understand what shadow lay between them. Time to build a partnership, not simply a union.

Until then, she would remain busy.

Pausing her quill, Gwen ran her finger over the line of verse, the paper soft beneath her touch, the ink just dry. She would not waste time in idleness. She would wait with purpose.

Cynthia prima suis miserum me cepit ocellis,
contactum nullis ante cupidinibus.

Gwen returned to her notebook, tapping the quill against her lips as she considered how best to capture the essence of the verse.

"Cynthia first captivated wretched me with her eyes, I who had never before been touched by Cupid."

The words fluttered in her chest like a heartbeat. She smiled, filled with the quiet joy of shared understanding.

"*Cuncta tuus sepelivit amor, nec femina post te ulla dedit collo dulcia vincla meo,*" she murmured aloud, breath held as if waiting for an answer from the room itself.

A soft chuckle stirred the silence behind her.

"Thy love has buried all others, nor has any woman after thee put sweet fetters upon my neck."

Aidan.

Gwen turned her head just enough to glimpse him peering over her shoulder. Her heart leapt with such a surge of warmth it nearly hurt. He was here. And not the distant man from the breakfast table, but her gentle, poetic husband. The man of the night before.

"You put me to shame, husband," she whispered.

"What need is there for my efforts if you translate with such poetic skill?"

He moved to take the chair beside her, and she felt the absence of his nearness like a sigh against her skin. His presence, steady and calm, enveloped her like a balm.

"I am naught but an ordinary man," he said, his voice deep and soft, "with a muse of great grace to lift my voice."

His gaze caressed her face, and she blushed, her smile widening until it ached across her cheeks.

"You are home."

His lips curved. "I am home."

She took in his appearance. His coat was a different hue from this morning, his linen crisp and clean. He smelled of starch and soft leather, not the sweat of a mount.

"You changed?" she asked, tilting her head with gentle curiosity.

His smile dimmed slightly. "I thought it would be dinner soon," he said. "So I scrubbed Valor's sweat from my skin ... that I might find you."

Gwen leaned back to glance at the casement clock. "I shall have to prepare for dinner myself, I suppose."

"Or," he murmured, his voice lowering into a rumble, "we can have a tray brought to your room."

His fingers brushed the back of her hand. Bare, ink-smudged, warm. The touch was light but adoring.

"Truly?"

His eyes roamed with undisguised appreciation. "Oh, yes."

Gwen beamed, shoving her chair back with eager delight. "Yes!"

Aidan rose in kind, but she halted suddenly, her hand suspended in midair as a remembered thought flared in her mind.

"Oh, wait!" She plopped back into the chair, skirts rustling about her ankles.

He paused mid-step, brow lifting with curiosity as he eased back into his seat. "Something amiss?"

"Your mother paid me a visit," Gwen said, folding her hands atop her notebook, the edge of her thumb smudged faintly with ink.

His brows rose slightly, but he said nothing.

"She told me about what happened with Lily."

A subtle shift crossed his features. It was barely perceptible, but Gwen saw it, the narrowing of his eyes, a faint tensing in his jaw. "Lily?"

"She thought I ought to be told now that I am family. About the footman who attacked her."

Aidan inclined his head slowly, though his expression remained carefully neutral.

"I was horrified," Gwen continued, voice low with feeling. "She is so small and kind. What sort of brute could think to harm her?"

Aidan's lips curved faintly, but the smile was shadowed. "Lily is far sturdier than she appears. She has borne all with admirable resolve."

"I can see that. One would never guess such a thing had occurred. Still, to hear it from your mother was a great shock."

He nodded, gaze drifting away for a heartbeat before returning. That familiar veil of distance flickered across his eyes again. "Was there more to the conversation?"

"Well …" Gwen hesitated. "She told me that you carry guilt over Lily's scandal. That she stepped forward to protect Lord Filminster by giving him an alibi, one that was not entirely true."

At that, Aidan straightened, rubbing a hand through his

hair in agitation. "That is rather a wealth of family confidence to be shared in a single afternoon."

"She spoke with love and concern," Gwen said gently. "Not gossip."

He exhaled sharply. "You do understand, I hope, that word cannot get out about what Lily did? Filminster was under heavy suspicion, but he could not have committed the crime. Lily witnessed enough to know he was innocent. She merely ... shifted the details to ensure the truth would be accepted. If anyone were to uncover the full truth, if she were accused of perjury, it could destroy her. And Filminster."

"She is safe with me. I have no desire to spread tales ... and no one to tell, even if I did." Gwen paused. "But your mother was right, was she not? You blame yourself for Lily's scandal."

Aidan's brown eyes fixed upon her, and Gwen saw his discomfort ripple behind them. He was clearly disconcerted by the bluntness of her question, but how else could she have asked it?

"I have felt regret," he admitted slowly, "that I chose to go out that night, carousing with friends. Had I been at home, I might have stood as Filminster's alibi instead."

Gwen's brows drew together. "So Lily does not wish to be married to Filminster?"

Aidan grimaced, the muscles of his jaw taut for several seconds before he spoke. "Lily and Filminster are in love. She told me only this afternoon that she has no regrets."

Relief swept through Gwen, bringing a soft smile to her lips. "I am glad. I was unsure what to think." Her voice softened further. "Is that why you insisted on marrying me?"

He blinked, surprise flashing across his features before he gave a decisive shake of his head.

"No. You and I ... we are nothing like Lily and Filminster. You are my Venus. My own Cynthia. The fetters upon my neck are sweet, Gwen Abbott."

Gwen inhaled sharply, her breath catching. The words curled around her heart like ribbon. Did he mean ... could it be ...?

She longed to ask outright, but the question lodged in her throat. It was too bold, too exposing, and her pride still bore the sting of this morning's uncertainty. Instead, she clung to what he had said. Words so lyrical, they could only be born of true affection.

Do not push him.

She recalled her whispered confession the night before, spoken half-asleep, and the regret that had shadowed her all morning. She would not risk their fragile connection by demanding more than he was ready to give.

Instead, she smiled gently. "Thank you."

Aidan's brow lifted, eyes warming with hope. "Now to bed?"

Gwen stood, her answer in the simple motion. They left the library hand in hand, ascending the stairs together in breathless silence.

Her heart brimmed with tenderness as she glanced at him. Tonight, he seemed almost carefree. But would he still be here tomorrow? Or would he retreat again into that quiet world of his thoughts?

When they reached her chamber, she fumbled with the latch, laughing as they tumbled through the doorway, mouths meeting in a fevered kiss.

"Uh ..."

Gwen jolted back. "Octavia!"

The lady's maid stood stiffly by the wardrobe, her gaze fixed to the floor as her hands fidgeted with the hem of her apron. A dull blush crept across her cheeks as she dipped into a swift curtsy. "I shall ... just ..." She gestured vaguely toward the door behind Gwen and Aidan, not daring to lift her eyes.

Gwen's own face flamed with heat. The air in the chamber felt thick, almost too warm. Her fingers tightened against her skirts as she stared somewhere just beyond Octavia's shoulder, her voice emerging with forced composure. "Could you arrange a dinner tray?"

Octavia nodded quickly, her cap ribbons fluttering as she edged toward the exit. Aidan stepped aside with gallant ease, inclining his head in a brief bow. Octavia gave a strangled nod, then darted from the room with the hurried rustle of muslin and the soft clink of the latch as the door clicked shut.

For a breathless moment, silence held them suspended. Then laughter spilled between them. Relieved, uncertain, and full of the awkward joy of shared understanding. It was the kind of laughter that unknotted lingering tension and made the world feel newly tender.

When their mirth had subsided, Aidan crossed the chamber to draw the heavy curtains, casting the room into softened twilight. Gwen blinked, her eyes adjusting as the carved furnishings faded into silhouette. A hush settled, the quiet echoing like a held breath.

He returned to her then, his hands firm but gentle as they found her waist and drew her toward him. Though she could barely see him in the dimness, she could feel the nearness of him ... his warmth, the quiet rasp of his breath.

She lifted her arms, curling them about his neck. Her fingers brushed the fine hairs at his nape as she leaned into the strong line of his frame. Their bodies aligned in perfect familiarity, a closeness that drew a sigh from her lips.

"I have been thinking about last night," he murmured, his lips brushing her temple, his breath stirring tendrils of her hair.

Her heart fluttered. "I ... have thought about it, too."

His hands glided along her waist in slow, reverent passes. She swayed gently in his hold, the muslin of her gown whispering against the wool of his coat. The chamber felt quieter still, as though the very walls wished not to intrude.

He drew her closer, and their foreheads met, a tender joining that felt sacred.

When he kissed her, it was not hurried. It was a question, an offering. Gwen answered with quiet conviction, her hands moving up to trace the breadth of his shoulders. She felt the tension there. The effort, the burden. And smoothed it away with a soft touch.

He stilled slightly as she explored and then caught her hands in his. His own trembled faintly as he pressed them to his chest, where his heart beat in steady cadence.

"Let me take care of you," he whispered.

Her reply was quiet, but certain. "Yes."

Together, they turned toward the inner chamber, the only sound the whisper of slippers on the polished floor and the hush of two hearts beating in gentle accord.

CHAPTER
FOURTEEN

"The energy of the mind is the essence of life."

Aristotle

Aidan winced in pain, catching Gwen's hands and pressing them gently to his chest, his breath held tight lest a sound escape. Her fingers had unwittingly found the worst of his bruises, and the flash of discomfort sent a wash of dizziness through him.

But the pain soon dulled to a manageable throb, and another fire, softer but no less consuming, rose to take its place. His thoughts turned to how he might draw Gwen close without revealing his wounds or alarming her.

When at last she rested in his embrace, her weight a welcome anchor upon his chest, Aidan exhaled a breath he had not known he held. He pressed a kiss to her damp cheek, his heart a tangle of awe and certainty. Around them, the chamber remained hushed, the scent of rumpled linen and lemon verbena lingering in the still air.

He tucked her close, her cheek against his shoulder, and buried his face in her hair. He thought of the future, not of battles or bruises, but of this. Her breath on his skin, her trust in his arms. Whatever challenge Smythe posed, he would meet it. So long as he could keep Gwen, he could face anything.

AUGUST 27, 1821

Aidan had held her close through the night, their kisses deepening into lingering embraces that blurred into the hush of night. In the darkness, they had discovered new ways of closeness, whispered laughter mingling between soft sighs and the rustle of linen.

When hunger beckoned, Aidan had risen to don his shirt and lit a single lamp across the room, casting a golden glow that danced upon the walls in shadows. He fetched the tray left in the corridor and returned with quiet steps, his smile gentle and knowing. The subdued light had rendered everything dreamlike. The meal, shared with hushed conversation and laughter, had tasted better for the intimacy of the moment. They had reclined in one another's arms beneath the shelter of quilts and dim firelight, speaking little, yet understanding much.

It was near dawn when sleep claimed them at last. They lay entwined beneath the canopy of the bed, arms and legs tangled as though separation would be a kind of grief.

Gwen had drifted into a dreamless slumber, cocooned in warmth and the steady rise and fall of Aidan's breathing.

When she stirred again, the sheets were cool beside her. Aidan was gone.

A groan escaped her lips just as Octavia whisked back the curtains, letting in the flat gray light of a cloudy afternoon. Buttercup lifted her head with a small affronted bark, as if the intrusion were personally offensive.

"What fresh hell is this?"

Octavia giggled from across the room. "It is the afternoon, Lady Abbott. I feared you would not rise at all if left undisturbed. And if you do not wake soon, you shall never find rest tonight."

Gwen sat upright, clutching the sheet to her chest. "Afternoon?"

"Indeed. Lord Abbott appears most committed to ensuring the succession," she remarked dryly.

Despite herself, Gwen let out a laugh, her fingers reaching to scratch Buttercup behind the ears. The terrier gave a low hum of pleasure and leaned in to the affection, all signs of indignation forgotten.

"Where is Lord Abbott?" she asked, though she already suspected the answer.

"He left some time ago. No word of when he might return."

Gwen fell back on her pillow with a heavy sough. "I planned on forging a true connection with him, but he turned my head with sweet words and ..." She gestured vaguely to indicate the mattress.

The lady's maid walked up to tower over her. Gwen suspected Octavia liked to do this because Gwen was so much taller. It was the only time that the woman was in a dominating position. Buttercup rose on her short legs, baring her teeth with a low growl to warn Octavia she was encroaching on her territory.

Octavia ignored Buttercup's posturing.

"What do you mean, true connection? I thought things were progressing well with your husband."

"I am no longer certain," Gwen murmured. "His mother warned me that he keeps secrets, and I believe her. At times he seems so present, so emotionally attuned, and then suddenly he becomes remote. He does not speak of his day or where he goes or what he does. And he said nothing of Lily's situation. Why?"

Octavia's brows lifted. "Lady Filminster? What troubles does she have?"

Gwen faltered, Aidan's warning ringing in her ears. He had been firm. Speaking of Lily's situation could endanger not only reputations, but Lord Filminster's liberty. She shifted uncomfortably against the pillows and looked away.

"I cannot say."

Octavia gasped with mock offense, lifting an open palm to her brow as though fainting from betrayal. "For shame, Gwendolyn Abbott! Do you not trust me?"

Gwen allowed a smile to tug at the corners of her mouth. "Not in the least. You are the most incorrigible gossip I have ever met. I would not entrust you with a piece of toast, much less a noblewoman's secret."

Octavia let out a peal of laughter, her sharp shoulders shaking beneath the tidy lines of her gown. "Well then," she said between breaths, "if it is to remain confidential, I would rather not carry the burden. Secrets cause indigestion."

Still grinning, Gwen watched as her lady's maid turned

away to gather the day's clothing from the wardrobe. She sat upright, adjusting the sheet to remain modest as she stared through the tall windows. A bank of clouds loomed beyond the panes, iron-gray and ominous, pressing down on the horizon with a heaviness that matched the turn of her thoughts.

She hesitated, then spoke. "How was he? This morning?"

Octavia froze in the wardrobe's doorway, her expression unreadable for a moment before she pursed her lips and said, "I would say ... distracted."

Gwen nodded slowly. That seemed right.

Whenever Aidan was near, she found herself enchanted by his presence. The light in his eyes, the curve of his mouth when he smiled. He made her feel cherished. But the moment he left her side, her worries returned like restless phantoms. What did she truly know of the man who had so quickly captured her heart?

He seemed to care for her. Of that she had little doubt. But his inner world remained a mystery. Where did he go? What weighed upon him? And why did he hide so much from her? She wished to be more than his bride in name only. She longed to be his confidante, his partner in truth as well as passion.

What burdens did he carry, and how could she convince him to share them?

Outside, the storm broke. Thunder cracked the sky with a violence that startled her, and the windows rattled as rain lashed the glass in heavy sheets. Gwen gave a soft gasp as Buttercup whimpered and dove beneath the pillows, trembling in fright.

"Oh, sweet girl." Gwen reached for the dog, stroking her quivering flank and smoothing her little head. "It is only the weather, Buttercup. You will be fine. We both shall be fine."

Her voice, soft and certain, rang more as a hope than a promise.

~

Rain roared down upon the roof of the hackney.

Aidan yawned widely and carefully kneaded the bruised shoulder he had landed on the day before. It was aching something fierce, and he was pleased with his decision to hire a driver rather than attempt to ride. Grabbing more than three hours of sleep would have been welcome under the circumstances, but he could not afford the time.

He had taken a page from Smythe's book, having decided that he could follow the Smythe carriage with less fear of being spotted if he was in a hackney that was indistinguishable from the next.

The rain made it more difficult to see, and his driver wore a battered hat and large, black overcoat with the collar raised to defend him from the elements. It further obscured any possibility that Smythe would notice he was being followed.

Aidan stretched his legs out, grimacing at the state of his damp boots, and hoped that Smythe would make a move again this day. He and the driver, Old Fred, had been observing the Smythe mews, he pulled on his fob to check his timepiece, for the better part of two hours.

Occasionally, they would traverse a block or two before taking up a fresh position to prevent rousing the suspicions of servants from the neighborhood. It was a boring and arduous process that made Aidan appreciate the tedious work of runners hired to retrieve stolen goods.

He rolled his shoulders, stretched his neck from side to side, and lamented that he had not brought a book to read while he waited inside the dim interior of the aging carriage. The thin squabs were flattened with the imprint of thousands of buttocks, and the upholstery had been mended dozens of times. The neat repairs spoke to the fastidious nature of Old Fred.

He did not envy the aging man. Sitting out on his box seat while the heavens poured water down in buckets. Even now, Aidan followed a trail of rainwater slipping down the interior of the aged carriage windows. He was grateful the driver had been persuaded to aid him for the day.

There was a knock on the window, and Aidan felt the pull of the carriage. Peering out the window, he saw the Smythe carriage exiting the mews. This was it!

Old Fred followed at a snail's pace, drawing to a stop at the corner to wait. The front door of the Smythe home opened and Aidan's father-in-law exited. At least, Aidan assumed it was Smythe, given the general size and gait of the cloak-covered gentleman running forward to climb the steps into the carriage interior while a figure dutifully held the door ajar. The steps were raised, the door was shut, and the servant climbed aboard.

Aidan's heart hammered in anticipation. He was prepared to see this to the end, having spent the morning catching hackneys until he had discovered Old Fred.

Today, there would be no reckless riders to cause him to be tossed from his mount.

He had instructed Old Fred to stay close when they reached the more congested streets. Aidan could not afford to lose Smythe again.

His only consolation on this dreary day was that Lily was in residence at the much larger townhouse of the duke, who had more footmen than Filminster in addition to the brawny guards that Halmesbury had hired to protect his guests.

Nevertheless, this investigation needed to progress before someone else was hurt ... or worse.

Old Fred nudged his horses forward, and soon they were following Smythe. Both carriages moved slowly as the wheels churned up mud from the puddled streets. Smythe was determined to reach his destination if he chose to brave such hard weather.

They trundled down empty streets, the citizens of London dissuaded from venturing out. When they reached the Strand, the traffic picked up. Riders were not to be seen, but carriages clogged the road as they moved tentatively through the downpour.

The journey to the London Docks took considerably more time than the day before. Pedestrians stood shivering beneath shop awnings and, on one corner, a wagon was mired in the slopping mud. Other drivers yelled impatiently from their perches, while the teams of men and horses toiled to unstick it, but Aidan only had eyes for Smythe's carriage.

Old Fred did an exemplary job of keeping it in sight, and Aidan felt proud of finding the man to assist him. It seemed that this would work!

Aidan caught sight of the London Docks down the street just as their quarry stopped to pull into an alley. Old Fred dutifully drew to a stop half a block away, and Aidan quickly pulled his hat down over his ears and raised the collar of the great overcoat he had borrowed from one of his father's grooms.

Opening the door, Aidan dropped to the ground, his riding boots squelching in inches of mud. Running forward with his hand holding his hat to his head to defend himself from the rain, Aidan reached the alleyway and carefully peered around the corner to see Smythe disappearing into a doorway.

Aidan studied the distance to where the carriage stood, then ran back down the block to the street parallel to the alley and found that the building was a tavern. He strode through the front entryway.

Inside it was dark, barely any daylight to shine in from the street and a few flickering oil lamps on the walls. Aidan carefully navigated through a maze of scarred tables and chairs, searching for Smythe. Dock workers in colorful linens, jerkins, and hardy boots sat in groups while sailors dressed in their merchant blues drank and talked loudly among themselves.

With great relief, Aidan spotted Smythe at a corner table. He was seated across from a rough man dressed in the style of a dock worker. He had the shoulders of someone who was accustomed to lifting great burdens of weight, and several days' growth of black beard on his unshaven cheeks.

Aidan quickly located a free table nearby and took a seat, careful to keep his hat down low and tugging his collar up to ensure it obscured his face.

He could not make out what they were talking about, but Smythe was leaning forward with an intense expression. He was knocking his hand down on the table as if his temper were piqued. The other man raised his hands in a gesture that implied he did not have an answer to what Smythe had said.

Aidan's heart hammered loudly in his chest. There was

no doubt that Smythe was up to no good. No gentleman met with dock workers and, as if to confirm his thoughts, Smythe reached into his coat and pulled out a small purse.

He placed it on the table and pushed it forward to the unknown conspirator. A hand covered in coarse black hair reached out to take it, and the rough chap swept his gaze about the tavern before peering inside. He nodded, putting the purse away in an inner pocket.

A tavern maid came up, interrupting Aidan's surveillance. He ordered an ale to get rid of her, relieved when she walked away quickly to serve another who had hollered out.

The meeting continued for a while, and Aidan wished he could overhear what they were discussing, but the tavern was engaged in a roaring trade because of the heavy rain, and Aidan could barely hear himself think in the chaos. He nursed his drink and observed what he could, waiting for the next development.

Fumbling about in his overcoat to find the pocket of his waistcoat, Aidan checked the time and realized he had been observing them for near an hour.

There was no more to learn from the position where he sat. He wondered whether he should wait it out and follow Smythe to the next destination. When he looked back up, it was to find that his father-in-law had finally risen to his feet, gesturing.

Aidan tossed a coin onto the table and quickly made his way out of the tavern. Swiveling his head around, he managed to pick out the figure of Old Fred bent over his reins. The rain had eased, but the day was still gray and dreary. Racing over to the hackney, the mud sucking at his boots, Aidan yanked the door open and embarked, knocking on the front glass.

Old Fred drove the carriage to the alleyway, where they waited on the main road. Then, slowly, the hackney entered the alley to follow Smythe's carriage out onto the opposite street.

Within three blocks, the Smythe carriage pulled into another alleyway. As before, Aidan assessed the position of the back door Smythe entered. Running out onto the parallel street again, Aidan found the corresponding door.

He hesitated, perplexed, before entering yet another dock tavern. This tavern was more shadowed than before, with no maids and only a man behind the bar serving to a thin crowd of brooding men.

Aidan hunched his shoulders down to appear shorter and ensure his figure was not recognizable. With fewer men patronizing the establishment, it would be easier for Smythe to spot him if he was not careful.

The table and chairs close to Smythe and his new cohort were not occupied, but Aidan did not dare approach lest he be spotted.

As before, Smythe gestured adamantly and leaned in to talk with yet another beefy dock worker. This one appeared to have not bathed in a week, nor any of the other patrons. Aidan breathed through his mouth to avoid the sour odor hanging about like an evil omen.

At the bar, a drunken argument broke out between two slovenly men, slurring as they gesticulated wildly. The sullen proprietor behind the bar came out, grabbing both men by the scruff of their collars to escort them out crudely. Aidan shook his head in amazement that he was sitting in such a place. He still could not overhear anything from the table where he sat, so instead he observed and seethed.

Smythe was a blackguard deeply involved in sinister schemes. There was no other explanation for why he would be visiting such blighted spots to converse with a criminal element.

Were these the ruffians who had attempted to break in to Ridley House? Had one of these men scared the wits out of his little sister? What gave Smythe the right to behave this way?

It was becoming more and more obvious that his father-in-law had visited the late Baron of Filminster on the night of the coronation and bludgeoned Brendan's uncle to death before running away into the night like a pathetic coward.

Aidan needed to find the evidence to end this farce.

Which means I will be forced to hurt Gwen when she learns of her father's perfidy.

This reminder of what lay ahead was unwelcome, so Aidan forced his attention back to the present.

After thirty minutes, Smythe took his leave and Aidan left the tavern to rejoin Old Fred. Once again, they trailed the Smythe carriage down the alleyway and onto the opposite street.

It was with some disappointment that Aidan realized they had turned and were headed back east.

Smythe must have completed his errands for the day, or the weather had dissuaded him from further activities, because they were headed back to the Smythe home across London.

If only Aidan could have caught him in the act of something. Frustration sizzled through his veins as he rubbed his hands up and down over his breeches and thought about how to bring this to a resolution. It was obvious that Smythe was guilty, as Aidan had thought from the beginning. But how to prove it?

It was excruciating to be this close to discovering the

truth, yet not know what to do to finish it and prove what he knew in his gut. He thought about the day Lily had been attacked, the marks on her neck from when the villainous footman had held her by the throat. He thought about how his little sister could have been killed.

And the more he thought, the more he seethed that Smythe could behave like an ordinary gentleman to his face, all charming grins and polite talk, while behind the mask was a cold-blooded murderer. He had hosted Filminster and Lily in his home, along with their family, and pretended to be a friendly face and a new relation, yet hurried about Town daily to plot his dastardly conspiracies.

It was up to Aidan to stop him.

CHAPTER
FIFTEEN

"The ultimate value of life depends upon awareness and the power of contemplation rather than upon mere survival."

Aristotle

~

When Aidan reached the Smythe home, ensuring he came in a good half hour after Smythe, it was to be met with another letter. Stalking over to the little drawing room off the entry hall, Aidan quickly unfolded the note to see what hellish report he was to receive.

After we left RH last evening, it happened again. Michaels is injured, but the doctor assures me he will recover.

Filminster.

Aidan's vision turned red as rage rushed through him. The butler had saved Lily's life! And if Lily had been at

Ridley House, she could have been hurt or killed, being such a tiny little thing!

Smythe was behind it! Aidan knew this was the truth. There was no other explanation for what he had witnessed this afternoon nor for the bills of sale he had found in Smythe's desk.

Aidan's hands were shaking with fury as he crumpled the page in his hand, attempting to quell the hot emotion causing his heart to race. He was panting with the sheer outrage that the killer was only dozens of feet away and he could do nothing about it.

It was beyond the pale! Completely untenable!

He stood here, helpless, while his family and their close connections were under attack.

The more he tried to hold his temper at bay, the hotter it simmered—*boiled*—until the appalling dishonor of this disastrous farce caused his feet to turn toward the door. In a blinding anger, Aidan stormed down the hall to throw open the door to Smythe's office.

His father-in-law's head shot up in surprise, then he frowned in confusion when he saw Aidan standing in the doorway.

"May I help you, son?"

Aidan stepped in, closing the door behind him with deliberation. It was time to end this, but there was no need for Gwen to overhear this confrontation.

"I know what you have done."

Smythe blanched before his eyes, and Aidan knew he had him cornered. He walked forward into the room, coming to a stop midway to glower at Smythe over his desk.

His father-in-law got to his feet. "I can explain."

Aidan could not believe his ears. The reprobate was

admitting it yet thought that Aidan would stand by him. "You can explain! Have you gone mad, sir?"

Smythe raised shaking hands to run them through his graying hair, his blue eyes stark in a face that had lost all color. "I beg of you, there is no need for this to get out. Not yet."

Aidan again could not believe what he was hearing. The man had no conscience. "I am afraid there is no delaying the news that you killed a man."

Smythe's jaw dropped open. "I did what?"

It was then that Aidan heard a rustle behind him.

Turning around, the horror of finding Gwen standing at the terrace doors swept through him in a wave. Seeing her red hair lit from behind, the sun peeking through the clouds for the first time that day, she was a glorious angel, and Aidan realized in that moment that his Venus had stolen his very heart from his chest the very first night he had met her. Which was unfortunate because her face was hard and pale as her expression firmed into a ferocious glare.

"What is he talking about, Papa?" Gwen's glare never wavered, even as she addressed her words to Smythe.

"I ... do not know. Who is it that I am supposed to have killed?"

Aidan swallowed. Losing his temper, and storming in here without a plan, just might be the costliest mistake he had ever made.

Ever.

He was supposed to have handled this with finesse. To ensure Gwen was not heartbroken in the process. To be here to support her when she learned the truth about her father.

All of which was currently a moot point.

He turned away to look at Smythe. There was no honor

to how Aidan had reacted to this muddle, so all he could do was proceed with his accusation. One step at a time.

"You killed the Baron of Filminster to secure your inheritance."

Smythe blinked his intense blue eyes before collapsing into his leather swivel chair. "I ... most certainly did no such thing."

"You just admitted it!"

Smythe's brows drew together, a heavy scowl marring his face. "I most certainly did not."

"What were you confessing to, then?"

"Not that! Why do you think I would kill the baron?" Smythe shook his head. "And why would killing him secure my inheritance? I did not even know the man that well."

Gwen's skirts rustled as she walked up to Aidan from behind. He was too ashamed to look at her, so he stared resolutely at Smythe, watching him like a hawk that had spotted its next prey. But it was he who was the prey to his bride's menace.

"When was the baron killed? Was it the night of the coronation?" Gwen's voice was melodic steel, and Aidan's chest tightened in response. If he had wrecked their marriage before it had even begun, he would never recover. He raised a hand to rub at the pain in his chest where his heart refused to beat.

"Yes."

"Then Papa could not have done what you accuse him of."

Aidan could scarcely breathe as he slowly admitted to himself, as if from a great distance, that he may have made a mistake. It never paid to lose one's temper. How many times had his own father repeated those words?

"How would you know that?"

"Because last month I contracted a terrible fever. Octavia and Papa were at my side night and day. The day of the coronation was when the doctor informed my father that I might expire before the night was over, and Octavia can attest that he kept vigil at my bedside all night long until my fever finally broke in the early hours."

Aidan blinked in horror, struggling to breathe at the awful accusation he had made. His gaze found Smythe's, who had an expression of sympathy on his face. "It is true, son. I do not know why you think I killed the baron, but I was at Gwendolyn's side all day and night. I could not bear to walk away lest she die while I was absent. It was such a blessed relief when her fever broke."

Behind Aidan there was once again a rustle of skirts, a hint of citrus teasing his senses, and the sound of a door opening and closing, then racing footsteps in the hall.

Aidan spun around to find he was alone with Smythe. Buttercup was at the door, pawing and scratching to be let out. She sat back and howled in distress, much as Aidan wished to do. Gwen had left without a word, taking his very heart with her so that he stood with his chest cracked open to reveal the gaping hole where it had once resided.

Aidan strode across the room to allow the distressed animal out, giving her a pat on the head, before whipping around to glare at Smythe.

"What the hell were you confessing to?" Aidan's cry was one of pure despair, his hopes for his marriage cracking into a thousand shards of glass as he realized he had ruined everything.

"Not that."

"Then what?"

"Take a seat, Aidan. I shall explain, but first you must calm yourself."

It was an excellent suggestion because Aidan felt as weak as a kitten. Lily Billy herself, his petite little sister, could overpower him in his current state.

He walked over to drop into one of the plump armchairs. He would race after Gwen if he had any notion of what to say. Given that he did not, he welcomed any assistance he could gain from Frederick Smythe to repair his egregious mistake in accusing his father-in-law of murder in front of his bride.

"Gwen thinks I married her because of this."

Smythe sank farther into his chair and nodded. "That is likely what she is thinking."

"But you did not kill the baron?"

"I did not. I find myself a little overwhelmed that you believe I am capable of such a vile action."

Aidan ran a trembling hand through his hair, an echo of Smythe's earlier distress. "It was all the assets you sold, and the fact that you were meeting with ruffians at the docks. It made perfect sense."

Smythe exhaled heavily. "There is an explanation for that which is far more innocent." He stopped, raising his gray brows. "This is such a muddle. I think we should sort this out one bit at a time. Let us begin with ... Why would I kill the baron?"

∽

Gwen held herself upright until the door to the study clicked shut behind her.

Then the tears broke through, silent at first, then spilling freely over her cheeks in hot, uncontrollable rivulets. Her vision blurred, and the polished wood floor beneath her slippers shimmered as if seen through a veil of mist.

It had all been too perfect to last.

She had known that, of course. And yet she had allowed herself to believe in her father's dearest hope. That the right man had come along and fallen in love with her, not despite her differences, but because of them.

Her skirts rustled harshly as she fled down the corridor, the hem brushing against the paneled walls in her haste. She barely registered Jenson's startled exclamation as she swept past him, only to collide with a tall figure at the foot of the stairs.

Lord Filminster's strong hands caught her gently.

"Are you well, Lady Abbott?" he asked, his tone shaded with concern.

Gwen looked up into his kind eyes and felt something within her give way entirely.

"I ... I liked you. And Lily. But you were all here to deceive us!"

She pulled her arm free, turned, and ran. Her breath came in hiccupping gasps as she climbed, one hand clinging to the carved bannister to keep her balance. Her glorious wedding day ... it had all been a masquerade.

Only Lady Moreland, gracious and kind, had seemed sincere. The rest ... the rest had been shadows in a play.

Like at school. Smiles masking jeers. Polite words cloaking disdain.

A sob rose in her throat and escaped her lips as her knees threatened to buckle. But she clenched her hands into fists and pressed on, half-running, half-stumbling toward the sanctuary of the family wing.

Her left slipper came loose and slid off, vanishing beneath a hall table, but she did not stop to retrieve it.

Her chamber door loomed ahead. She burst inside and slammed it shut with a resounding thud. Her hands shook as she turned the key, the metal cold beneath her damp fingers.

Then she crumpled to the floor. Silk and sorrow pooling around her in a tangle of crushed fabric and wracking sobs.

She had dared to believe.

She—Gwen, Gwen the Spotted Giraffe—had foolishly let herself hope that a man like Aidan could love her.

A soft scratching came at the door, followed by a low, anxious whine. Buttercup.

Dragging herself upright, Gwen unlocked the door. The little dog scrambled in with a flurry of claws on polished wood and nestled immediately beside her, whining low in her throat.

Gwen locked the door once more and slumped against the wall, her back cold against the paneling. She stroked Buttercup's silky ears, seeking comfort in the familiar weight at her side.

"Do not worry, girl," she murmured. "You and I will be all right."

But even as she said it, her eyes flooded again, and the first tears traced a fresh path down her already swollen cheeks.

It had all been a cruel trick of the moonlight.

Aidan was still trying to gather his thoughts, to piece together what might be said to Smythe to begin righting the wrongs he had wrought, when a knock interrupted.

Jenson entered with his customary precision. "My lord, Lord Filminster is here to see you."

Aidan froze.

The delicate hope that had only just begun to stir within his chest fell still. Cold dread took its place.

Something has happened to Lily! Why else would Filminster call upon me here?

His mind conjured horrors in rapid succession. Had his sister been injured? Was she ill again? Had Michaels—gallant, cantankerous Michaels—succumbed to the wounds he had received while defending her?

Beside him, Smythe stirred. "Show Filminster in."

Jenson bowed and withdrew.

"I shall leave you to your conversation," Smythe added quietly, already moving toward the door.

Aidan barely managed a nod, so fixated was he on the fear gnawing at his insides.

Moments later, Filminster entered the room, his face unreadable. Smythe departed in silence.

"What is it?" Aidan rose. "Has something happened to Lily?"

Filminster shook his head, stepping forward. "No, it is not Lily."

Aidan's lungs filled with air again, but the reprieve was brief.

Filminster took the chair opposite and leaned forward, reaching into his coat. "But something may have happened to Trafford."

"Trafford?" Aidan repeated, frowning.

His brother-in-law nodded, withdrawing a page folded into quarters. "A woman brought this to the duke's townhouse not long ago. The butler knew nothing about her. Only that she had fair hair, and he believed she was young.

She wore a heavy cape with the hood drawn, obscuring her features. She did not give a name. Only this."

Aidan accepted the missive with a growing sense of foreboding. The note was written in hurried strokes with a lead pencil, the lines faint and uneven.

Blast. If he never received another letter again, it would be too soon.

It is not Smythe. 1 of the other 3. Do not inform Peel until you hear from me.
—Traf ...

THE NOTE TREMBLED in Aidan's grasp. The handwriting was erratic. A scrawled mess devoid of Trafford's usual flourish. He had trailed off mid-signature, as though he had lacked the strength to complete his own name.

Aidan squinted at the paper. "Is this ... blood?"

Several reddish-brown droplets stained the page, dried but unmistakable.

Dread coiled tightly in his gut. Was Trafford grievously wounded? Or worse?

Filminster exhaled heavily and scrubbed a hand down his face. The weariness in his manner spoke volumes. "We believe it is blood. Briggs and his men are already searching for him. I came here to learn whether you might know his whereabouts. No one has seen Trafford since early this morning, and his father's townhouse was locked, with only the servants in attendance. The Earl of Stirling left for the Continent on Crown business at first light."

"By George," Aidan breathed. "What the devil happened?"

Filminster leaned back, eyes drifting to the ornate crown molding above them. "He was incensed to hear of Lily's encounter yesterday. Deeply frustrated. Said our investigation was too cautious, too slow. He wanted action, something decisive to flush the villain out. I think ..." He trailed off, grim. "I think he attempted something rash. And it went poorly."

"But he is alive."

"For now," Filminster replied soberly. "He was well enough to write and to send the girl with the note. But his condition is uncertain. And Trafford is not a man who easily concedes weakness."

Aidan paced a few steps, the words striking like hammer blows. "Do we alert the authorities? Speak with Peel?"

"I asked Halmesbury. The duke urges caution. Without knowing where Trafford is or how compromised he may be, it would be unwise to act hastily. Trafford's note pleaded for discretion. We must respect that ... for now."

Aidan clenched his fists. "Devil take this entire farce! I accused Smythe, and Gwen overheard every word."

Filminster winced. "So I gathered. She nearly ran me down in the corridor, poor thing. Said Lily and I had deceived her. And ... well, she is not wrong. I never meant for any of this to hurt her."

He lowered his gaze, regret heavy in his voice. "When I found my uncle lying dead in his study, I knew nothing would be simple. But I never imagined it would ensnare so many. Least of all your wife."

Aidan shook his head slowly. "You are family now, Brendan." The name still felt foreign on his tongue, but it was time. "You did not draw us into this. We stepped in willingly. And no matter how you felt about your uncle, he deserves justice. Someone murdered him in cold blood."

Filminster nodded gravely.

Aidan walked to the window. Beyond the glass, the afternoon wore a sullen, gray expression, the drizzle continuing despite the faintest glimmer of light behind the clouds.

"I wonder," Filminster said softly, "if we were wrong to take this on ourselves. Should I have gone to Peel the moment I found that letter?"

"Perhaps," Aidan murmured. "But it is far too late for regrets. Trafford asked us to wait for word, and so we shall. You focus on your men. I shall do what I can to repair the damage I have done with Gwen ... and with her father."

"You will let me know if you require anything?" Filminster asked, rising and smoothing his coat. "Lily and I are still entrenched at the duke's townhouse. Anything at all, Aidan. You have risked much on our behalf."

"I shall send word if I require aid," Aidan replied quietly. "And keep me informed of the search for Trafford. He is ... more than I expected."

Filminster chuckled. "That is his way. One day, you realize you cannot imagine life without him."

Aidan gave a weary nod. Despite Trafford's absurdities, his insight and peculiar wisdom had become unexpectedly indispensable. His tutelage, particularly regarding certain conjugal matters, had proven quite effective on Aidan's wedding night.

The scoundrel had better survive whatever misadventure he had pursued. The world would be colder without his irreverent cheer.

"I must go," Filminster said, moving to the door. "There

are a few places I wish to search. Send for me if you require anything further."

Aidan watched him depart, then turned as the door reopened and Smythe stepped inside.

They regarded each other across the study with long, unspeaking gravity, until Aidan broke the silence.

"I cannot reveal the details surrounding the baron's death nor the reasons I suspected you. Too many lives are entangled. It is safer you remain uninformed."

Smythe gave a slow nod and returned to his chair. "Very well. But my daughter is upstairs in a state of profound distress. The servants are concerned."

Guilt stabbed through Aidan's chest like a blade. Gwen —his Gwen—had fled in tears, and he had not followed. He had not known what to say.

He swallowed. "What have you been doing, sir? If I may ask. Even though I cannot answer your questions, I must know."

To Aidan's astonishment, Smythe leaned forward with a conspiratorial grin lighting his face. "Ships!" he whispered, eyes twinkling.

Aidan blinked. "Ships?"

Smythe nodded, his grin spreading wider. "Around the docks, they call them clippers. I have been selling off anything that I can to invest. Ships that can move commodities faster than before. Souchong and Congo teas, for instance. I aim to profit."

Shaking his head to clear his thoughts, Aidan attempted to understand. "Why were you meeting with those brutish ruffians in the taverns?"

"I have been gathering information about the conditions of the ships and crews. Information I can use to negotiate the best arrangements for myself. I have limited funds, so I cannot afford to make any errors."

"But sir ... your behavior—"

"Appeared suspicious," Smythe finished for him. He glanced down at his hands, his voice quieter. "I am the third son of a minor baron, Aidan. My claim to any true influence is tenuous. When it becomes known that I sold off my land to invest in trade, polite society will be appalled."

Aidan's breath left him in a rush. "They will say you are no longer a gentleman."

"Exactly. My children may find it more difficult to marry well. We shall be relegated to the edge of society, and many of my peers will call me mad. But I am determined my family will never lack. I would rather be a scandalous success than a respected failure."

Aidan shut his eyes. The guilt was unbearable now. He had accused an honorable man, misled his wife, and failed to see what was plainly before him.

He had been a greater fool than Trafford.

Smythe bobbed his head slowly in assent. "I shall be, horror of horrors, a man of trade."

Aidan rolled his shoulders, wincing at the soreness that gripped him still, no doubt intensified by the tension strung tight through his frame as he calculated how he might ever make amends to his bride.

"But why?" he asked, voice hoarse with weariness. "Why are you doing all this?"

Smythe rose, pushing his chair back with a soft scrape of mahogany on carpet. Clasping his hands behind him, he moved to the fireplace and stared into the cold hearth, where only the charred remnants of earlier warmth lingered.

"My estate income was declining. When I inherit the title from my brother ... he is a man stuck in the past. His estates are out of date, run with the same methods as our father and our grandfather before him. The Americans have unlimited lands for growing and export. I have seen the future, and it is grim unless I take steps to build a secure future for my son. Gareth will have nothing left unless I take action."

At the mention of Gwen's younger brother at Eton, everything fell into place for Aidan. The driving ambition Smythe had exuded on their wedding day was not mere personal ambition. It had been desperation. A frantic need to secure Gwen's future before society caught wind of his commercial ventures.

"You wanted Gwen married before word spread."

Smythe turned from the hearth, his familiar grin flickering back into place. "Precisely! She is now the wife of a future viscount, allied by marriage to the Earl of Saunton and the Duke of Halmesbury. My daughter is somebody now. The *haut ton* will not dare ridicule her again."

Aidan frowned. "Ridicule her? What are you talking about?"

And then Smythe told him.

Of how Gwen, shattered by her mother's death, had been sent to school. A decision Smythe had believed to be sound, thinking the company of other young ladies would help his daughter heal. But grief, paired with Gwen's height, her freckles, her quiet and bookish nature, had made her an easy target. The other girls, cruel in the way children often are, had taunted her mercilessly. Letters home had not given away the truth, for Gwen had borne her torment in silence, determined not to trouble her grieving father.

It was not until she returned for good, two years later, that the truth emerged. But by then, the damage had been done. Those very same girls made their curtsies during Gwen's first Season. And society, following their lead, had found Gwen odd, unfashionable, and altogether too peculiar.

"Year after year, she faced their disdain," Smythe said, his voice rough. "Their whispers. Their smirks. And always, she smiled. Always, she endured."

Aidan sat back, stricken. It was so easy to look at Gwen and see fire, spirit, intelligence. He had never realized how much of that courage had been forged in loneliness.

And now ... now she believed he had married her not for who she was but as part of a scheme.

He closed his eyes, despair threatening to drag him under once more.

"She must think I am just another one of them."

Smythe gave a solemn nod.

"Gwen is a lovely girl," he replied softly. "And the elder matrons of the *ton* have long adored her, though the young wretches who followed the schoolroom herd were less kind. When you declared yourself overcome and offered marriage, I thought ... this was her chance. To finally become the woman she was meant to be. To rise above the barbed whispers. The doubt."

He paused, eyes searching Aidan's face. "Tell me true ... did you lie? Did you marry her only to investigate me?"

Aidan's breath caught, the weight of shame as heavy as a wagon of stones. Gwen. His brilliant, kind, whip-smart Gwen. He had seen her strength but had not grasped the wounds she carried, the years of solitude and whispered cruelty that had shaped her quiet resolve. And now ... this.

His betrayal must have ripped the scab from every one of those old wounds.

How deeply she must be hurting.

He clenched the arms of the chair. "Never. Gwen was never a scheme. She was the unexpected gift the Fates bestowed upon me. The moment I saw her in your receiving line, I was struck dumb. And when she quoted Manilius, I knew—I knew—I had found the other half of my soul."

Smythe huffed a mirthless laugh. "Aristotle."

Aidan smiled faintly. "I was thinking Plato, but Aristotle would agree."

Silence stretched between them for a moment, thick with the memory of what had passed and what must now be mended.

"Are we settled, then?" Smythe asked. "You are convinced I am not a murderer?"

"I believe Gwen implicitly," Aidan said. "But I also received confirmation from one I trust."

Smythe nodded slowly. "Then we are in a fine pickle indeed. Gwen has always harbored a skeptic's soul when it comes to her own appeal. You will find that convincing her of your sincerity now will be no easy task."

Aidan leaned back, exhausted. His bruises throbbed, but it was the ache in his heart that all but unmanned him. "She is more than I deserve after the havoc I have wrought."

Smythe lifted a brow. "That is the lot of all men where their wives are concerned. But you must find a way to restore her trust. She needs to know that you are, in fact, the man you seemed to be."

CHAPTER
SIXTEEN

"Suffering becomes beautiful when anyone bears great calamities with cheerfulness, not through insensibility but through greatness of mind."

Aristotle

Gwen sat still as stone, her fingers buried in Buttercup's soft fur, absently stroking the spaniel's silky head as sorrow dulled her senses. She felt as though she had been hollowed out, the fire in her chest reduced to brittle ash.

Footsteps approached in the corridor. They slowed, then came to a halt just beyond the locked door.

"Gwen?"

His voice.

Lord Aidan Abbott. Her husband. Her betrayer.

Gwen did not respond, nor did she turn her head. A tear slipped down the slope of her cheek, cool against her skin, and she dashed it away with the back of her hand. A part of her wanted to rise and throw open the door. To demand answers. To hear some explanation that might lessen the ache.

But she was not ready.

Her delicate, precious dreams had been crushed, and all she could do was sit amidst the wreckage and mourn.

"I am so sorry, Gwen," came the muffled voice again. "Please ... let me in so we can speak of what happened."

Buttercup shifted in her lap, lifting her head with a worried whimper, brown eyes searching Gwen's face for reassurance. Gwen shook her head slowly, whispering, "Not today, girl. Not today."

"Gwen?"

His voice—low, coaxing—scraped raw along her nerves. How easily he had lied to her, all soft-spoken charm and ardent glances. Aidan Abbott was no hero. He was Hades, spinning poetry as he lured her into the underworld.

And she, Gwendolyn Smythe, the Spotted Giraffe, had been fool enough to believe him.

Footsteps retreated down the corridor. Buttercup huffed quietly and tucked her head against Gwen's ribs once more.

Outside the window, the storm rolled away in slow procession. Golden light spilled across the floor in stripes, growing more vivid as the clouds thinned. The sky bloomed with color. Dusky violet, burnished rose, fire-bright orange. A wound bleeding beauty into the twilight.

The handle of the door rattled again.

Gwen did not stir.

Then came another knock.

"Gwendolyn Smythe, are you in there?" Octavia's voice was hushed with worry. "Are you well?"

Gwen remained where she sat, her fingers lost in Buttercup's silky ears. She offered no answer. The door handle rattled again.

"Let me in. Please. I only wish to know that you are well."

Still Gwen made no reply. She could not be expected to soothe others when she herself felt splintered down the center. Whatever came next could wait. This moment belonged to grief.

The wreckage of what might have been, the dreams she had dared to nurture, lay strewn about as so much debris in a field after a tempest. She would gather the pieces come morning. But tonight ... tonight was for mourning what she had believed was true.

A beat passed. Then another. At last, the gentle echo of retreating steps marked Octavia's departure.

Darkness embraced the room. The sunset had faded, leaving no trace but a dusky gray. Shadows softened the furniture, and Gwen sat unmoving save for her hand gliding over Buttercup's warm back. The little dog curled in her lap like an ember of comfort, and Gwen clung to that flicker of warmth with quiet desperation.

She considered rising. Perhaps she ought to light the lamp or change into her night rail. But the effort seemed monumental. Instead, she turned her cheek to the velvet cushions of the chair, letting memory carry her to a time when she had been a girl with a mother who brushed her curls and promised the world held joy and love in abundance.

She longed for her mother's arms. For the balm of that soothing voice and the scent of lavender water and linen.

You cannot hide forever, Gwendolyn, her mother would

have said with gentle command. *The world may break your heart, but you must always rise.*

Gwen exhaled, the breath long and weary. "You are right, Mama," she whispered. "I cannot stay buried in this sorrow."

She kissed the top of Buttercup's head and set the little dog on the rug. The floor was cold beneath her feet, the kind of cold that reminded one to move.

Crossing to the bellpull, Gwen rang for Octavia, then moved about the room to light the lamps. The soft glow pushed the darkness into corners, and with it, the ache in her chest began to ebb.

The stars blinked faintly beyond the windows. No moon tonight to enchant or deceive.

The world would not pause for a broken heart, nor did it care for love betrayed.

She was no longer the girl with stars in her eyes.

She was a woman, and it was time to choose her future.

AIDAN STOOD in Smythe's study, rolling his stiff shoulders as he contemplated the molten sky spilling through the terrace doors. The sunset, glorious and unyielding, seemed to mock the turmoil lodged beneath his ribs. The bruising along his side, an unwelcome reminder of recent events, throbbed with each breath. After his failed effort to speak with Gwen, he had spent the last hour mentally rehearsing his apology. Not for the pain he carried, but for the pain he had caused.

He awaited a final knock at the door, pivoting as it came at last.

Jenson stepped inside. "The Duke of Halmesbury and Lord Filminster."

Smythe rose behind his desk, gesturing to receive them. Jenson held the door wide for the duke and Aidan's brother-in-law to enter, then withdrew, closing the door with a muted click.

The study bore signs of preparation. Extra armchairs had been summoned from other parts of the house. Aidan's eyes swept across the room, noting who sat where. His father had arrived first and occupied the seat nearest Smythe. The Earl of Saunton had appeared shortly thereafter in response to Aidan's urgent summons and now leaned casually against the mantelpiece, declining the chair intended for him. The Duke of Halmesbury, always imposing, was folded into a chair far too small for his long frame, and Lord Filminster balanced on the edge of his own, his expression unusually grave, his gaze flicking repeatedly toward Smythe.

"For those of you not yet aware," Aidan began, his voice measured, "Mr. Smythe did not kill the baron."

Lord Moreland let out a breath. "Thank the Lord. The notion of informing your mother … it was …" His words drifted into silence, and he simply shook his head.

Clearly, Aidan's father had not yet been briefed on the news of Trafford and the others. Saunton, Halmesbury, and Filminster exchanged quiet nods, already privy to the truth. Filminster, no doubt, had relayed the message to Saunton earlier in the day. Aidan suspected the earl was even involved in the manhunt. His younger brother's longstanding friendship with Stirling's heir made it likely.

Aidan resumed pacing. Speaking to such elevated company unsettled him. Though his recent marriage had tied him to such important noblemen, familiarity had not yet bred ease. And what he was about to ask, he knew it was not a small thing.

"My wife has informed me," he began, carefully, "that Mr. Smythe was with her on the day of the coronation. All through the night, in fact, owing to a grave illness." His voice faltered, the import of the statement anchoring in the room like a weight. "We have since received a note … confirming this." His glance met Smythe's, and he caught himself just in time, stopping short of revealing what could not yet be spoken aloud.

Given the number of individuals already privy to the details surrounding the baron's death, it seemed wisest, for Trafford's sake, to refrain from further disclosures. Especially with his whereabouts still unknown and no resolution yet in sight.

Aidan raised a hand to his brow, pressing his fingers briefly to the skin as if he might calm the storm within. His mind had been occupied with thoughts of Trafford, their uneasy friendship and the looming uncertainty coiling through every waking hour. And yet, he had forged ahead, preparing for this evening with a singular purpose. To support both Mr. Smythe and the young woman who had come to mean so much to him.

"Mr. Smythe has explained his actions to me," Aidan began quietly. "The reasons behind the sale of certain holdings. Once I understood the truth, I felt it my duty to arrange this meeting before the ladies join us."

Smythe sat stiffly, hands worrying the objects strewn upon his desk. Papers, an inkpot, a pocket watch slightly askew. The habitual grin that usually softened his features was notably absent. Aidan had pressed him for this meeting, insisting it would bear fruit. Even so, he knew how difficult it had been for the older man to agree.

"Aidan assures me that I may place my confidence in all of you," Smythe said at last, his voice grave. "That what I share here will remain within these walls. And perhaps, that you may even offer your counsel."

The Duke of Halmesbury inclined forward, the light catching the blond strands threaded through his hair. "You have my word. Nothing spoken here will travel beyond this room. We are family now, and family must hold one another steady."

Smythe offered a tight nod and slowly lowered himself into the armchair near the fireplace. "I had long imagined the moment I would explain myself. I thought I would feel prepared. But instead ..." He hesitated, staring at the fire as though it might offer him courage. "I find I am more anxious than I had anticipated."

Aidan moved to stand beside him, his posture strong and quietly supportive. "Mr. Smythe is preparing to enter trade," he said, voice steady. "And I hoped to ask for your assistance in smoothing the way."

Silence settled across the room like a silken drape, weighted by implication. For a long breath, no one stirred. Then, from his place near the fireplace, the Earl of Saunton shifted, adjusting his cravat as though it had grown inexplicably tighter.

"I ... must admit something," he said, voice low. "I already engage in trade."

Aidan's eyebrows shot up. "What?"

The very notion contradicted everything he had been taught. Gentlemen, especially those of noble birth, did not stoop to commerce. Such matters were for merchants and shopkeepers. A gentleman of standing derived his income from land, rents, and investments executed at arm's length through agents. And yet, none of the men before him seemed remotely scandalized.

Saunton raised both hands, surrendering to the truth. "What choice did I have? I inherited a crumbling title, with estates so neglected I scarcely knew where to begin. My father, God rest his soul, was a menace in the eyes of his tenants and addled by the end. I could not right things without capital. So I engaged a proxy and entered trade. Mills. Steam. Whatever turned a profit. How do you think I tripled my holdings in such a short time?"

The Duke of Halmesbury leaned forward, tugging his coat into better alignment. "When Saunton confided in me, I made a similar choice. A proxy acts on my behalf, but I have investments in ventures reaching as far north as Scotland. It has brought my interests unexpected breadth."

"A gentleman is permitted, by the unwritten rules of society, to invest outside of his estates," Aidan said slowly, his tone contemplative as he resumed pacing.

Saunton gave a rueful tug at his shirt collar. "Yes, but we are ... rather more involved than the occasional idle investor."

Aidan cast a look toward his father, uncertain what to believe. Lord Moreland rose from his chair and crossed to the window, folding his hands behind his back with the air of a man deep in thought.

"I have been exploring similar possibilities," he admitted. "My solicitor has conducted inquiries on my behalf. I have not yet committed to any one course, but ... it is heartening to know others have made similar considerations. It is not a topic easily discussed."

Filminster spoke then, his tone steady. "Halmesbury and Saunton have both provided valuable guidance as I navigate the beginnings of such ventures."

Across the room, Smythe rose from his desk and moved toward a nearby cabinet. In silence, he selected a decanter and poured a modest measure into a tumbler. With a steady hand, he drank, then replaced the glass with a decisive clink. When he turned back, he was transformed. Confidence radiated from him, his eyes glinting with humor.

He was the smallest man in the gathering, yet in that moment, he stood the tallest.

"Well," he said, voice rich with satisfaction, "then it seems I am speaking to precisely the right group of gentlemen."

Aidan chuckled softly. "So it would seem. I had expected far more resistance. But"— he gestured toward Smythe with an encouraging smile—"please, go on."

Smythe inclined his head. "Aidan and I have discussed the merits of forming a syndicate. A business arrangement to acquire a fleet of fast ships. I have already compiled a list of clippers in sound condition with experienced crews. I intend to approach the owners with offers to purchase."

Lord Moreland returned to his seat, his expression sharpening with interest. "You mean to control the means of transport, not the goods themselves. That would allow for flexibility in responding to demand. A clever strategy. Tell us, what is your full plan?"

Smythe adjusted the front of his coat with a sharp tug, his posture now firm with conviction. "My plan is to establish a shipping company centered on swift voyages, reaching the Orient and returning in under a year. We would specialize in highly profitable goods, such as Chinese tea. If we pool our resources, we can purchase the fastest vessels available, and commission new ones built to our exact specifications."

"What of the East India Company?" Aidan asked. "They still hold dominance in trade with India."

Smythe inclined his head in acknowledgment. "Indeed. But I have contacts within the company, and I have broached the idea quietly. There are routes they do not serve effectively ... paths that could be turned to our advantage. Our strength will be speed and adaptability. The East India Company is immense, but precisely because of its size, it cannot pivot quickly. We, on the other hand, are unencumbered. With the changes brought on by Napoleon's fall, opportunities abound."

The Duke of Halmesbury leaned forward, his elbows resting on his knees. He exchanged a glance with Saunton, who offered a brief, approving nod. The duke then turned back to Smythe. "We are interested. Naturally, I would like to review the proposed routes and examine the specific opportunities you have identified."

"Would it be possible to operate through a proxy, Mr. Smythe?" Aidan asked, the question earnest. It seemed unnecessary for Smythe to risk his standing in society, given how Halmesbury and Saunton had managed their own affairs discreetly.

Smythe shook his head in dissent. "I have decided I must be the headman to make this venture a success. There are connections I have cultivated these past few years, in Parliament, within the shipping companies themselves, and I have cousins in the navy, so I know the right men. High society might be scandalized, but the men I do business with will be impressed to work with me."

Halmesbury rose and crossed the room. He extended his hand. Smythe blinked, startled by the gesture, but recovered swiftly and grasped it in a firm handshake.

"You have earned a fine reputation for negotiating on

your brother's behalf at the Lords," Halmesbury said warmly. "Saunton and I will examine your proposal. If it holds merit, you shall have our support. Financial, strategic, and confidential."

Saunton joined them, clasping Smythe's hand in turn. "It sounds like the start of something remarkable."

From his chair, Lord Moreland cleared his throat and leaned forward slightly. "I, too, am intrigued. Once I see the particulars, I may be persuaded to lend my support."

Filminster gave a quiet nod. "I shall follow Halmesbury and Saunton in whatever course they recommend. They are seasoned in such matters, and I am still learning the intricacies of managing my estates."

Aidan felt one weight lift off his shoulders. The first part of his plan was a success. Smythe had a pledge from powerful peers to back him as he moved his interests into trade. Their support would be invaluable over the coming days, especially within the *beau monde*, where Smythe would need support once he made his scandalous move into business dealings.

When the meeting concluded, the gentlemen moved onto the terrace, where a cooler breeze stirred the heavy air. It was a brief respite, a pause before the evening took its next turn. The more delicate matter involving Gwen.

Filminster and Aidan stepped away from the others, finding a quiet corner. It offered both privacy and a moment to collect their thoughts.

"Any word of Trafford?" Aidan asked, his voice low. Unexpectedly, he had grown fond of Julius Trafford and his eccentricities, despite his earlier resolve to keep the man at arm's length.

Filminster tapped a thoughtful rhythm on the stone balustrade. "Yes. It appears Lady Astley is missing someone as well. She had intended to collect Stirling's ward this afternoon, but the rain delayed her. By the time her carriage reached Trafford's family home, the young lady was nowhere to be found."

Aidan's thoughts returned to the bloodied note received earlier. "The young woman who delivered the letter to Halmesbury's house?"

Filminster lifted his shoulders in a slow shrug. "Perhaps. Miss Audrey Gideon, I believe her name is. No one seems to know much about her, but it is too coincidental to be ignored. Two people vanishing from the same household on the same afternoon? Still, we must tread carefully. We risk endangering them both if we act too publicly."

Aidan studied his brother-in-law's features and saw the worry that lingered beneath his composed expression. "Trafford is clever. He will find a way to send word soon."

"I hope so. It unsettles me, knowing a friend placed himself in danger for my sake. I keep thinking about the events, wondering whether there was a better way to handle everything."

Aidan shook his head. "What is done is done. All that remains is to deal with the present. Trafford was adamant about helping, and he is no fool."

Filminster burst out laughing despite his anxiety. "That is not true. Trafford would be the first to insist that he is, indeed, a fool."

Chuckling, Aidan shook his head at the ridiculous assertion he had just made. "I meant to say ... he is an enterprising and gumptious fool."

The two men fell into silence, their thoughts drifting toward their absent friend. Each, in his own way, admired the peculiar loyalty of Julius Trafford.

After a time, Aidan stirred. "And Michaels? You mentioned he had sustained an injury?"

"My butler," Filminster replied with a sigh and a wry twist of his lips, "is a cantankerous old creature. The doctor advised rest, but he has taken that as a personal affront and is already back to patrolling the household, keeping everyone on edge."

"What happened?" Aidan asked, curiosity piqued.

Filminster raked a hand through his hair, his movements taut with tension. "The stubborn fellow tackled an intruder, someone half his age, when the scoundrel forced entry into my study through a window. Michaels heard the glass shatter and, rather than call for help, ran straight in. He hurled himself at the villain and earned a solid blow to the face. And yet, somehow, he managed to strike the brute with the same sculpture used to kill the baron. Only then did he raise the alarm. Alas, the miscreant escaped before anyone could catch him."

Aidan shook his head with admiration. "Michaels is a good man. A belligerent old goat, but a loyal one."

Filminster leaned against the stone balustrade, his gaze turned toward the darkness beyond the gardens. "I owe him everything for what he did that day ... for saving Lily. I cannot imagine what I would have done if ..." His voice faded, unable to complete the sentence.

Aidan exhaled slowly, then lifted a hand and gave Filminster's back a quiet pat. "I know, Brendan. Believe me, I understand."

They stood in silence for a moment, the air between them thick with unspoken obligations.

"Do you suppose Trafford will be all right?" Filminster asked, his voice barely above a whisper.

Aidan felt a pang of dread twist through him, but he

answered with conviction. "He must be. If ever there was a man capable of looking after himself, it is Julius Trafford."

Filminster nodded slowly, yet his face remained shadowed with concern as he stared into the gloom where the garden dissolved into night.

GWEN WRAPPED her fingers around a warm cup of tea and tried to see recent events from a fresh perspective. The fragrance of the steeped leaves brought some measure of comfort to her wounded spirit. The dull ache in her chest lingered, a quiet echo of recent heartbreak, but at least now her thoughts moved with some clarity.

She cast her mind back to Lady Moreland's visit and the dreadful revelation that Lily had been attacked in the wake of the baron's murder.

Given the circumstances, she could understand why Aidan might resort to desperate measures in order to protect those he loved. It stung, deeply, that she had been unwittingly caught in those schemes. And yet, when she looked past the pain, she could grasp the fear that had driven him. Desperation could twist even the most honorable of men into untenable choices.

Still, understanding did not erase the hurt. It did not quiet the knowledge that she had been used as a piece upon a board in a game of misdirected revenge. But Gwen refused to allow those thoughts to drag her back into despair. She took another sip of her tea, letting its warmth seep through her limbs. It had taken time to chase away the chill she had acquired from sitting by the window during the storm, but now, slowly, she was thawing. Body and heart alike.

"This is a good cup of tea," Octavia murmured from the bench at the foot of the bed, her saucer nestled near her chest.

"That sounds suspiciously like self-congratulation."

Octavia shrugged, unrepentant. "A fact is a fact. Just because I made it does not mean it is not true."

A soft, reluctant laugh escaped Gwen. "I wish I possessed even a fraction of your certainty."

The lady's maid frowned into her cup. "You do, Gwendolyn Smythe. Just not when it comes to yourself."

Gwen sighed and set her cup down gently on the table beside her mother's old armchair. "It is clear Aidan did not marry me for my sake. He did so to reach my father."

"I do not believe that," Octavia replied, her tone brimming with conviction. "I have seen how he looks at you. That is not the gaze of a man bound by duty."

"Come. Let us not quarrel. I need to think about what comes next. I did not wish to trap Aidan in this marriage, but I think we are stuck with each other now. Annulment will not be possible, considering we have consummated the marriage."

Octavia snorted in surprise, spewing drops of tea. "You certainly have done that!"

Gwen flushed at once, the heat climbing all the way to the tips of her ears. She pressed a hand to her cheek and looked away, waiting for the warmth to subside before she spoke again.

"I do not know what happens next," she said quietly. "It is our duty to produce an heir, of course, but I have begun to wonder ... perhaps I should remain here, at Papa's house. Give Aidan the freedom he clearly desires. He could visit now and then, and when we know whether or not I am increasing, he could choose to return ... or not."

Octavia shook her head at once. "He will not agree to that. I tell you now, Gwendolyn, Lord Abbott is in love with you."

This time, it was Gwen who snorted. She stared at her maid in disbelief. One would think Octavia were the one who read novels, judging by the fanciful nature of her conclusions.

"I cannot indulge in hopes that will only make me weep," Gwen replied, folding her hands tightly in her lap. "It is time to be practical."

Octavia slapped the bench with her open palm. "I am being practical. True love is not a fantasy. Perhaps Lord Abbott did attend that ball because of Mr. Smythe, but no one made him kiss you. That he did of his own accord."

Gwen narrowed her eyes. "Perhaps he only did so to gain entry to our household. Perhaps he thought seducing the daughter was the surest path to uncovering whatever secrets Papa kept."

Octavia drank down the last of her tea, then set her cup and saucer down with a decisive thunk. "You must fight for your happiness, Gwendolyn Smythe!"

"If my husband is so distressed by our quarrel," Gwen said bitterly, "why did he make only one feeble attempt at a reconciliation earlier? He knocked once, twice at most, and then disappeared. Buttercup is more persistent when she wants to be let in from the garden!"

Octavia slapped the bench again, this time hard enough to rattle the tea set. "Mr. Smythe is not upstairs with you either, yet I do not hear you complaining of his absence!"

"My father is quite possibly defending himself from a murder accusation," Gwen snapped. "I think he can be excused for not calling on me this evening. His regard, at least, is not so easily shaken."

The two women glared at one another across the room, their emotions flaring too brightly to be concealed. Then, quite suddenly, Buttercup shot to her feet from her sprawl in the middle of the floor. The little dog dashed to the window, barking furiously, her entire frame rigid with tension.

"What on earth is she doing?" Gwen asked, her voice nearly drowned out by the shrill yapping.

Octavia and Gwen exchanged alarmed glances. Their quarrel vanished in an instant as the terrier transformed before their eyes into a ferocious guardian, her bark rising to a snarl as she trembled with excitement.

AIDAN GROWLED UNDER HIS BREATH. "The ladder will not hold. The ground is far too sodden. Look what it has done to my boots!"

Smythe, puffing from exertion, threw up his hands. "Burn my buttons!"

The Earl of Saunton doubled over with laughter, clutching his sides. "Did I ever tell you about the time my brother tried just such a thing to woo his wife? Last year, in the dead of winter—"

Filminster began to chuckle as well. "I was there. We were trapped in the mud for days."

Aidan cast a warning scowl at the lot of them and motioned for silence. "Hush, all of you! Buttercup is already barking loud enough to wake the neighborhood. Gwen will hear and catch us at this ridiculous business."

From his post against the garden wall, the Duke of Halmesbury sighed deeply, arms folded across his chest as he surveyed the muddied chaos before him. "We may need to revisit this plan. Your intentions are noble, Abbott, but this ..." He gestured toward the ruined ladder and the churned earth at its base. "This is hardly a dignified approach."

Aidan straightened, releasing the ladder with a defeated clunk as it struck the side of the house. "Agreed. Let us return to the terrace before we rouse suspicion."

The men trudged back up the garden steps, carefully wiping their boots before reentering Smythe's office through the terrace doors. The fire crackled within, a quiet counterpoint to their muddy endeavor.

Aidan had entertained a fleeting notion of climbing to Gwen's window and offering some poetic declaration—something Shakespearean and suitably romantic—but in truth, the thought had never quite sat well with him. And now, covered in mud and thoroughly humbled, the idea had been laid to rest with appropriate finality.

Once they had reclaimed their seats, they resumed their discussion, sorting through possibilities with renewed determination. Suggestions were made—some clever, others outlandish—but none seemed to suit.

Aidan shook his head with each new offering, his fingers laced together as he searched the depths of his mind for the right course of action. Something heartfelt. Something worthy of Gwen.

Anything.

As suddenly as it had begun, Buttercup's barking ceased. With a huff of smug triumph, as though she had vanquished some dire intruder, the little terrier strutted back to her place on the rug, flopped down with exaggerated drama, and rested her chin upon her paw. Her eyes found Gwen's, watchful and judgmental, as though she alone held the answer to some unspoken question.

Octavia and Gwen exchanged a frown, neither willing to hazard a guess about the cause of the dog's fit. After a moment, Octavia shrugged and returned to the matter at hand. "I think you should give Lord Abbott a chance to explain himself. Speak to him plainly. Resolve this ... before it becomes permanent."

Gwen gave a weary sigh. "Aidan has a strong sense of duty. That much is undeniable. He will tell me what I wish to hear if it means easing my distress. But that does not mean it is true. He married me under false pretenses, believing Papa guilty, and now that he knows the truth, I imagine he regrets everything. He must. What man would not?"

Octavia rose abruptly and began pacing. "Oh, for pity's sake! Why can you not believe he might care for you—truly care for you? You stubborn, infuriating girl!"

The pain surged in Gwen's chest, sharp and hot. She pressed her hands together, willing herself to stay composed. "Because there is no evidence," she whispered.

Octavia halted in her tracks, eyes blazing. "What about the way he looked at you? The tenderness in his voice? The words he spoke? That was not performance, Gwendolyn. It was affection."

Gwen swallowed hard and hardened her heart. "It was an act," she said, her voice as brittle as glass. "A necessary illusion to accomplish his goal."

"Have you no faith?" Octavia asked, her voice cracking with disbelief.

Tears stung Gwen's eyes. Her lips quivered, but she forced the words out. "Not in this."

Octavia turned sharply, her voice shaking now with something akin to fury. "Not in you."

Gwen turned away from the condemnation and crossed the room to the window. The garden beyond was cloaked in blackness, the sky moonless and clouded, offering no light. The sight felt symbolic, a perfect representation of what she felt within. Her hopes for love, for partnership, for a future filled with mutual trust, had faded into shadow.

Partners do not keep secrets from each other.

"I do have faith in myself," Gwen said, her tone quiet but steady. "As a person, I know my worth. But I am not a great beauty ... not the sort to inspire a man like Aidan to fall in love. I simply do not believe that a man could see me in that way after all these years. When I met him, I was all but on the shelf."

Octavia let out an incredulous grunt, throwing her hands into the air. "The men you met were pompous, pea-brained fools who were frightened by a tall, intelligent woman. You are too original, too brilliant for the lot of them."

"Will you help me discuss what comes next," Gwen asked, rubbing at her temple, "or must we declare this conversation over for the evening?"

Octavia gave a long sigh. Her shoulders sagged, the fire in her voice dimmed by fatigue and affection. "Perhaps, once you have rested, you will see things more clearly. For now, let us speak of something else."

Gwen nodded and sank back into her chair. "I had high hopes, you know. For once, I thought things might change. But now ... it is ever so lonely. Aside from Papa and you, I have no one with whom I can truly speak."

Octavia let out a soft chuckle. "And what of Lady Hays and Lady Astley? They always make a point of conversing with you at every gathering."

Gwen groaned and dropped her head into her hands. "I wish they would not. Lady Hays is sweet but forgets her own thoughts midway through them, and Lady Astley is a spiteful harridan. If her husband were not so wealthy and well-connected, society would never tolerate half the things she says."

Octavia returned to the bench, her voice lifting with quiet confidence. "It will all work out in time. I truly believe you will find real friends, good friends, if only you allow yourself the chance to hope again."

Gwen pressed a hand over her aching heart. It was fragile tonight, brimming with memories of what had been and dreams already fading.

Only the night before, she had felt the promise of something new and extraordinary. Held close in Aidan's arms, warm and cherished, their connection undeniable.

Now she sat here, shrouded in shadows and silence, arguing with her lady's maid.

"I did give it a chance," she said softly. "I opened my heart. And all it earned me was a reminder ... that I am still *Gwen, Gwen the Spotted Giraffe*."

CHAPTER
SEVENTEEN

"The roots of education are bitter, but the fruit is sweet."

Aristotle

~

Aidan was still pacing mentally, desperate for an idea—any idea—that might convince Gwen of the depth of his regard. His thoughts remained a tangle, the fragments of half-formed plans refusing to coalesce. When Jenson entered the room to announce that the wives of the guests had arrived for dinner, Aidan nearly groaned aloud.

Another interruption. Another moment stolen from his already slipping grip on the problem.

The gentlemen moved to the smaller drawing room, where his sister, cousin, mother, and the Duchess of Halmesbury had gathered. The atmosphere was lively. Gowns rustled, laughter floated, and in the center of it all stood Lily hopping with anticipation, something odd clutched in her hands.

The moment her gaze caught his, she darted toward him with barely restrained glee.

"Aidan! I brought something for you," she declared triumphantly. "Annabel found it in her attic. It took us the longest time to uncover. There was a whole crate of them, but we only brought the one. We thought it might help."

Aidan stared at the strange object she held aloft, temporarily silenced by both her excitement and the peculiar contraption in her hands. "What is it?"

With great ceremony, Lily held it up and twisted her hands to reveal that the object expanded, telescoping into a paper sphere, light and intricate.

"It is a Chinese lantern," she explained with pride. "Annabel had them strung across the garden for a ball a few months past. Look!" She spun it slowly, the delicate paper catching the lamplight. "We thought it would be just the thing to show Gwen that you love her."

She paused then, frowning thoughtfully at the paper decoration. Her head tilted, her expression sharpening. "You do love her, do you not? That is the reason we are all here?"

Aidan could not help smiling despite the clamor in his head. He lifted a hand to gently tap her chin in that familiar brotherly gesture. Lily's thoughts often tumbled out faster than most people could follow, but Aidan had learned long ago to listen for the truth buried within her words.

"Of course I do," he said, his voice firm, the certainty finally taking shape in his chest.

Lily beamed. "I knew it! It was plain as day at the wedding. You claimed it was all a matter of honor and doing what was right and all that, but I told Brendan then ... You wore the expression of a man in love. I watched you closely. You flinched, just a little, when Gwen hesitated during her vows."

Aidan glanced around and realized every eye in the room was fixed on him. The heat crept up his neck. *Blast it all!* How did he find himself laying bare his soul in rooms full of people? Men and women both! Even his mother, and Gwen's father, were present, watching with undisguised interest.

"I do love her," he said at last, voice low but steady. "It will not be easy to convince her of that, which is why I asked for everyone's help."

Lily bounced on her toes, eyes alight, and caught his arm. "This is so exciting! What do you think? Do you see it now ... what it could be?"

She lifted the lantern again, stretching to her full height, though she barely reached his chest. The delicate sphere spun gently in her grasp, casting shifting patterns of light across the walls. Aidan tilted his head, studying it. Slowly, a glimmer of possibility took hold.

He looked again at the lantern, truly looked, and began to understand Lily's excitement.

Around the room, everyone was still watching, breath held as though waiting for a pronouncement. His cousin Sophia stood with her husband's arm around her, chewing her lower lip. The Duchess of Halmesbury nibbled on a fingernail while her towering husband stood beside her, his expression unreadable but warm.

His mother stood at the back, her handkerchief delicately pressed to her lashes, as though she were already overcome. Lord Moreland remained by her side, posture formal but eyes softened with something Aidan could not name. At the door, Filminster and Mr. Smythe stood shoulder to shoulder, the latter grinning broadly, his eyes tracking the swaying of the lantern as though he, too, saw its potential.

Aidan straightened, his chest expanding with sudden certainty. A grin spread across his face.

"It is absolutely perfect," he said.

Gwen's stomach gave a most unladylike growl, and she clapped a hand over it, scowling. "Why is the maid taking so long with my dinner tray? It is dreadfully late already."

Octavia, who was methodically preparing the bed for the night, turned back with a shrug. "I ate hours ago."

"That is hardly helpful."

The lady's maid stifled a laugh behind her hand. "It was helpful to me."

Gwen pulled a face. If the tray did not arrive soon, she would be forced to leave the sanctuary of her room, and she could not bear the risk of encountering her husband. Not yet. Skipping a meal would only leave her wretched and irritable come morning, and she was set to endure a night of troubled sleep.

Every time her thoughts drifted to the confrontation in her father's study, her heart gave a sharp twist, and her eyes stung with tears she refused to shed. No. She would not think about it. She would not break again tonight.

Octavia had made a wise suggestion. Rest now and face the day anew with clearer thoughts. Still, her body would not be silenced so easily.

She briefly considered taking the back stairs to the kitchen to fetch something modest, a bit of bread and cheese, perhaps. The teapot was long since emptied, and the room had grown quiet and cold in its solitude. Surely, if she took the back route, she would avoid running into Aidan.

And yet ... her feet remained still. Her heart was not ready. Not for explanations. Not for apologies. Not even for kindness. Octavia and Buttercup were the only souls she could endure tonight.

Thump, thump.

The knock shattered the quiet, and Gwen let out a startled squeal. She had been so lost in her thoughts, she had not heard anyone approach.

Her eyes flew to Octavia, who merely shrugged. Gwen's pulse quickened. If it was Aidan ...

Octavia made a silent offer to open the door, but Gwen shook her head quickly, her breath caught somewhere between dread and longing.

"Gwendolyn?"

The voice beyond the door was unmistakable.

She exhaled in relief and crossed to the door.

When she opened it, her father stood there grinning, his white teeth gleaming in the dim light of the corridor. His good spirits caught her off guard. The last time she had seen him, only hours earlier, he had been under immense strain.

"Papa?"

"It is time to come downstairs, Gwendolyn."

She shook her head at once. "I do not wish to see ... him."

Her father's smile dimmed, softening with understanding. "I would like a word with you, and I promise it will be just the two of us. Aidan is ... elsewhere."

"I am not ready," she murmured, voice low and frayed.

His grin faded, and he tipped his head, a gesture of

sympathy rather than argument. "Time and tide wait for no man."

Gwen folded her arms. "It is not yet noon. I shall face him tomorrow."

Her father blinked, bemused. "Your mother always had the uncanny ability to redirect any conversation, and I see you have inherited that devilish trait."

She gave a weak wave of her hand. "It is simply what Chaucer meant by that line, is it not?"

"I am no scholar, my dear. I have not the faintest idea what you are talking about. Is this one of your attempts to be clever?"

She sighed, her resistance wavering. "Chaucer was speaking of noontide, not the tides of the sea. I was merely stating that I would confront this muddle in the morning. At noon, perhaps."

Her father let out a quiet chuckle. "Well, it is an amusing rebuttal. I will grant you that."

"Yet it did not work."

He smiled again, showing those familiar teeth. "No, I am afraid not. It is imperative we speak."

He held out a hand, palm up, gesturing toward the hallway and the grand staircase beyond.

"You will not run into Aidan."

"You swear it?"

"On my honor. Not until you are ready."

Gwen hesitated, then stepped out into the corridor, leaving the door ajar for Octavia. She slipped her arm through her father's, comforted by his presence.

"Well, then," she said with a sigh. "Lead the way."

Despite her father's assurances, Gwen could not help casting nervous glances down the hallway as they walked. With every step, she half-expected Aidan to appear. His presence always managed to catch her off guard. She was not ready for that yet. Not tonight.

On the main floor, they passed the closed door of the small drawing room. Her eyes lingered on it. Was Aidan within?

They reached the study. Gwen sank into a deep, upholstered armchair by the hearth, the familiar shape of it cradling her weary form. The fireplace stood empty, but it remained the most comforting spot in the room, far preferable to the formal space across her father's desk.

Papa settled into the matching chair beside her, tapping his knee lightly with one hand as he gathered his thoughts.

"These past few weeks have been quite the whirlwind," he said at last.

Gwen thought of the illness that had nearly claimed her life, of waking up with a sense of clarity and determination to make something meaningful of her second chance. She had wanted to adopt, to mother a child who needed love. And then everything had changed.

One moonlit night, she had found herself enchanted by a stranger's poetry. Only to discover he was a man of startling beauty who would soon steal her first kiss and, shortly thereafter, her entire life's course. A scandal, a rushed marriage, and then the shattering truth that it had all been founded on a deception.

So yes. A whirlwind indeed.

She merely nodded.

"I have spoken to your husband at length," her father said carefully, "and we have resolved our misunderstanding."

"That may be," Gwen replied, her voice tight, "but it does not change the fact that he was dishonest with me."

Her father moistened his lips before replying. "I think it

does, Gwen. Aidan is a man caught in a tangle of duty and desperation. His sister was attacked in her own home mere weeks ago, and he believes she remains in danger. He was frantic to uncover the truth, and he made a mistake. He accused the wrong man."

Her father leaned forward, resting his forearms on his knees, his gaze steady and full of quiet reflection. "But here is what matters … I was not forthcoming either. I had secrets, too. Had I spoken plainly, much of this might have been avoided. My own silence made things worse."

"You mean about the artwork and the properties?" she asked.

"I do. I have plans, Gwen. My income had plateaued, and I saw a chance to build something new. Something lasting. I am going into business."

"The shipping company."

He blinked, clearly startled. "You knew?"

Gwen nodded. "After you sold the northern estate, I became concerned. I needed to know whether you had taken leave of your senses."

He huffed a laugh. "And how did you work it out?"

Gwen gestured toward the desk. "I went through your office. I found the notebook in the bottom drawer. You had written down details about the ships. Load capacities, journey dates, information about captains and officers. I concluded you were evaluating them for purchase."

Her father blinked in surprise. "And yet you said nothing?"

She lifted one shoulder. "What was there to say? I approved of your plan. You seemed to have everything well in hand."

"And the consequences?"

"There will be a scandal," she said evenly. "That is why

you insisted we host the ball. You wished me to marry before society discovered you were lowering our family's standing by entering trade."

He inclined his head. "Aidan noted certain inconsistencies ... enough to suspect I might be the man he was seeking. But once he learned the truth, he took action. He arranged for support. The Duke of Halmesbury, Lord Saunton, Lord Moreland, and Lord Filminster have all pledged to back me. Quietly, of course. It means I can proceed with greater ambition and far less risk. Their involvement is more than I could have hoped for, and Aidan made it happen. Because he is committed to this marriage."

She turned her face away. "He has no choice. He is bound to me now."

Her father gave a quiet sigh. "A man always has a choice, Gwendolyn. And Aidan chose you."

Gwen fidgeted with the edge of her sleeve, her fingers twisting the fabric in agitation. "I have tried to imagine what it was like for him ... to be caught in the middle of a family crisis. I can even appreciate the desperation that drove him. But it does not erase the lies."

He sat forward, his expression firm. "And I believe you have allowed your past to cast a long shadow over your future. Those cruel words at school, the senseless mockery, they do not deserve this power over you. You are no longer that girl." His voice softened. "Those girls are gone. Their opinions matter not at all. What matters now is your life. Your marriage."

Tears stung her eyes. She swallowed hard and blinked them away. "How can I believe he chose me of his own accord?"

Her father's eyes crinkled with a hint of a smile. "I think

you should allow him the chance to prove it. Use that brilliant mind of yours to see what is right in front of you."

Papa rose and crossed the room, opening one of the terrace doors and standing aside.

Gwen frowned, peering past him into the dark. The sky beyond was a sweep of velvet black, twinkling with distant stars. Without a moon to cast its silver glow, the night appeared especially deep, profoundly still.

Her father tilted his head toward the doorway in a silent invitation.

She hesitated. Her hands clenched, then unclenched at her sides. She wanted to see Aidan. And she did not. Her heart wavered between longing and dread.

Several moments passed.

"Go to him, Gwendolyn," her father urged gently.

With a sigh that was more resignation than agreement, she rose and moved across the room. She paused in the doorway, casting her gaze down to her slippers, seeking strength.

"You will never do anything in this world without courage," her father said, his voice low and firm. "It is the greatest quality of the mind, next to honor."

She glanced back at him, a reluctant smile tugging at her lips. "You are not such a terrible scholar after all, Papa. Quoting Aristotle at such a moment."

"There is always time for Aristotle," he replied in a falsetto that mimicked her mother's tone so precisely that Gwen gave a startled laugh, even through her nervousness. It was an echo of the past, one that warmed her heart and gave her strength.

With a deep breath, she stepped onto the terrace.

The door shut quietly behind her.

She was alone.

Looking about, she found no sign of Aidan. The terrace stretched out before her, washed in the soft hush of night.

Then she saw it.

Down at the far end of the terrace, near the very place where she had first encountered Aidan, hung a softly glowing orb. A lantern. It swung gently from the eaves of the house, lit from within, casting a serene golden light.

Gwen took a step closer.

The lantern was round, delicate, and unmistakably fashioned in the likeness of the moon. Along the balustrade, dozens of candles flickered, mimicking the scatter of stars across the heavens.

And suddenly, she understood.

The entire terrace had been transformed into a reflection of the night they first met.

She raised her hands to her mouth, emotion breaking through her chest in a soft, stifled sob. The beauty of it, the thoughtfulness, it reached a place within her that had been locked in sorrow.

Then, a voice carried across the still night air. Low and steady.

> *"She walks in beauty, like the night*
> *Of cloudless climes and starry skies;*
> *And all that's best of dark and bright*
> *Meet in her aspect and her eyes:*
> *Thus mellow'd to that tender light*
> *Which heaven to gaudy day denies."*

Gwen choked back another sob, her breath catching as she turned, and found Aidan kneeling behind her. The glow of the moon-shaped lantern bathed him in golden light, and she could scarcely breathe for the ache in her chest.

Byron's words still echoed in the air, but now she needed Aidan's.

He reached for her hand, pressing it to his cheek.

"I am so sorry, my love," he said, his voice steady but rich with emotion. "I am sorry I deceived you. But more than that, I am sorry I never said what was in my heart."

He drew in a deep breath, his eyes never leaving hers. "From the moment you recited that verse of Manilius, I knew. I had found the other half of my soul. A woman who would challenge me, who would keep me honest, and whom I would cherish until my final breath. I could not walk away. That is why I kissed you in the moonlight. I love you, Gwen Abbott. With everything that I am."

Tears slipped silently down her cheeks, tracing her chin and neck, but she did not brush them away.

"How can I know it is true?" she whispered.

Aidan stared pensively back up at her, biting his lip. "What if I told you a secret? An embarrassing secret that a man would only tell his beloved wife ..." He hesitated. "And perhaps a very close friend."

Gwen used her palms to wipe her cheeks, and nodded, intrigued to hear what he might tell her. Would she finally learn something tangible about her moonlight visitor?

Aidan rose up, peering over his shoulder before leaning down to whisper in her ear. "You are the only woman I have ever lain with, Gwen. The only one who ever tempted me."

Gwen gasped, pulling back to gaze up into his face. "Is that true?"

Aidan peered about again, as if afraid of being overheard. "It is."

"You mean the other night when we ..."

Her husband's brows shot up, and he swiftly raised a finger to press her lips shut. "Shh ... and yes."

Gwen pursed her lips while she thought about his confession. Slowly, a warmth began to spread through her body, sending shivers down her arms and legs. Even her head felt giddy. Pulling his hand away, she leaned in and whispered into his ear. "I was your first?"

He bobbed his head, murmuring close to tickle her hair with his warm breath. "I left that afternoon to receive lessons on what to do. I ... did not want to disappoint you."

It was not the sort of secret a gentleman would typically share, especially not with the woman he adored.

Gwen threw her arms around his neck, her heart overflowing at the trust he had shown her. "Oh, Aidan," she whispered. "I love you, too!"

He drew her into his arms, and under the gentle glow of the moon-shaped lantern, their lips met. The kiss was tender and deep with meaning. A sealing of hearts laid bare with no more secrets to come between them. In his embrace, Gwen felt as though she had summoned a dream to life beneath the stars.

She barely noticed the soft creak of the terrace doors behind them, so absorbed was she in the moment. When they finally broke apart, breathless and smiling, Gwen glanced toward the sound.

A small crowd stood there, illuminated by the warm light spilling from the house.

At the front, Lily and Filminster beamed with delight, Lily's impish smile positively glowing. Behind them stood the duke and duchess, arm in arm. The Earl and Countess of Saunton stood together in quiet happiness, and Aidan's parents stood just beyond, their expressions carefully composed though their pride was evident.

Then, with quiet joy, Lily stepped forward and threw out her arms. "Welcome to the family, Gwen Abbott!"

Aidan gently urged her forward. One by one, each member of his family stepped close to greet her. Offering warm embraces, kisses to her cheek, and kind words that wrapped around her like a protective cloak.

Even the duke, typically more reserved, enveloped her in a brief but sincere hug. "Welcome, Gwen. I apologize for the deceptions that brought us here. But we are proud to have you join us. We shall do our best to make amends."

Gwen was overcome by an incredible warmth. Outside of her own family, she had never known such open affection and certainly not from people of such stature. It felt overwhelming and tender all at once.

Tears welled again, spilling freely as her emotions overcame her.

Lord Moreland stepped forward with a handkerchief in hand. "I am so relieved to learn your father's true plans, young lady," he said kindly. "I look forward to a successful future with Frederick Smythe."

She nodded, dabbing at her face, then gave a grateful blow into the cloth. She finally accepted the truth. Her father had been right. Aidan was the right man.

A sudden growl from her middle made her gasp in dismay. Her eyes widened, mortified. Papa, who had come up behind her to offer a quick hug, chuckled.

"I think it is time to eat, everyone. My daughter has been expecting her supper for quite some time but I had instructed the maid not to bring it."

Lily immediately seized Gwen's hand. "I am hungry,

too! I have not eaten since breakfast. That was at eight o'clock, and Annabel and the duke are early risers, so now I am, too! But it is difficult, going such long hours without a meal."

Gwen giggled, caught in the whirlwind of her sister-in-law's chatter as they walked inside. She marveled at how wonderful it would be to build connections with each of Aidan's family members. Her brother Gareth would surely adore them. He and little Ethan would get along famously, especially over a chessboard. She smiled, imagining the fierce and enthusiastic matches they were sure to enjoy.

As they crossed the threshold, Gwen glanced over her shoulder and found Aidan directly behind her.

"Are you going to tell me," she asked lightly, "why you thought my father had murdered a man?"

He winced, clearly discomfited. "Must I?"

Gwen paused mid-step, and with the spark of courage she had been nurturing, she looked him squarely in the eye.

"Yes," she said firmly. "You must."

CHAPTER EIGHTEEN

"Wishing to be friends is quick work, but friendship is a slow ripening fruit."

Aristotle

Aidan watched as Gwen brought the spoon to her lips, her posture elegant even in the simple act of eating. Though she might not favor this particular soup under ordinary circumstances, tonight hunger rendered her unusually enthusiastic. The gentle clink of silver on porcelain punctuated the hum of conversation around the long dining table, accompanied by the occasional chime of crystal or faint rustle of silk.

It was a profound joy to witness her in this light. No longer guarded, but surrounded by ease and laughter. On their wedding day, there had been warmth, certainly, but a heaviness had hovered above their gathering. Tonight, by contrast, the air itself seemed lighter, as though the burdens of doubt and suspicion had finally been swept away. Gwen's cheeks were tinged with a natural flush, and her gaze remained bright as she listened to the tale being retold by Saunton and Filminster. Her contented expression was a balm to Aidan's tightly strung nerves.

The story was, apparently, a well-embellished retelling of how Saunton's brother had managed to win his bride. Gentle laughter echoed around the table, mingling with the mellow glow of candlelight that flickered against the crystal decanters and polished wood. Beneath the tablecloth, Aidan slid his hand toward Gwen's and covered it lightly. Her fingers tensed a moment in surprise, then relaxed. She turned toward him just enough to grant a small sidelong smile before returning her attention to the tale.

Even in this moment of tentative harmony, Aidan's thoughts drifted toward Julius Trafford. The nagging worry remained. Where was the devil-may-care heir? Was he hurt? Alone? The bloodied note haunted him still, its crimson mark etched into his thoughts. It seemed almost a betrayal to sit in comfort, dining on roast and puddings, when Trafford might be in mortal danger. Yet, glancing around the table, he saw similar shadows behind the smiles. The fear for their missing friend was shared, though unspoken.

"And then Trafford said he could attest that Perry was an irreparable idiot to all who were present."

The punchline prompted Gwen to cover her mouth, her eyes dancing with amusement. "Little Julius has always been a bit of a scoundrel," she said lightly, her tone teasing.

The laughter fell away with astonishing swiftness. Silence pressed in. All heads turned toward her with collective surprise, forks pausing mid-air. The ticking of the clock upon the mantel became suddenly audible.

Even Smythe, who had been entirely absorbed in his soup, looked up with an uncomprehending glance before realizing the shift in mood.

Aidan cleared his throat, voice low. "Do you ... know Lord Trafford, Gwen?"

Gwen's brow furrowed at the attention. "No, but Lady Hays tells stories about Little Julius all the time. He frequently snuck into her home to wreak havoc on her household as a boy."

Saunton's hand moved to adjust his cravat, a small frown forming. "Lady Hays?"

"She resides near her niece's house in Mayfair," Gwen replied. "We are speaking of the heir to the Earl of Stirling, are we not? Little Julius was a regular visitor in her home."

The name had barely left her lips when a flicker of recognition sparked in Aidan's mind. He turned to Filminster, whose subtle shake of the head confirmed it. No one had considered Lady Hays's home.

Then, the final piece fell into place.

"You mean ... Aunty Gertrude?"

Gwen smiled gently. "That is correct ... Lady Gertrude Hays. She was recounting a story about him at the ball where we met. After our betrothal was announced, she sought me out. Said it was a great pity I had not met her great-nephew. I believe she had hoped we might take to each other."

The implication lingered. Lady Hays had once envisioned a match between Gwen and Lord Trafford.

"She told me he needed an intelligent woman to bring him up to scratch."

Aidan exchanged a look with Filminster.

"And ... is Lady Hays in London at present?" he asked.

Gwen shook her head. "She left with her husband shortly after the ball. She told me they would not return until Christmastide, but that we might expect an invitation to a house party before then."

Hope surged through Aidan. If Lady Hays's townhouse was near the Stirlings' London residence and if she had left just after the ball ... then perhaps that was where Trafford had taken refuge. And if Miss Gideon was with him, it could explain her sudden disappearance.

But riding up to knock on Lady Hays's door in broad daylight was out of the question, not with the real culprit still at large, possibly watching their movements. They would need to proceed with caution, not give away the game.

At the head of the table, the Duke of Halmesbury gave a genteel cough into his hand. "Smythe, the wine this evening is quite fine. Where did you come by it?"

Aidan glanced down. The duke's goblet was full. It was a subtle cue. Halmesbury was deflecting, giving cover. Around the table, there was a flutter of movement as the conversation turned obligingly.

Lord Saunton raised his own glass with a bright smile. "Indeed, remarkable flavor." He had barely touched his portion, as Aidan recalled. None of Sophia's immediate family, a gesture of solidarity, knowing the pain spirits had brought to her kin.

Talk turned to the meal, to the quality of the fish and the freshness of the herbs. Aidan returned to his own plate, only to find Gwen watching him closely. Her gaze lingered, thoughtful and steady, her soup momentarily forgotten.

She leaned in just a little, her voice low. "When we are

alone," she murmured, "you must explain what that was about."

The scent of citrus clung to her skin, and the soft press of her shoulder brushed his coat. Aidan swallowed hard. For a moment, he imagined brushing a curl from her cheek, telling her everything. About the note, the fears for Trafford, the possible safehouse nearby.

But her nearness stirred other thoughts too—simpler, deeper ones. He smiled, letting just a touch of mischief reach his eyes. "When we are alone, we may find ourselves rather occupied."

She tilted her head, cheeks faintly pink, but her voice was steady. "We will make time for both."

Her confidence delighted him. Under the table, he squeezed her hand lightly where it rested in her lap. She offered him a subtle smile and turned her attention back to her meal. He, in turn, focused on his, though the gentle blush rising in her cheeks stayed with him.

There would be time. Time for secrets. And time for love.

∽

"What was that about?" Gwen asked the moment they stepped into her bedchamber, her voice firm but not unkind.

Buttercup, clearly sensing her mistress's agitation, leapt from the bed and scurried across the floor, barking furiously at Aidan as if he were a villain in a stage play. Her tail stuck out like a quill, her little body quivering with defiance.

Aidan blinked in surprise at the ferocious display, and

Gwen could not help herself. Laughter burst from her chest until she had to clutch her sides.

"The trials of winning the affection of a protective guardian," Aidan said wryly, his mouth twitching into a lopsided smile.

Still giggling, Gwen motioned toward the door. Aidan obliged, opening it just long enough for her to scoop Buttercup gently into the corridor. The dog gave one last protesting bark as the door closed behind her.

Gwen took a breath to calm herself, then stood tall, her hands planted firmly on her hips. "Now. No more evasions. I am your wife, Aidan Abbott, and I insist on being included. I deserve to know what is happening."

He looked at her for a long moment, then took a step closer, cupping her cheek with gentle fingers. His kiss was soft and reverent, not seeking to distract, but to affirm. "You are my family now, Gwen. You have every right."

His voice, low and steady, curled around her like velvet. She stepped closer, her heart beating faster as the warmth of his nearness enveloped her.

"Then do not try to charm your way out of this," she said, tilting her head up to meet his gaze. "Why is Lord Trafford the subject of such furtive whispers?"

Aidan sighed and pressed another brief kiss to her forehead before stepping back, his expression sobering.

"Trafford was following a lead," he said carefully. "He believed one of the other suspects might be guilty, and he went to investigate. Alone. We received a note from him clearing your father of wrongdoing ... but it bore bloodstains. And no one has seen him since."

Gwen's lips parted, her breath catching. The words made sense, yet the situation felt unreal. "That sounds very grave," she said quietly. "Start from the beginning. Please."

Aidan nodded and began to pace, his steps slow and measured as he recounted the sequence of events that had brought them to this moment. He spoke of the baron's murder. So sudden, so senseless. Of Lily's terrifying attack. Of Filminster's discovery, the cryptic note that hinted at motive but fell short of naming the villain. And finally, of the men they had scrutinized, the narrowing of the field to her father and three others, and the startling developments at Ridley House.

Gwen listened in silence, her brow furrowed, her hands clasped tightly in front of her as if to brace herself against the weight of each revelation.

When he fell quiet, she released a breath she had not realized she had been holding. "You have all taken such grave risks," she said softly. "Did you know the baron personally?"

"No." Aidan's voice was low, tinged with regret. "But his death touched everyone around him. And Lily ..."

Gwen's gaze softened at the mention of his sister. She leaned back against the door, absorbing the tangle of implications. "Perhaps ... Trafford is hiding at Lady Hays's townhouse. She and Lord Hays often leave it in the care of their oldest servants when they are away. Some of them practically raised Little Julius."

"I pray that is the case," Aidan replied. "But we cannot simply call at her door. If the murderer is watching our movements, we risk leading danger straight to Trafford."

She nodded slowly. "Do you think he found something? Some proof?"

"There is no way to be certain. Not until we speak with him. Until then, we are navigating blind."

Gwen lifted her chin, her voice calm but certain. "That is not quite true. You told me the list of suspects is fixed.

That means every effort should now focus on those three men. You are not as lost as you believe."

Aidan stopped pacing, his brows rising in surprise at her clarity. He studied her for a long moment, struck by the precision of her reasoning.

"You are right," he said after a moment. "Your insight is ... exactly what we need."

Gwen rolled her eyes and folded her arms over her waist, a firm tilt to her chin. "I know I am right. The evidence is plain to see. Trafford's note named three men. He did not hedge or speculate. If he is now in hiding, it is because he uncovered something real. Something dangerous. Your investigation has achieved more than you realize. It has narrowed the truth to a definite few."

Aidan's expression shifted, the furrow of concern easing into something far gentler. "You make me wish I had spoken to you about all this much sooner," he said. "You offer a clarity that eludes even the most seasoned among us."

She softened slightly. "I am a scholar. I weigh what is before me. Emotion has its place, but facts guide decisions."

With a slow step, Aidan approached. He slid an arm around her waist, drawing her close until they stood chest to chest, the space between them narrowing to nothing. "And what of you?" he murmured, his voice low and intimate. "Have you accepted the truth about yourself?"

Her breath caught as his hand brushed lightly against her temple, tucking back a strand of her hair. His gaze, so intent, searched her own, and her heart stuttered beneath it.

"Gwen, Gwen the Spotted Giraffe?" Her father had confessed after dinner to revealing her youthful secrets earlier that day in the interests of reconciliation, so she knew Aidan was aware of her past troubles.

Aidan leaned in to brush his lips over her freckled cheek. "I happen to like your spots, Gwen Abbott." He rose to nuzzle at her temple, teasing her hair with his hot breath to make her shiver. "And I appreciate your height." He raised his head to stare deep into her eyes. "And your name is exquisite poetry." Aidan stroked her mouth with the pad of his thumb. "Gwen." He leaned in to steal a kiss. "Gwen." He tilted her chin with his forefinger to gaze into her soul with impassioned chocolate brown eyes. "Gwen."

Then he fell silent, giving her space to respond. Gwen opened her mouth, searching for words, but they slipped away beneath the weight of what he had just spoken ... and how he had said it. His voice wrapped around her like a silken ribbon, gently binding her heart.

A breath escaped her lips. "I ..." Her voice wavered, featherlight, as affection pooled and spread through her limbs. "I have realized that perhaps those girls ... might have been wrong about me. About my ... appeal."

"Very wrong," Aidan murmured, his voice husky with emotion. His gaze fell to her lips, and before she could gather her next thought, he dipped his head and captured her mouth in a kiss that was soft, searching, and full of longing.

Gwen responded instinctively, her hands rising to grip his shoulders, leaning into his embrace. But just as quickly, Aidan pulled back with a strangled groan, his face a study in conflicted anguish.

"What is it?" Gwen frowned, breathless. "Please do not tell me this is another secret."

He stepped back again, rubbing the bridge of his nose as

if trying to summon the courage to confess. "I may have been ... thrown. From Valor."

She blinked. "May have?"

"I was," he admitted with a sheepish grimace. "The street was narrow and full of commotion. Valor was startled, and I took a rather hard tumble."

Concern furrowed her brow as she stepped toward him. "That sounds terribly dangerous."

Aidan's face flushed. He could not quite meet her gaze. "It happened yesterday."

"Yesterday?" Gwen's voice rose slightly in disbelief. "That explains why you insisted we sit in the dark. You were hiding something from me."

He gave a guilty nod.

Gwen bit back her irritation. "Let me see, then," she said, gesturing pointedly at his coat.

Aidan sighed, his movements deliberate as he rolled his shoulders and eased the garment off, folding it neatly and laying it on the bench at the foot of the bed. He then unwound his cravat with practiced fingers, placing it beside the coat. When he untucked his shirt from his breeches, Gwen's breath caught. It was not scandalous, not exactly—he was her husband, after all—but it was still unfamiliar, still enough to send a flush creeping up her throat.

Her breath stilled the moment he drew the linen over his head.

"Aidan!" she cried, horror stealing into her tone.

His shoulder and upper arm were marred with vivid bruises. Deep red, dusky blue, and the sinister shade of dark plum. Gwen circled him swiftly, her hand covering her mouth. The contusions were worse along his back, a brutal smear of injury that covered nearly a quarter of his back.

"You could have been killed," she whispered.

He cast his shirt aside and reached for her, drawing her close. She leaned into him, heedless of the bruises, laying her cheek against the warmth of his chest, grateful for the steady beat of his heart.

"Would that have been a bad thing, Gwen Abbott?" he murmured against her hair.

She lifted her eyes, blurred with unshed tears. "A very bad thing."

"Then I shall be far more careful in future," he promised solemnly.

Gwen reached up to touch the curve of his jaw, memorizing the planes of his face as though to anchor him to her world. There was a pause, heavy with feeling, before she asked, "Is it true? That I was the first?"

Aidan gave a small nod, his voice quiet. "It is."

Gwen held his gaze. "You seemed ... very certain for a man unfamiliar with such matters."

Aidan gave a soft laugh, the corners of his eyes creasing. "Trafford was determined I should not shame myself ... or you. He offered his instruction with all the seriousness of a military campaign."

Gwen smiled in return, her heart lifting despite the heaviness of the moment. "Then we must ensure his safety. For that guidance alone, he has earned our eternal gratitude."

Their foreheads touched, and Gwen closed her eyes, letting the quiet hush of the room settle around them. The ache of what might have been still lingered, but so too did the reassurance of what was. The warmth of his arms around her, the promise of a future they would face together.

He covered her hands with his, drawing them to his lips to press a kiss to her knuckles. "You undo me, Gwen," he murmured. "Completely."

She smiled shyly, the moment suffused with quiet intimacy. In the quiet that followed, Aidan drew her into his arms and held her close, their bodies cocooned in the softness of the bed.

"It is better with no secrets between us," he said softly, his lips brushing her temple.

Gwen sighed, utterly content. "Much better."

"Shall we pledge never to have secrets again?"

She hesitated, then laughed. "If that is how it must be, then I confess ... When you asked me about Papa selling the property, I told you he had not discussed it with me. That part was true, but ... I did suspect what he had planned and chose not to say."

He lifted his head with mock reproach. "Gwendolyn Abbott! You deceived me."

She grinned, her cheeks flushing. "To be fair, we were not yet married, and I had not decided whether you were to be trusted."

His chuckle rumbled against her ear. "No more secrets, nor half-truths, nor carefully worded answers intended to misdirect?"

"Unless I am planning a surprise," she added with a teasing smile.

He tucked her against his side, one hand tracing idle patterns on her arm. "When this is over, when we find Trafford and bring the truth into the light, shall we take that trip to Italy together?"

Her breath caught, and her heart fluttered. "You meant that? That you would take me to Florence?"

"Of course. But at the rate we are going, we might need to travel soon. If you are with child, we will have some time limitations."

Gwen stilled, her heart swelling with quiet joy. He had laid her most sacred wishes of love, family, and discovery gently at her feet. He was no longer a mysterious visitor from the shadows. He was her partner. Her future.

"Then we have no choice but to solve this murder swiftly," she whispered, her voice thick with promise.

EPILOGUE

"Well begun is half done."

Aristotle

AUGUST 29, 1821

Gwen pulled the edge of her hood down, careful to hide any evidence of her red hair beneath it. Her unusual height could not be helped, but she would keep her knees slightly bent and her shoulders hunched as she walked down the street.

Old Fred brought the hackney to a stop by the main square, and Gwen carefully disembarked, keeping the hood down and holding her skirts so she would not tumble. Old Fred had been told not to assist her, or do anything out of the ordinary.

The men had argued at some length against involving her, but she had stood her ground and reasoned it out.

If there were ruffians about, searching for Trafford or his father's ward, they would not think twice about a woman walking by.

It was the only way to safely approach Lady Hays's townhouse without rousing suspicion, considering how close it was to Trafford's family home.

There could be men watching, so it must be a woman.

It had been three days and still no word from Trafford.

Something had to be done.

Aidan had finally acquiesced when she had agreed that Old Fred would be the driver and remain within a few feet of her. The hackney driver had apparently been in the army, so her husband had provided him with twin pistols to hide within pockets of the massive overcoat he wore.

Gwen reached for the large covered basket on the passenger bench. She was pretending to make a delivery, and they hoped that no one would be aware Lady Hays and her husband had already left London. Nevertheless, the remaining servants on duty might receive a delivery in the owner's absence.

Hoisting the basket up, she turned and headed toward the townhouse, making for the tradesman's entrance.

She rang the bell and waited. It might take some time to attract the attention of the old couple who took care of the house when the household packed up and left for the country.

After a few minutes, Gwen rang the bell again, gnawing on her lip while she waited with bated breath.

Trafford could be right there, dozens of feet away. And he could know the identity of the man who had murdered the baron.

She wanted so much to help. To bring home good news. Any news.

Her new family was so worried, waiting for word of Little Julius.

But despite her eagerness to help, all Gwen could do was wait for someone to come to the door.

∽

Next in the Dazzling Debutantes series:
Miss Gideon and the Incident
A daring lord and a young woman find themselves in peril, igniting a possible romance as they escape to stay alive.

DOWNLOAD A FREE BOOK

Enjoyed the story? The adventure isn't over yet ...

Subscribe to Jarrett's newsletter to receive a book—absolutely free!

The Meddling Duke: A determined duke. Three unforgettable women. And a meddling hand in each of their lives that may just lead to true love.

Join thousands of Regency romance readers who love exclusive content, behind-the-scenes peeks, giveaways, and early access to new releases. Your next favorite story is just one click away.

AFTERWORD

While gentlemen of the Regency were certainly permitted to invest without sullying their reputations, engaging in trade was an entirely different matter.

In fact, if a man built up his wealth and wished to become a gentleman, he did so by purchasing estates and then severing all financial ties to the business that helped him achieve his wealth.

This was to remove the stain of trade from his family so they would be accepted within the new social strata they had ascended to.

Frederick Smythe's choice to pursue trade would have been insightful from a financial standpoint, but would certainly lower his family into a different class.

Hence, the willingness of Halmesbury, Saunton, Filminster, and Lord Moreland to assist on the condition that their involvement was to remain a secret. To be fair regarding their discretion, by remaining unknown parties, they would offset the damage to Gwen's status, so Frederick would want to keep their involvement unknown.

The Kama Sutra was available in many versions across

AFTERWORD

the Indian subcontinent. However, it was not published in Britain until 1883, when Sir Richard Francis Burton found a way to circumvent censorship laws. It soon became one of the most pirated books, being copied and reprinted and even republished.

Trafford is the sort of enterprising man of leisure who would know the right people and be able to obtain a copy of the notorious book in its original Sanskrit sixty years earlier.

If you enjoyed this story, I would be incredibly grateful if you'd consider leaving an honest review. Your words help others discover the book and support future stories.

Speaking of Julius Trafford, he is missing along with Miss Audrey Gideon. There is quite a scandal brewing, not to mention risk to life and limb. If he manages to survive this murder investigation, Trafford will be faced with doing the right thing to save the young woman who has been inadvertently ruined by his misadventures.

Find out what happens in *Miss Gideon and the Incident*, the third book in the Dazzling Debutantes series of Regency mystery romances.

ABOUT THE AUTHOR

C. N. Jarrett started writing her own stories in elementary school but got distracted when she finished school and moved on to non-profit work with recovering drug addicts. There she worked with people from every walk of life from privileged neighborhoods to the shanty towns of urban and rural South Africa.

One day she met a real-life romantic hero. She instantly married her fellow bibliophile and moved to the USA where she enjoyed a career as a sales coaching executive at an Inc 500 company. She lives with her husband on the Florida Gulf Coast.

Jarrett believes in kindness and the indomitable power of the human spirit. She is fascinated by the amazing, funny people she has met across the world who dared to change their lives. She likes to tell mischievous tales of life-changing decisions and character transformations while drinking excellent coffee and avoiding cookies.

Stay in touch by signing up for the C. N. Jarrett newsletter!

ALSO BY C. N. JARRETT

DAZZLING DEBUTANTES

Book 1: Miss Ridley and the Duke

Book 2: Miss Hayward and the Earl

Book 3: Miss Davis and the Spare

Book 4: Miss Davis and the Architect

Book 5: Mrs. Brown and the Christmas Gift

The Meddling Duke: a Collection of Regency Romantic Short Stories

RELUCTANT RECKONINGS

Book 1: Miss Abbott and the Suspect Lord

Book 2: Miss Smythe and the Midnight Lord

Book 3: Miss Gideon and the Incident

Book 4: Miss Bigsby and the Aristocrat Next Door

Book 5: Miss Carter and the Baron's Heir

TREACHEROUS TREASURES

Book 1: Lady Slight and the Visitor

Book 2: Miss Bigsby and the Very Short Courtship

Book 3: Miss Fairfax and the Secret Symphony

Book 4: Miss Metcalfe and the Romantic Blunder

Book 5: Miss Caraway and the Encrypted Heart

CLEAN REGENCY ROMANCES FROM ROGUE PRESS

Beneath the silk and satin of Regency England ... something stirs.

From C. Karloff comes a collection of clean romantic tales where genteel drawing rooms hide ancient secrets, and true love must face the most chilling of curses.

In this sweeping new series, intrepid heroines and haunted heroes collide in tales of mystery, longing, and redemption. Where the monsters are real, but so is the hope of a happy ending.

SEASON OF SHADOWS

Duke Undying

Earl Lunar

Viscount Refracted

Baron Electrified

Marquess Unwrapped

Made in United States
North Haven, CT
01 December 2025